THE
REVENGE
OF THE
HOUND

THE REVENGE OF THE HOUND

MICHAEL
HARDWICK

WITH ILLUSTRATIONS BY
STERANKO

A BYRON PREISS BOOK

VILLARD BOOKS • NEW YORK • 1987

ALSO BY MICHAEL HARDWICK
Prisoner of the Devil
The Complete Guide to Sherlock Holmes
Sherlock Holmes: My Life and Crimes
The Private Life of Sherlock Holmes
The Private Life of Dr. Watson

Text design by Alex Jay/Studio J

Special thanks to Peter Gethers, Mollie Hardwick, Edmund Preiss, Esq.,
Jon Lellenberg, and Randall Reich.

Grateful acknowledgment to Dame Jean Conan Doyle
for permission to use the Sherlock Holmes characters
created by Sir Arthur Conan Doyle.

Library of Congress Cataloging-in-Publication Data
Hardwick, Michael, 1924–
   The revenge of the hound.

   I. Title.   II. Title: Sherlock Holmes mystery.
PR6058.A673R4   1987   823'.914   87-40188
ISBN 0-394-55653-4

Manufactured in the United States of America
2   3   4   5   6   7   8   9
First Edition

Based on the characters of
Sherlock Holmes and Dr. John H. Watson
created by Sir Arthur Conan Doyle

THE
REVENGE
OF THE
HOUND

I have never been able to decide, to this day, whether or not Sherlock Holmes knew my intentions. That he had some inkling of them, I cannot doubt; his inquiring hints were so obvious, while the tactics by which he sought to trick me into revealing all were almost totally transparent.

It was early summer, 1902. Although Edward VII had been our sovereign since the death of his mother, Queen Victoria, in January of the previous year, he was yet to be crowned. State ceremonial and rejoicing had been out of the question while our less-than-triumphal war in South Africa dragged on, but now that the war was to all intents and purposes over, the way was clear at last for the Coronation. All Europe's royalty massed dutifully in London. Two days before the ceremony, the King was stricken with abdominal pains. He was operated upon at once by his surgeon, Sir Frederick Treves. His recovery was swift. Within two weeks he was quite better, and appendicitis became all the fashion; but by then the impatient royal guests had gone home.

On the first day of July, I returned to Baker Street from a delicious sortie into Bloomsbury. I sank gratefully into the cane-backed chair before our smouldering parlour fire and put up my aching leg and hot and throbbing feet upon the brass

3

fender rail. The weather had turned sultry, and if my sensation had been as of walking upon air, the reality was that I had been treading London pavements, which seem to be of a peculiar hardness and to carry a heat of their own. Sheer elevation of spirits had prevented my taking a cab. I was proud to parade my aura for all to recognize, like Trooping the Colour, along streets whose every building still sported its Coronation bunting against the postponed day.

At my entry, Holmes glanced up from his armchair, where he sprawled with his dressing gown draped loosely about him. Closing the fat album of newspaper clippings he had been perusing, he ran his gimlet eyes over me until his gaze came to rest on my boots. His curiosity about my recent comings and goings had been plain enough. His ultrasensitive antennae must have enabled him to deduce a certain amount, but his cold pride would not allow him to seek direct confirmation. Before asking an important question he preferred to know most of the answer already.

"But why Turkish?" was his oblique greeting.

I determined to take a little revenge for that amusement which he chose so often to indulge at my expense.

"English," I answered, waggling my feet. "I got them at Latimer's, in Oxford Street."

"The bath, not the boots!" said he. "The bath! Why the relaxing and expensive Turkish rather than the invigorating home-made article?"*

"Because," I said, "for the last few days I have been feeling rheumatic and old. A Turkish bath is what we call an alternative in medicine—a fresh starting-point, a cleanser of the system."

---

* The reader who is acquainted with the chronicles of my long association and friendship with the greatest private detective that ever lived will recognize this exchange. It is that which opens my narrative, *The Disappearance of Lady Frances Carfax.*

I added that, while a connection between my boots and a Turkish bath might be logical to him, it was not to me. More than twenty years' experience of his methods had taught me to be able to see through the airy reply that followed.

"The train of reasoning is not very obscure, Watson. It belongs to the same elementary class of deduction which I should illustrate if I were to ask you who shared your cab in your drive this morning."

Now this was nothing short of snooping. Had I been in lesser spirits I should have objected strongly. Holding the upper hand for once, however, I could afford to lie back in my chair and watch him try to lure me into showing my cards.

From the splashes which he claimed to see on my left sleeve and shoulder he inferred that I had shared a hansom-cab seat with someone. Had I been alone, he stated, I should have occupied the centre of the seat, and escaped splashing.

I did not trouble to point out that the streets, for once in that miserable summer of '02, were dry. I asked instead, "But the boots and the bath?"

"Equally childish."

He gestured with his pipestem. "You are in the habit of doing up your laces in a certain way. I see they are fastened in an elaborate double bow, which is not your usual method. You have, therefore, had them off. *Who has tied them?* A bootmaker, or the attendant at the bath? It is unlikely that it is the boot-maker, since your boots are nearly new. Well, what remains? The boy at the bath. Elementary, is it not?"

He proceeded to mask his attempt to learn my secret by lighting his worn briar and puffing forth clouds of smoke. My refusal to take his bait had confirmed that I was harbouring a secret, and he evidently had a strong inkling that it concerned himself. It did, but its disclosure could wait. I was not ready to tell him that a certain young American lady had just consented to become the third Mrs. John H. Watson.

"Т here, John," my dear Coral had said, as she pulled tight the last of the double bows. She smiled up at me from her kneeling position beside the upholstered stool upon which my boots rested. "Those won't come unfastened in a hurry."

"I shall keep wearing them all evening," said I, "because you have tied them."

The episode, still less than an hour old, had taken place in the house which she and her Aunt Henrietta were occupying in Russell Square. Although they were situated just round the corner from the British Museum, their coming from the United States a few months earlier, in unseasonable February, had not been for scholastic reasons. Aunt Henrietta had come over to inspect her two racehorses, which had preceded them by some weeks to be trained up in readiness for our season.

She was Mrs. Henrietta Wilmington Atkins, of Omaha, Nebraska. Her husband owned land scattered halfway to Kansas City, most of it leased out to small farmers. I had met her in May, on the opening evening of a military tournament. I had gone alone, under the privilege of a complimentary ticket, sent to Holmes by a grateful military client and tossed across the breakfast table to me with contemptuous murmurings about the fatuity of martial pomp in the aftermath of the South African fiasco.

My seat turned out to be one of the best in the Grand Agricultural Hall, Islington. It was made more so by the proximity of a fetchingly dressed woman in handsome middle age. She smiled at me as I sat down, then introduced herself with that American forthrightness which one may either welcome or deplore. Her accent was the wholesome one of the Midwest. Her manner had the self-assurance of wealth.

"And this," she added, indicating her younger companion, "is my niece, Miss Coral Atkins."

I bowed and shook hands across her, introducing myself to them both. Miss Atkins appeared to be about seven-and-twenty. She, too, was expensively tailored, and of a fresh beauty of face and form that distinguished her among the fashionable ladies present. She had copper-coloured hair, a delicate porcelain-like complexion, and those remarkably glistening white teeth one notices so much in American women. I wondered that she was not married, but her aunt had referred to her distinctly as "Miss."

"Coral is my favourite girl, aren't you, dear?" Mrs. Atkins confided. "It's her first time in England. I come back every year. My hubby brought me first, in '86. Oh, isn't he just too awful, Coral, your Uncle Gabriel? You know what he said?" she added, turning her blond head to me. I thought she was going to nudge me in the ribs as she laughed and broadened her slight accent: "London ain't so bad, but Nebrasky fits me best."

Her niece shared her laughter and I allowed myself a deferential chuckle.

"Your husband is not with you, then?" I asked.

"Oh, no," said his wife. "He never comes any more. But that doesn't keep me away. I just love it here. Don't I, dear?"

Miss Atkins gave me a warm affirming smile.

I was on the threshold of fifty. I had been a widower again some ten years, since losing my dear Mary in 1893, so long before her time. My desolation had been joyously relieved in the following year by Sherlock Holmes's "return from the dead." Unknown to me, in common with the rest of the world, he had been wandering incognito in Europe and parts of Asia throughout the three years following his "fatal" combat at the Reichenbach Falls in Switzerland with his archenemy, Professor James Moriarty, the "Napoleon of Crime." Upon his return I was content enough to resume our comfortable sharing of the old rooms at 221B Baker Street. The possibility of marrying yet again had scarcely presented itself to my thoughts. It was Mrs. Henrietta Wilmington Atkins—Henry, as she prefers to be known—who must bear the sweet responsibility for introducing it.

While the cavalry horses dashed and pranced around the arena of the vast hall, and the commands and the trumpets' cries echoed off the lofty iron roof, she plied me with questions about what was going on. My military knowledge appeared to impress her deeply, as she exclaimed constantly to Coral. Their eyes shone with admiration at my passing mention of my part in the Afghan campaign of '80, of which they had not heard. In answer to their anxious inquiry, I was compelled to admit that I had taken a Jezail bullet in a shoulder at the height of the battle of Maiwand, and a further one in the leg during the retreat. Mrs. Atkins laid a sympathetic hand on my arm, insisting that I join them for supper afterward and tell them all about the awful Maiwand massacre, which I had been so lucky to escape with my life.

We went to the Hotel Russell, just across the way from their rented house in Russell Square. In the carriage back from Islington, Mrs. Atkins kept asking me to name the sights of London that we passed, for Coral's benefit. It was the same all through supper: "Dr. Watson, why don't you tell Coral . . . ?"

"Darling, ask the doctor to explain . . . " "I just want to get your opinion, Doctor, for Coral to hear . . ." "John—your name *is* John, isn't it? This is Coral, you know. And you *must* call me Henry, short for Henrietta."

The waiters had greeted the ladies familiarly, and two bottles of champagne had appeared at once. Clearly, they were used to doing themselves well. I was willing enough to fall in with this, and went gladly across the road with them after supper for a nightcap. The house was very grand, but they were obviously at home in rich surroundings. I thought what a merry, unbridled pair they were, entertaining at this late hour a man whom they had met only that evening.

"Well, Miss Atkins," I said to the girl, while her aunt was briefly absent from the room. "How are you liking it over here?"

"Please do call me Coral, John," she replied, coming to share the sofa. "I think England's just wonderful. I know why Aunt Henry keeps coming back and back."

"Perhaps you might wish to return as well," I suggested, but it occurred to me that this visit might be some form of vacation treat before marrying and settling down in America. She wore no engagement ring on her small hand, but I was not versed in the conventions of the Midwest.

In fact, as she went on to tell me, she was not really from that region at all. I had noticed that Coral's almost nonexistent accent was quite different in nuance from her aunt's.

"I was born and raised in Philadelphia, Pennsylvania, you know? I lost both my parents two years ago. A railroad accident."

"I am so very sorry," I said, much moved by the way she faltered and bent her head for a moment. She recovered quickly, though, and glanced up with her sweet smile.

"Thank you. Uncle Gabe was Daddy's brother, though no one would ever have thought it. A rough diamond, as they say, but a heart of gold. He and Aunt Henry took me in to live with them. They've been so sweet and kind and generous . . . "

"Nonsense!" We heard her aunt's voice from the doorway. "She's had nothing more than she deserves. John, I've been thinking."

She shooed Coral from the sofa with a gesture and sat down in her place, to address me forthrightly.

"She's the best-natured gal in Omaha, but she's no Midwesterner when it comes to horses. I've seen her yawn even when they're neck and neck in the straight."

"Oh, Aunt!" protested Coral, laughing, but Henry ignored her.

"We're fixed to stay in your country till the end of the Season. My trainer has entered the nags for a couple of events apiece. I mean to take in all the big races. This poor gal has to drag around with me or stay in this house with no one but the servants."

"I'll be all right, Aunt," Coral protested. "Truly."

"If I might suggest it," I put in, "I know two or three families with daughters at home. I'm sure they'd be delighted to take Coral under their wing whenever you go out of town."

"I appreciate the suggestion, John." Henry nodded. "Only, if I know my girl, she'd sooner stop here. All she needs is somebody to take her about. You know, to theatres and places, where a gal can't go on her own. Maybe on a trip or two."

I was about to assure her that my friends would do that, too, but she forestalled me.

"How about you, John?"

"*Me*, Henry?"

"Who better? You don't practise medicine any more. You're a gentleman of leisure—and I can tell a *real* gentleman from the other kind. You know all about London. If you would spare the time, the dear child would be just thrilled to go around with you wherever you want to take her. Wouldn't you, darling?"

"I couldn't possibly impose on John's time, Aunt."

"Charged up to me, of course," Henry added to me, almost casually.

"My dear madam . . . !" I began, but the protest died. My wound pension and small dividend income would not nearly have accommodated the costs, yet the invitation was one scarcely to be declined. Henry read my thoughts and gave me a beaming wink that would have come shockingly from any English aunt.

"Never mind what's *proper*. Good old Teddy's on your throne now. Things are set for change over here. Anyway, Coral's not the kind for chaperoning. She's a good, straight gal. Any four-flusher who tries to put something over on her has a big surprise coming. She doesn't need an old hen like me clucking around her. So, what do you say, John?"

"I say whatever Coral would like me to," I answered.

"And I say, yes, please!" said she.

It marked the start of a joyous time for me. Each morning I arose eager for the day. Holmes was between cases and keeping his boredom at bay by composing one of his works of esoteric scholarship. He was withdrawn and silent, scarcely seeming to notice my comings and goings. He was almost invariably in bed by ten o'clock, while his habit of rising late spared me his scrutiny across the breakfast table.

The days passed in an increasing whirl. I went round to Russell Square each morning at eleven, and from there escorted Coral to the Royal Parks, the Tower of London, the Zoological Gardens, the museums. We went to the Crystal Palace, to Greenwich and to Blackheath, where I showed her the ground on which I used to play for the local Rugby football club in my days as a medical student. We watched a late-season match. I noticed some of the hearties eyeing Coral. I was surprised at the feeling of possessiveness of her that their glances aroused in me.

We travelled as far afield as Ramsgate, Margate and Brighton in excursion trains, and up and down the Thames by pleasure steamer, matching our mood to that of the carefree throngs about us. We joined our voices to the banjo and mandolin:

> Let's all be merry,
> Drinking whisky, wine and sherry,
> On Coronation Day . . .

I had behaved to her throughout as I would toward a daughter. A man will think his thoughts, however, and it was thus that the gap between our ages came into my reckoning.

When Mary Morstan had entered my life, bringing Holmes his celebrated *Sign of the Four* case, I had been thirty-six, and she eight years my junior. We had loved each other instantly, and, both being alone in the world, were free to marry, I for the second time. Coral was now the age at which dear Mary had been then, while I had recently notched up my half century. She was also, I imagined, wealthy in her own right. I was decidedly not. Such notions about her as had developed in my mind were thus easily, though wistfully, dismissed.

Her aunt returned to the house in Bloomsbury at intervals, and all three of us were happy together. Mostly, though, Henry preferred to go her way alone and leave Coral and me to ours.

One warm, lazy June afternoon I took her for a gentle row on Regent's Park lake. She sat straight-backed in the stern facing me, her big, flower-decked hat, pale lilac dress and matching long gloves and fringed parasol the ideal complement to her handsome features and figure. Admiring whistles from some lads in another boat made her smile. When she gave the youths a little wave, and they cheered back and doffed their hats, my stomach churned. This was man's work, I resolved. I pulled toward one of the miniature islands.

By the time we had touched the soft bank, under the overhang of tree branches, with the brown ducks fluttering and splashing about us, I was determined to do or die.

"Coral, my dear."

"Yes, John?"

"You must be contemplating marrying sometime."

She had removed her left glove and was dabbling her hand in the water. She lifted it out, to watch the crystal droplets run down between spread, ringless fingers.

"I've contemplated it," she answered, still looking at her hand.

"And?"

"I guess I just never met my husband."

My heart seemed to leap skyward and the hot blood tingled in my cheeks.

"I hope you have now."

"I was hoping so, too, dearest John," came her reply.

T hus I came to be engaged to be married
for a third time. In my state of overwhelming joy I gave no
thought to its possible repercussions upon the unique career of
my friend and fellow tenant, the world's greatest detective,
Sherlock Holmes.

Mrs. Atkins was out of town upon a horsey expedition.
Coral and I agreed to interview her together upon her return,
to seek the blessing of Coral's guardians. The meeting was
planned for the morning of Saturday, June 28. A slight contretemps prevented it, however. On the Friday afternoon I was
shot by the notorious American criminal, "Killer" Evans.

I have related the circumstances in my chronicle entitled
The Three Garridebs. It was another of those cases of a covetous
dupe being lured away from his usual habitat by a criminal
wanting to get possession of something hidden on the premises. Few of Holmes's investigations placed either of us in actual danger, or required us to brawl or use weapons. For a man
who took no exercise, Holmes showed himself remarkably pro-
ficient in a variety of martial arts when he needed to be, but
it happened rarely in my experience. His weapon was his
brain, that supreme coordinator of observation, inference and
accumulated data, culminating in deductions and forecasts

that seldom failed to astonish his friends and confound his enemies.

"Killer" Evans, our quarry in the Garrideb case, had more at stake than most. He had shot men in America and England. Tricked and cornered by Holmes and me, he pretended to surrender, then whipped out his revolver. The wound I sustained in consequence was only superficial—I did not even fall. It necessitated a couple of days' lying up, though, and it was not until the following Tuesday, July 1, that I was able to go to Russell Square for the postponed meeting with Aunt Henry.

The good lady gushed sympathy upon me from the generous fount of her American heart. Brushing aside my protestations that a grazed thigh was a mere nothing, she insisted I rest my legs on a footstool. Coral herself brought it forward, and lifted my limbs tenderly.

"Take off the poor man's boots," commanded Henry. "Do you good to waggle your toes, John."

I demurred at that, having no slippers to put on. "Perhaps I might sit with them just unlaced?" I suggested. Coral knelt at once to attend to it.

She had promised me she would tell her aunt nothing of our understanding until we could do so together. Knowing this made it all the more astonishing when Henry sent her from the room on some errand and came to take my hand herself.

"Why don't you ask her, John?"

Amazement made me begin to stammer. She waved me impatiently to silence.

"She's the gal for you, and you couldn't be righter for her. Why wait? Ask her straight out."

It seemed superfluous to tell her the question had been answered already.

Thus it came about that I returned to 221B Baker Street an officially engaged man, and my fiancée's mode of retying my bootlaces before I left her house at the end of that enchanted afternoon gave Sherlock Holmes the opening for the interrogation he had been seeking.

I could understand his concern. He was a creature of habit. He was used to my company, and, I daresay, my always-unstinting praise. Our set of rooms with its professional clutter, Mrs. Hudson's superlative cooking and domestic attention, and the quiet regularity of our way of life suited his unsocial ways perfectly. My leaving for a home of my own would upset it all for him.

Finding me obdurate in refusing to tell him what he was trying to discover, he changed tactics. First, he flung himself down into his armchair and smoked furiously, the slate-gray clouds from his strong shag darkening the room. I lit up my own pipe of lighter Arcadia mixture and puffed away, letting agreeable thoughts roam freely.

Gradually, Holmes became less agitated. He ceased to re-light his pipe every few minutes, finally letting it rest unheeded in his lap while he stared blindly before him. Then he suddenly sprang up, to lean upon the mantelpiece, one slippered foot on the fender top.

It was now some hours since my return from Russell Square. The evening was well advanced, and it was becoming dark outside. Our lamp was lit and the fire had been allowed to smoulder through into a subdued blaze. As Holmes stared into the grate, its flickering light emphasized the gauntness of his features. One of his hands was plunged deep into a pocket of his mouse-coloured dressing gown. His brow rested upon his arm, which lay along the mantelpiece among the litter of pipes, matches, spills, dottle of half-smoked tobacco, lenses, photographs, envelopes, unanswered letters transfixed with a jackknife, and those many other small objects for which this was his repository. Mrs. Hudson, our admirable landlady and housekeeper, was under injunction never to tidy nor dust there.

"My mind is made up," said he.

"About what, Holmes?"

"I resolve to retire."

"*Retire*, Holmes?" I echoed. "*You?*"

"You cannot imagine why?"

"No, I can't think why," I said. "Frankly, I really don't believe it."

After so many years watching him at work, his act failed to deceive me. So accustomed was he to getting what he wanted out of his suspects, among whom he seemed now to include me, that he would not stand to be thwarted. He would use any means, however melodramatic, to wheedle out what he wanted to know.

He withdrew his foot from the fender and let drop his arm before slumping into his chair. With a significance Beerbohm Tree could not have bettered, he rallied briefly, to make a few forlorn jabs with the poker at the coals, letting it clatter into the hearth as he sank back.

"My time is out of joint," he declared, in a hollow tone befitting Marley's ghost. "Life, Watson, has passed by me. It is high time I ceased meddling in other people's affairs like some venerable household quack."

"Your 'household quack' is the salt of the medical profession, Holmes."

"Oh, yes. The dear old healer, held in awe by people whom he had brought into the world, at whose tongues he has peered at intervals before prescribing his unvarying panaceas. His patients' faith in him is what cures them, not his medicines. The law of averages must catch up with him, though. The longer he carries on, the greater the risk that he will make his fatal mistake."

"Nonsense! Anyway, you are not a doctor, quack or otherwise."

"I have come to dread a similar decline in my powers—my entire reputation wrecked by a single failure. Ghastly!"

He uttered a deep sigh.

"You have failed before," I reminded him.

He sent me a sharp look.

"Once or twice," I amended.

A further silence followed, while he smoked his pipe moodily.

"Put it this way, Watson," he resumed at last. "You recall that railway journey which we made together once to Dartmoor? We were going to Tavistock and the King's Pyland racing stables."

"In '89 or '90," I recalled.

"In your account of the case, which I seem to recall you entitled *Silver Blaze* and in which you made several gross errors regarding the rules of horseracing, you recorded my observation that the speed of our train was exactly ascertainable from the rate at which we were passing the telegraph poles, spaced sixty yards apart."

"So you claimed at the time, Holmes."

"All life, Watson, is a journey. To be precise, a *series* of journeys. We are born, we set forth; we live, we travel; we succeed, we arrive. But there comes a time when the telegraph poles seem to be set wider. We are slowing down. The terminus is almost within sight . . . "

"What mawkish twaddle, Holmes! You are two years younger than I. You don't hear me carrying on about telegraph poles and termini."

He shook his head gravely. "We must all come to it."

"Balderdash!" I had to cry. "If you are so jealous, why don't you get *yourself* a wife?"

Holmes sat up and slapped his thigh triumphantly.

"I was in no doubt, of course!" he exulted. "Your eager spirits. Your daily outings in leisure clothes. Your intonings— if that is the correct term—of some of the more turgid romantic ballads while you are at your toilet. It could add up to only one thing."

"Holmes, you are some sort of demon incarnate!" I protested. "I can spot your tricks a mile off, yet I still fall for them. Very well. I *am* to be married. Now that that is cleared up, I'll thank you to mind your own business."

He leaned toward me, gripping his chair arm.

"Permit me to remind you that it *is* my business. A change in your domestic arrangements implies a corresponding one in mine. Out with the sordid details, pray. Tell me the worst!"

There was no point in refusing. He would coax it out of me anyway. I told him everything, pausing only to rebuke him for the groans and sighs with which he punctuated my narrative.

"For heaven's sake, Holmes, stop making those sepulchral noises! You have managed well enough without me before. When it suited you, after the Reichenbach episode, you went off for three years, callously leaving me to suppose you dead. You know you will manage again."

The rebuke brought yet another silence. Holmes sat motionless, staring straight before him. When he spoke again, he sounded more in earnest.

"Then I have come to my terminus at last."

"*Terminus?*"

"The curtain's fall. The actor must respond to his cue."

"Might we dispense with the railways and the theatre, Holmes, and face the fact that I have come to one of the most important junctions—I mean junctures—of my life?"

"You don't think that a few days' reflection would help? For instance, how would Lausanne suit you? First-class tickets and all expenses paid on a princely scale?"

"I fail to see what a trip to Switzerland can possibly have to do with my arrangements."

"Purely professional, I assure you. Lady Frances Carfax, the sole survivor of the late Earl of Rufton's family, has disappeared on the Continent. Scotland Yard seem reluctant to act, so I have been retained to find her. Her last known whereabouts was Lausanne. You know that I cannot possibly leave London while Old Abrahams is in such a mortal terror of his life . . . "

" 'Old Abrahams'? I have never heard of any such person."

Holmes regarded me with that vague expression with which he feigned forgetfulness.

"I thought I had mentioned him to you. Dear me! But, with your being out so much lately, perhaps it is inevitable that one or two things should slip my mind. The poor old fellow! I dare not desert him just now. Besides, on general principles it is best that I should not leave the country. You know that Scotland Yard feels lonely without me, and it causes an unhealthy excitement among the criminal classes. I beseech you, my dear Watson, to undertake this one brief errand on my behalf, if only for old times' sake."

"I shall have to consult Coral," I replied, causing him to wince and draw a hand over his brow. "You had better let me hear the details, meanwhile."

His recital kept us up well past Holmes's accustomed bedtime. It was after eleven o'clock before I poured our nightcap. I had just sat down again when there came a knock at our door. Mrs. Hudson looked in, in her dressing gown and curlpapers.

"Beg pardon, Mr. Holmes, but you've a caller."

"Old Abrahams in person?" I could not resist suggesting. Holmes gave me a scowl.

"No, Dr. Watson. Nobody of that name. It's Inspector Lestrade, from Scotland Yard."

Holmes, who had frowned at the prospect of receiving some agitated client at so late an hour, exclaimed with relief.

"Lestrade!" he called to him on the landing. "Come in. You'll join us in our last glass?"

"Pleasure, Mr. Holmes," said the little plainclothes officer, standing aside for the landlady to leave. "Beg pardon for troubling you gentlemen at this hour."

I had known Inspector Lestrade for almost as long as I had known Holmes, which was twenty-one years. He had been one of the stream of mysterious visitors to our rooms who had so intrigued me in those first days before Holmes revealed his unique profession to me. The sallow hue of his ferret-like features had yellowed further with late middle age, and the lank hair had become thin and tarnished. He had never risen higher than a senior inspector in the Criminal Investigation Department. Holmes's private opinion was that Lestrade's dogged honesty had been his professional handicap. The lack of imagination that characterized his work had precluded him from feathering his nest.

"Good health, gentlemen!" said he, when I had given him his drink, then addressed himself earnestly to Holmes.

"Mr. Holmes, if I hadn't seen you, with these very eyes, shoot that hound on Dartmoor, I'd believe what they're saying about it up Hampstead way."

"Hound? Hampstead? What on earth has either to do with the other?"

Lestrade wagged his head in agreement.

"That's what you or I or the doctor here would ask. What, indeed? It's not what *they're* asking up there tonight."

"Up where? Hampstead? Has something happened there?"

"They're saying the Hound of the Baskervilles has come back."

"*What!*"

"Running free on the Heath, as we sit here."

"Utter piffle!" I exclaimed. Lestrade turned to me, nodding sagely.

"I know it's piffle, Dr. Watson. *You* know it's absurd. *Mr. Holmes* knows. . . . But you try telling that tonight to anyone living next to the Heath—even supposing they'd open their door long enough to give you a hearing."

"Lestrade," Holmes interposed, "are you saying that someone claims to have seen the Hound of the Baskervilles—or rather its ghost, for that is what it would have to be—this evening on Hampstead Heath?"

"Mark my word, Mr. Holmes, tomorrow morning will see a run on every locksmith's in North London."

"There has been nothing in the papers," I pointed out. "Rubbish like that would be certain to get in."

"You may bet Fleet Street is ablaze this very moment, Doctor." He held up a hand dramatically to his ear. "Listen! Isn't that a newsboy calling 'Special!'? No? Well, it soon will be."

"This evening, you say?"

"A couple of hours ago. A strange, eery sort of business, and a nasty—'specially for the poor devil they've got in Hampstead Hospital."

Holmes shifted impatiently.

"What poor devil? For heaven's sake, man, out with the details!"

"I came straight from there to tell you, Mr. Holmes," answered Lestrade reproachfully. "One of the tramps who sleep rough on the Heath got attacked by the beast. If the officer passing on his beat hadn't reached him in time he'd have been a goner."

"Great heavens!" cried I.

"Here's the queerest bit, though, Dr. Watson. In some soft ground just nearby there was—"

"Not . . . !"

"Yes, Doctor. *The footprints of an enormous hound!*"

Within little more than half an hour of hearing Inspector Lestrade's news, we were upon the wild fastness of Hampstead Heath. The undulating expanse of two or three hundred acres of sandy earth, wiry grass, bracken and great ancient trees spreads between the high-up villages of Hampstead and Highgate, constituting London's Northern Heights. A four-mile climb from the levels of the West End necessitated a four-wheeler and two nags. Lestrade directed the police driver to a part near the Spaniards inn and tea gardens, immortalized by Charles Dickens as the scene of Mrs. Bardell's arrest upon Pickwick's suit.

It was quite dark by now, and chilly. It was almost midnight. There was no breeze, and the only sound was the distant stir of the metropolis, tossing like a troubled sleeper. Nothing moved along or beside the Spaniards Road. The Heath had been for centuries the haunt of footpads and highwaymen, among them the ladies' man Claude Duval, Sixteen-string Jack, Robert King and even the notorious Dick Turpin, who was said to have possessed keys to the Spaniards, giving him an escape route through the stables.

Nowadays the Heath was a favourite venue of courting couples (and others not exactly courting). On fine evenings, especially Sundays, it was thronged with servant girls, office clerks, shop assistants, seamstresses, soldiers, sailors and every other type of person thankful for brief escape from weary and monotonous toil. They came by railway, by Underground, by bus and on foot, seeking the only privacy most of them ever got. Sitting or lying on the high slopes, out of reach for a while of acid smoke and unceasing din, they could dream of ultimate escape from that vast, gray, grim prison of their bodies and souls that occupied the river plain below.

Tonight, though, as we got down, there was not a soul to be seen save the uniformed constable who had been looking out for us. His lantern winked its yellow glass eye against the background of looming thickets separating the roadway from the Heath. He was lanky and young and nervous-mannered. He had not been long enough in the force to have acquired the portly complacency of that unique type of being, the London bobby.

"Anything more doing?" Lestrade asked him. I sensed the man's relief at being no longer alone.

"Not sign nor sound, sir."

"No more howling?"

"Thank Heaven, no, sir. It's not half creepy, this, compared to the beat. Be glad to feel me boots on proper streets again."

"Where your boots get sent, you'll go in them," Lestrade reminded him brusquely. "Show the way for Mr. Sherlock Holmes."

"The senior local sergeant, Roberts, is at the spot," Lestrade told us, as we made our way onto the heathland itself. "Out of his uniform, though. There was a little police supper this evening, along the road at Jack Straw's Castle. One of the old North London inspectors, Blenkinsop, retiring. I was there on behalf of the Yard, which is how I came to be on the scene. Some of the tramps from the Heath came bursting into the taproom, full of tales of a hound."

"Had they all seen it?" Holmes asked.

"Hard to tell. You know those sort of people—say anything for a free drink."

"Had *any* of them seen it?" persisted Holmes.

"Some swore they had. Some weren't so sure. We didn't waste time on questions. Roberts and I hurried here."

"The Heath certainly seems deserted," I said. "Extraordinary!"

"That's right, sir," put in the young constable leading us through bush and thicket. "There's usually hordes of 'em sleeping hereabouts, men and women. It's a reg'lar stopping-off place for them as are on the tramp northward, and them coming south."

"Are we to take it that tonight is the first time this so-called hound has put in an appearance?" Holmes asked him, not troubling to hide disbelief.

"First we've heard of, sir. There's plenty of stray dogs out here. They sometimes run in packs and create a bit of bother. The rangers pick a few off, and then the rest seem to know to keep away for a while. I never heard talk of a hound of any sort. Ugh!" he added, indicating revulsion.

"All right!" Lestrade reminded him of his office. "Just get on shining the way."

He himself had shared some dramas with Holmes and me, but never any more horrendous than that one in a lonelier and vaster wilderness than this. None of us would ever forget the wild-eyed onrush of the Hound of the Baskervilles from out of that Dartmoor fog. My description of its appearance as it sprang toward us remained ineradicably word-for-word perfect in my memory. It had seared itself there as I chose the most exact words by which to convey it to my readers, comfortable and secure in their fireside chairs:

A hound it was, an enormous coal-black hound, but not such a hound as mortal eyes have ever seen. Fire burst from its open mouth, its eyes glowed with a smoulder-

*ing glare, its muzzle and hackles and dewlap were
outlined in flickering flame. Never in the delirious
dream of a disordered brain could anything more savage, more appalling, more hellish be conceived than
that dark form and savage face which broke upon us
out of the wall of fog.*

I myself had fired one of the shots that left the Hound of the
Baskervilles dead at our feet. I had examined its corpse. It
proved to be nothing more unnatural than a great hound,
starved to savagery, whose muzzle had been painted with some
substance to present a spectral effect. Still, there was something
chilling about even the remote possibility that anything like it
might be lurking in the hushed, dark uncertainty into which
we were now advancing in an eery silence, broken only by the
occasional snap of a dry twig under our feet.

After we had trekked across coarse wiry grass and between
clumps of sparse undergrowth, we were beckoned to our destination by another lantern's glimmer. It guided us into an area
of deeper grass, under looming trees. A young but burlier uniformed officer awaited us, with a big man in middle age, wearing civilian clothes but every inch a policeman. Lestrade
introduced him as Sergeant Roberts.

"Anything more doing?" Lestrade asked him.

"Nothing, Inspector. I reckon . . . "

Roberts checked himself in mid-speech, cocking his head
to listen. A wailing cry seemed to come from away toward
Highgate, rising and falling mournfully, like the moan of wind
through an ill-fitting window sash.

"That's it!" exlaimed the thicker-set constable, the man
who had evidently been first upon this scene. "That's what I
heard before!"

"Listen!" Lestrade ordered. The sound was repeated twice
more. We stood in silence for some minutes, but did not hear
it again.

I had supposed at first that it was a night bird. I was sure now that it was not; but neither did it resemble any dog's howling that I had ever heard. I could not settle upon a likeness for it. The distant moaning which we had heard upon Dartmoor had been quite different. That had proved to be the death cries of moor ponies, sucked into the depths of the great Grimpen Mire. There were neither deep bogs nor wild ponies upon Hampstead Heath.

Lestrade sounded equally puzzled as he asked the constable, "You're sure that was it?"

"Positive, sir," replied the officer. "Only it was a lot closer before. I mean, it came from here, where we are now, as I was passing along the road."

"Sounded to be over Highgate Ponds way," observed Sergeant Roberts. "Wouldn't be the first time anyone'd drowned in them."

"Never," said Lestrade, with Scotland Yard assurance. "That wasn't the sound of someone drowning—was it, Mr. Holmes?"

He got no reply. Looking round, I found that Holmes, who had been saying very little, had strayed away from us. He must have taken the other constable's lantern silently from his hand. He was casting its rays around where a large old tree's thickly leaved branches had kept the sun from drying a broad belt of grassless earth encircling its gnarled roots.

"That's where he was lying," the constable called across to him.

"So I observe," came the preoccupied reply.

We went over to join Holmes there. The earth was sandy and moist, with many traces impressed in it. I made out boot prints among the blur of smudges and scourings. Then, in the yellow glow, I saw the clear outlines of the biggest paw marks that I had ever seen.

I had not myself seen actual prints made by the Hound of the Baskervilles. I had witnessed, though, what it had done to

the escaped convict Selden, whom it had caught upon the
Moor. What now lay before us astounded and horrified me.
The outlines in the soft clay seemed to me more likely to have
been made by some strange beast than by any breed of dog.

"You're *sure* a dog made those?" I asked him.

"That's what the poor fellow who it attacked says, Doctor,"
answered the inspector.

"You weren't in time to catch sight of it yourself, presumably?" Holmes questioned the constable sharply.

"No, sir," came the firm reply. The heavy-set young officer
looked the reliable type who might relish an excuse for a scrap,
though not necessarily with a gigantic hound. "I was proceeding in an easterly direction along the Spaniards Road on my
beat and heard a man screaming. The drink takes them funny,
or sometimes they get set on by their mates."

"Yes, yes," said Holmes impatiently. "What about the animal's howling? Did you hear that?"

"Yes, sir. Like we heard just now, only closer by."

"What did you make of it?"

"Some of them have dogs that go about with them. I didn't
stop to think much. I went to find out what was going on."

"Did you blow your whistle then?"

"Not at first, sir. I reckoned I could handle a bit of bother
without help."

"Good lad!" put in Lestrade.

Holmes paid no attention. He went on addressing the
constable.

"Everyone but the victim ran away from the Heath, we
gather?"

"Real panic, sir. I shouted to some to stop, and tried to
grab hold of one or two, but I couldn't make them stay. I
thought they'd been in the fight. I'd have chased after them,
only the chap was still screaming, so I thought I should get to
him quick."

"Quite right," approved Lestrade. Holmes ignored him still, giving the constable all his attention.

"The man lay exactly here, I fancy?"

"That's right, sir. He was staggering about when I came upon him. Then he fell down."

"He was alone when you reached him?"

"Why, yes, sir!"

"I thought as much," commented Holmes, to the young officer's surprise. "Just let me look at your boot soles, if you please."

The man lifted his feet in turn. The sergeant shone the light for Holmes to glance at each.

"Thank you. I see from the traces of your boots in the clay that you entered onto the soft ground just over here. You did well not to tramp all over it, as is too often the case. Was the victim able to talk?"

"I didn't bother him for a statement there and then, sir. He could only say that he'd been woken up suddenly to find this great hound all over him, howling and snapping at him. I blew my whistle for help, while I made sure he didn't bleed too much."

"That was the first occasion you used your whistle?"

"Yes, sir."

"It could not have scared off an assailant, then?"

"He was alone when I got to him. The thing must have heard me breaking through the bushes, and run off."

"Ah, to be sure. Was the man bleeding badly?"

"Not so much as I feared, sir. I reckon it might have finished him off if he hadn't turned a shoulder and taken the worst of it."

"Never mind opinions," Lestrade told him. "Always stick to facts. I can answer you, Mr. Holmes. They say at the hospital that it's severe scratches and lacerations to the neck, chest, hands and shoulders. Nothing broken and no muscles torn."

"No bites?" said I.

"Not as such," Lestrade answered.

Holmes was glancing about, shining the lantern this way and that. He asked the constable, "Did he indicate where he had been sleeping?"

"Yes, sir. When they helped him to the ambulance he signalled me to fetch his bundle for him. It was over here, sir."

The young officer led us all to the edge of a wide area of long grass and ferns, some twenty or more paces from where we had been standing. It bore clear indentations in the form of smooth, hollowed-out cocoons, rounded and compressed from use by a nightly succession of tramps and other wanderers through that economical world in which bedding made up by one man serves all subsequent comers.

"That one, sir."

The constable pointed down the yellow beam of light. Holmes swung it around, his eyes darting with it.

"You're quite sure of the spot?" Holmes demanded.

"Positive, sir."

"*Absolutely* sure?" Lestrade pressed him officiously.

"I remember it particularly, sir."

Holmes turned to Lestrade at last.

"In that case," said he loftily, "there is nothing for me to do. The details are straightforward enough. This young officer has given an excellent account of what occurred. All the evidence is here to see. It is also long past midnight. Perhaps we might return to town, Inspector?"

At that he made off swiftly in the direction by which we had come, the beam from his borrowed lantern swinging with his stride.

"But Mr. Holmes . . . !" Lestrade began to protest; then, remembering his dignity in the presence of junior ranks, contented himself with murmuring to Sergeant Roberts that, as the local man, he had better carry on as he saw fit. Lestrade and I hurried after Holmes toward our carriage.

"I must say, Mr. Holmes," panted the inspector when we caught up with him, "I might have expected this business to set you on your mettle. After that Baskerville case I'd think anything with a hound in it would be food and drink to you."

The chilly tone of Holmes's reply, flung over his shoulder without a turn of the head, embarrassed me on behalf of our old Scotland Yard friend.

"On the contrary. I no more cherish the memory of that experience than you do. For Watson, here, of course, it is a different matter."

"I don't know what that is meant to imply, Holmes," said I.

"I refer, of course, to the extravagant impression which your highly coloured narrative of our Dartmoor adventure has clearly made upon gullible minds. A man has only to be set upon by some stray dog for a rumour to begin that the spectre, or reincarnation, of the Hound of the Baskervilles must be responsible. Really, it behooves you authors to take more thought for the consequences of your fancies."

It was my turn to smart under this gratuitous injustice. Holmes's sneering reference to literary fancies was as inaccurate as it was uncalled-for. I had had no recourse to invention. Given the highly dramatic sequence of events, in a setting charged with such brooding menace, I had needed merely to present the facts. Holmes knew it. I saw his jibe as a further sign of his rancour at my earlier news, together, no doubt, with resentment at having been called out unnecessarily and detained long past his bedtime. My best response, I decided, would be silence.

We re-joined the carriage. Lestrade, who was not without his feelings, which must have been bruised by Holmes's scathing reference to "gullible minds," addressed him huffily: "As we'll be passing by the hospital, I thought you might care to step in and see the chap."

Holmes sighed offensively and mounted the carriage step.

"A good idea, Inspector," said I. "I'd like a look at the fellow, and to hear anything he has to say."

Holmes sniffed and settled silently into a corner of the cab.

We were soon rattling along toward Jack Straw's Castle, the highest situated of Hampstead's many public houses, standing on the place where the crowds used to gather to see highwaymen hanged in chains. Its windows were ablaze with light, but outside it was deserted. Even at this hour of the early morning one would have expected to see any number of people there.

"I see what you mean about people keeping off the streets, Lestrade," I said. "There's scarcely a soul to be seen."

"Mr. Holmes may think what he likes," he answered pointedly, "but that story of yours has taken a powerful hold, Doctor. The Heath isn't exactly Dartmoor, but it's a lonely enough place by night. It stands to reason that talk of a hound would scare some folk stiff."

"You reckoned the rumour would be all over North London by now," I reminded him. "Do you really think it could have become so widespread?"

He nodded confidently. "As that bobby said, there would be dozens of homeless folk bedded down there on the Heath. Word runs like wildfire amongst that sort. Good for a free pint or two in any pub, to be first with a tale like that. You bet they were off smartly when they heard what was happening. Jack Straw's had half-emptied by the time Roberts and I left." He laughed out loud. "There'll be talk of whole packs of hounds by now, all over North London. Flaming muzzles, too!"

We soon halted before the small hospital in Heath Street. In his present silent mood it would not have surprised me if Holmes had declined to budge from the carriage and go in with us. However, he did, and we were soon beside the victim's cot in a curtained-off slip ward, where he was the only occupant.

He was much bandaged, but conscious and able to be propped up for us by the attendant. I could see that he was still shaking from shock. He regarded us balefully from between bandages on his forehead, chin and throat. His hands were swathed, too, and one shoulder under the flannel nightshirt was bulky with wadding.

He looked typical of the vagrants who wandered restlessly from town to town, living rough or in parish wards. They sustained themselves by occasional work, while altogether lacking the application or desire to stick to it for long; though, to do them justice, there was precious little of it available to them. They filled in by begging and, in many cases, stealing. They were a perfect nuisance to householders, with their whining stories, backed with truculent demands when refused. The police preferred to turn a blind eye to their petty offenses. Rather than give them a night's free board and lodging in a cell, having to put up with their noisome presence and disagreeable habits, they would boot them across the boundary into another parish, where the same thing happened. Thus, they kept moving to and fro, south and north and back; and Hampstead Heath was one of their pedestrian equivalents of Crewe or Clapham Junction. Their kind is almost extinct now, but they were very numerous at the time of which I write.

From what was visible of the man's features he appeared to me to be in his forties, although emaciation and deeply lined and weatherbeaten skin added to his actual years. His grizzled hair was a clump of spiky tufts, growing afresh after compulsory shaving in some charitable institution. The tattoos on his arms, above the bandaged wrists, were military in theme, making me feel extra compassion for him. His was the too-common lot of the former soldier or sailor who had served his country, only to be jettisoned to fend for himself, on a pittance of discharge money, in a world alien to the disciplined, comradely life he had known. I had myself experienced being alone and unwanted in that uncaring world, with my funds running low and no prospects. My chance introduction to Sherlock Holmes in '81, through an old Bart's Hospital colleague, had saved me. With fresh happiness now before me I could feel for the poor fellow. Given a worse spin, something like his circumstances might have been mine.

"Now, my lad," said Lestrade to him sternly, "just tell these gents again what you say happened up there on the Heath."

The victim regarded the inspector and me suspiciously. Holmes stood behind us, seemingly inclined to hang back, as though determined to dissociate himself from the proceedings.

"It was the 'ound," replied the man at length. He spoke, understandably, with difficulty, his voice weak and croaky from his throat injuries. His accent marked him for a North-countryman. "It coom for me jugular."

"Lucky to be alive, eh?" said Lestrade laconically.

The trembling, bandaged hands were held up.

"Reckon I am, that."

"You did well to fight it off," said I.

"Reg'lar wrestle with it, I had."

"Not to be envied, waking up to an attack like that," I was surprised to hear the apparently disinterested Holmes say. His easy tone brought the slightest of appreciative nods from the man. "You were unlucky that it picked upon you," Holmes added. "And it seems that no one came to your aid."

A resigned shrug was the response.

"Can't blame 'em. I'd ha' run like them if I'd had t'chance. That 'owling! Enough to curdle your blood, it were."

"It was howling as well as attacking you, was it?" asked Holmes with a cluck of sympathy.

"Something 'orrible."

"But it heard that bobby coming, and ran off before he reached you?"

"Must ha' done, sir, or I'd not be here now."

"No," Holmes agreed finally. "You've had a fortunate escape, but you're in good hands now. Good night to you."

I had hoped to see him fish a coin or two from his pocket and place them on the victim's little side-table, but he made no such gesture, only turned on his heel and, without a word of consultation with Lestrade or me, strode out through the door. The inspector and I exchanged glances. There seemed nothing to be done except follow him.

"Somebody from the local nick will come and talk to you in the morning," Lestrade told the man. "We'll leave a full statement until then." He went out after Holmes. I hung back briefly.

"Good luck," said I to the poor fellow, and put down a half sovereign for a fellow-soldier in a bad way. He raised a bandaged hand in a gesture of salute.

"It would be a ghastly experience for anyone to undergo," I remarked as the carriage took us back toward Baker Street, on Lestrade's way to Scotland Yard. "It must surely have been some wild dog."

"The constable was most definite on the howling," said Lestrade. "He's positive as to a hound."

"In that case, he was lucky indeed to survive. You didn't see what the Baskerville hound did to Selden, the convict, Lestrade. Holmes will confirm that he was quite dreadfully mauled. Wasn't he, Holmes?"

Holmes had remained silent from the time we had left the hospital. He slumped in his corner of the vehicle, head back and eyes shut. He did not open them now.

"Do tell your driver to whip up, Lestrade," came from him in a drowsy tone. "I hold you personally responsible for wasting half my night's sleep."

CHAPTER
FIVE

A s Lestrade had predicted, next morning's newspapers were full of reports of "The Hound of Hampstead," as they naturally chose to term it. Their versions differed widely. The single hound was mutiplied to packs, many strong, each roaming its own section of the Heath and prepared to fight to the death against antagonists, animal or human. The rangers who cared for the Heath and enforced its bylaws were reported to be virtual prisoners in their cottages. People whose homes adjoined it were advised to keep doors and windows secured. Outdoor excursions should be confined to busy main streets, and on no account should household pets be allowed out. This led to reports of the disappearance of domestic animals in the vicinity, attributed to the hounds' undiscriminating appetites.

Holmes, who was in distinctly better mood at the breakfast table, laughed aloud at the reports, in particular "eye-witness" sightings of enormous beasts with burning eyes and flaming jowls, and hides impervious to bullets.

"The irresponsibility of journalists, and their readers' capacity for sensational claptrap, complement each other perfectly," he crowed. "The public gets the press it deserves."

"It is all very well for you to mock, Holmes," said I. "I

39

have had three approaches from reporters already, seeking my comparison with the Hound of the Baskervilles situation. One editor has invited me to accompany a photographer to the Heath, to make an exclusive assessment."

"Bravo, my dear fellow!" He positively beamed across the toast rack. "The remuneration will swell your marriage fund significantly."

"On the contrary, Holmes." I was able to confound him for once. "You have invited me to go to Lausanne tomorrow, so I have referred the editor to you in my place. He was dubious about your literary experience, but I suggested that you might give your views to a reporter, who could write them up. I thought that 'The Hound's Revenge' might make a good title."

It gave me the satisfaction of making him splutter into his coffee.

I had reached my decision about Lausanne shortly before this. We had had the telephone installed at Baker Street for a mere matter of weeks. The principal instrument was in Mrs. Hudson's parlour downstairs, attached to the wall beside her door. It was a wooden box contraption, with a small crank handle protruding from one side and the handpiece on top, under a large bell that our worthy landlady declared affected her "like a cat jumping out of its skin" whenever it "went off." She answered all incoming calls, putting some through to the portable instrument in our parlour, where it had its own table beside my chair. In many cases, though, rather than risk losing the connection, she enjoined the caller to wait, while she laboured up to ascertain whether either of us was "at home." Most calls were for Holmes, who was already doubting the desirability of so easy a means of intrusion into his jealously preserved privacy.

No formal etiquette for the telephone's use had been laid down by this early stage. While I should not have dreamed of calling in person at Russell Square before eleven o'clock, the instrument tempted me. I knew that Coral and her aunt were experienced telephonists, so, with an eye on the door for Holmes's entry, I obtained their number. Coral herself answered and declared it was both a delightful surprise and a coincidence to hear my voice. Only moments earlier she had been contemplating telephoning me, but had feared that it might disturb Mr. Holmes at his meditations. I answered that he had not yet even had breakfast, let alone begun cerebrating. After an exchange of endearments and resumed avowals, I mentioned the trip that he had asked me to make.

"Of course, I shall not go," said I. "I had rather spend every minute with you."

"That's sweet of you, John," came the dear voice, "but, you know, you'll have all the time in the world with me soon. You must be a bit pulled down by your wound. Why not go?"

Clearly, I had not fully appreciated the quality of wife I was getting.

"You wouldn't mind?"

"It would do you good. Anyway, Aunt Henry is going to Berkshire tomorrow to stay a few days with distant cousins. I know how much they want to see me, too. I'll tell her I'll come."

"I look forward to the day when I may take you to Switzerland with me," I answered tenderly, and our conversation ended much as it had begun.

"So you have condescended to go," said Holmes, ringing our bell for Mrs. Hudson.

"I couldn't place 'Old Abrahams' in jeopardy," answered I.

When Mrs. Hudson appeared, with a questioning look and a fresh pot of coffee, just in case, Holmes sternly gave her instructions that he was at home to no one, particularly journalists. He was all the more vexed when, no more than five minutes after she had left us, our street bell's distant ring was soon followed by the landlady's reappearance.

"Inspector Lestrade, Mr. Holmes," she announced without apology.

"Mrs. Hudson, I distinctly said—"

"He says it's urgent, sir. Scotland Yard business."

She stepped aside as Lestrade rushed in. He did not pause for apology.

"What do you think, Mr. Holmes?" he cried.

"What I think and what I allow myself to say are not necessarily entirely the same." Holmes scowled from the table. He picked up a newspaper and disappeared behind it.

"How's that, sir? Ah, I see you have the papers in. Didn't I tell you what today's headlines would be? Only there's one item that the mornings didn't get in time."

"What is that, Inspector?" I asked.

"It's about that vagrant from last night, Doctor—well, perhaps I ought to say this morning. Name of Chapman, by the way. Old soldier . . . "

"Royal Mallows," I heard muttered from behind the newspaper. Lestrade blinked in that direction, then went on.

"He's gone. Done a bunk from the hospital. They don't know when he went, being that he was in that little ward alone, and they had left him to sleep. I knew Mr. Holmes would be interested."

The eloquence of Holmes's silence was lost on the inspector. He gave me a perplexed look.

"Holmes has rather a lot on his mind this morning," I explained. "Naturally, half of Fleet Street wants his opinion upon your hound."

"Aha! I might have known. You've formed a theory, then, Mr. Holmes?"

A strangulated exclamation was all the response.

"Ah, well," went on Lestrade blithely, "it's early days yet, and I haven't much to offer, either. I don't say that this Chapman making off so fast has any meaning, but I've always been a believer in passing things on, which is more than might be said of *some* people."

Still Holmes returned no answer. I placed a finger to my lips and ushered the inspector to the door. The newspaper was not lowered even when he was gone. Shortly afterward I took my own hat and cane and crept out, to spend the day with my brand-new fiancée before our first, brief parting.

It was early evening when I came back. Mrs. Hudson's door at the foot of the stairs was ajar. She had been listening for me to come in, and hurried into the hallway to greet me. "Mr. Holmes left a message for you, Doctor. He said that if you can spare the time, you should step round to Marble Arch."

"Marble Arch?"

"You have to be there before seven o'clock, or it would be too late."

It was approaching six already. The traffic was as heavy in Baker Street as was usual at that time of day, but a cab should get me to Hyde Park inside a quarter of an hour.

"Is there some sort of trouble?" I asked our landlady, wondering whether it would be worth going upstairs for my service revolver.

"I'm sure I can't say, sir. There was a note came by hand this afternoon. When Mr. Holmes came in, an hour or so ago, he read it and hurried straight out again."

I decided to dispense with the weapon. I went back into the street and immediately saw a hansom cab letting its occupant down. I was at Marble Arch in precisely fifteen minutes.

The reason for the summons had occurred to me on the way. A few days earlier I had read out to Holmes a newspaper item relating to roadworks about to be undertaken at the junction of Oxford Street, Park Lane and the Edgware Road, close to where the Arch stands. I had drawn his attention to it solely because of the exceptional traffic jams it was certain to cause, but his interest proved superior to that.

"The Deadly Never-Green!" he had surprised me by crying. "The Three-legged Mare. The Triple Tree. Tyburn, Watson! That is the very spot!"

I myself had once read the inscription on the small bronze tablet affixed to the park railings near the place:

> *TYBURN TREE*
> *The triangular stone in the road-*
> *way, sixty-nine feet north of this*
> *point, indicates the site of the an-*
> *cient gallows known as Tyburn*
> *Tree, which was demolished in*
> *1759.*

Holmes had pointed it out to me, risking our limbs, if not our lives, by dragging me into the maelstrom of traffic to look down upon the marker stone itself.

"Perkin Warbeck, Claude Duval, Jack Sheppard, Jonathan Wild, Earl Ferrers, Dr. Dodd!" he had exulted, as we stood there amid the rush and clamour of wheels and hooves and drivers' oaths. "All ended their careers at this very spot."

"And almost Sherlock Holmes and John Watson," I gasped, after bustling back to safety.

His morbid interest in the history of capital punishment naturally embraced the grim annals of Tyburn, to which he had referred me that same evening, with the aid of his vast accumulation of commonplace books. These scrapbooks, which he indexed scrupulously, contained all manner of information, preserved in the form of clippings from newspapers and learned and popular journals, pages torn from books, items of ephemera and notes in his own hand, both cryptic and detailed. It was a large part of his method to view any new case in the light of past occurrences offering points of similarity. He was a firm believer in reserving his brain for reasoning rather than for remembering: "A man should keep his little brain-attic stocked with all the furniture that he is likely to use, and the rest he can put away in the lumber room of his library, where he can get at it if he wants it." The commonplace books were his "lumber room," a formidably comprehensive and unique aide-mémoire.

"See here, Watson," he had said, pointing to a printed transcript. "This copy of Henry III's order in 1220 to the sheriff of Middlesex calls for two good gibbets to be made in the place where the gallows were formerly erected. Those had been known as the 'King's gallows,' because they were used for political offenders."

"Why not the Tower?" said I.

"Royalty and noble traitors only. Execution had its degrees of privilege, as it does still."

"But so far out of the City? It must have been a considerable journey for all concerned."

"In particular, the wretched victim," said Holmes. "It was part of the ordeal. The longer the route, the more the torture of apprehension, the humiliation under the jeers and missiles of the howling rabble. The procession took anything up to three hours. Hence the expression 'to go west'—to be taken westward to Tyburn Tree, sharing the cart with one's coffin, or dragged backward on a hurdle; upon arrival to be burned, hanged, mutilated, drawn and quartered, beheaded . . ."

"Do stop, Holmes!" I had implored. "Great heavens, I wonder that anyone should memorialize such barbarity."

"It is the barbarousness of it which is memorialized," replied he gravely. "We do well to acknowledge the place of so much shame and suffering. Not but"—he sighed—"if public executions were brought back tomorrow, thousands would turn out for them, as they did two and three hundred years ago. The scenes of depravity, drunkenness and violence which accompanied them would surely be repeated. Depend upon it,

Watson, there are deplorable elements in human nature that have only been submerged."

It was this sordid topic which returned to my mind as I travelled again to that place on this July evening. When I had read out to Holmes the news that the roadway was to be dug up, and he had reminded me of the significance of the site, he added eagerly: "This time they will surely get down to the bones."

"Is it an old burial place, too? A plague pit or something?"

"I suppose you might call it that, if you regard many who perished there as having been plagues upon society. It was the custom for those who had relatives or friends to have their remains carried off immediately after execution. It saved them further ignominies, such as being dissected by students. (You recall how difficult it was at Bart's to get hold of complete specimens, even in your time?) Some optimists, indeed, had surgeons standing by to attempt resuscitation—or resurrection, as it was called—after hanging. There are recorded instances of success."

"You don't say!"

"Hangmen were not experts. Anyone could volunteer, for the fee of a few pence and such perquisites as the wretched victim's clothes, not to mention the hope of a bribe to make a botch of it to give the resurrectionists a chance."

"Did the authorities *let* them?" I asked.

"They did not always trouble to notice. The executioner was liable to find himself in trouble if caught, though. The remains of those who were not rescued, or had no family or friends to claim their corpses, were simply thrown into a pit under the gibbet itself. The old principle, you know, of burying malefactors at crossroads. Some of their bones came to light forty or fifty years ago during works in Connaught Place. The chief body of the remains, for want of a happier term, has never been uncovered. I fancy we shall have them this time."

"You sound as though you have an interest in them, Holmes."

"You know my compelling curiosity, Watson. Mortality is the greatest mystery of all. My life's work has been to deal with scoundrels. I have been responsible for sending a few to the gallows, though never, I am happy to say, to a punishment so fearful as Tyburn's. I have never exulted over their fate. I have acted as society's agent, not its prosecutor or judge. There have been times when I have questioned privately its right to take away life, for whatever reason.

"Occasionally, though, in the dark hours, I have pictured the ranks of the executed, waiting silently upon the far shore as the ferry carries me near. In nightmare, I have scanned their wasted faces for some indication of what to expect from them. Forgiveness? Understanding? Or some horrible retribution? '*Exoriare aliquis nostris ex ossibus ultor*: Arise, avenger, from out my bones.' The notion of Virgil at Marble Arch may be a trifle farfetched; but if those bones are revealed, I must see them. They represent the mortal relics of that court of tormented souls before which it might prove my ultimate lot to conduct my defence."

In consequence of this sombre notion, he had sent a note to an old acquaintance, the inspector in charge of the police post that is housed high up inside Marble Arch itself. He begged the favour of instant word if the Tyburn remains should come to light. It was from this obliging official that the summons had come to 221B Baker Street this afternoon.

I expected to find crowds at the place. However, the roadworks congestion was so great that the constabulary were moving everyone on. My cabby was waved away, but Holmes's high-pitched "Holloa!" from nearby, and the sight of him and the uniformed inspector gesturing approval, was enough to satisfy the officer into letting me get down.

A low tarpaulin wall and roof hid the excavation. Notices

prohibited pedestrians from coming near. Holmes and the inspector were standing just within the enclosure, which I entered through a gap in the canvas. Workmen were passing in
and out with barrows of earth, cobblestones, tarry wood
blocks, and other roadbuilding materials. There was a reek of
clay and sewage, and some more objectionable smell. I took
out my handkerchief, ready to hold it over my nostrils.

"My dear Watson!" Holmes greeted me. His eyes shone
with that almost boyish excitement which he made no effort to
suppress when something novel and intriguing had come his
way. "You have not met Inspector Arkwright, in charge of the
Marble Arch office?"

The officer stepped forward with a salute and a handshake. He was one of that massive build of London bobby, less
often encountered up west than down the City way and in the
East End.

"Pleased to make your acquaintance, Doctor." He grinned
through black whiskers as he reduced my hand in a ferocious
grip. "Seems like your hound's come back to roost among us,
in a manner of speaking."

I wondered for a moment whether there had occurred yet
another manifestation of it, here in Hyde Park, but I saw that
it had been merely the inspector's notion of pleasantry.

"So glad you got my message, Watson," said Holmes. "I
was not at all sure how long your, er, business might be likely
to keep you from home. Since you are off abroad tomorrow,
now is your only chance to see what has come to light."

"You mean those bones, I suppose?"

Holmes nodded. "We are indebted to Inspector Arkwright
for an unique glimpse into the past. Come along."

He strode off into the workings, the inspector stepping
aside to let me follow. It was a curious sensation, walking
through this vast, low-ceilinged tent whose pitch was one of
the busiest and best-known confluences of people and traffic
in all the world. The entire road surface had been removed and

was being prepared for re-laying. Dozens of men were at work, hacking, picking, shovelling, hoisting and wheeling, perspiring copiously from the effort in such stuffy confines.

"We had to order the screens to go up because of the bones," said the inspector behind me. "Wouldn't do to have every Tom and Jack coming to stare. But it makes it even harder for these poor chaps, so they've been offered extra pay to carry on through the night."

"I was told that seven o'clock was the latest time," said I.

"For any visitors, that is, sir. No reporters. No photographers. Naturally, we have to allow access to a few scholars and genuinely interested parties, like Mr. Sherlock Holmes and your good self. Lord Belmont's here now. He's with Dr. Garside, who's in charge. But there has to be a limit to who's let in. There will be one last viewing, for an hour first thing tomorrow, then the remains will be covered in again."

"By the by, Watson," put in Holmes aside, "if Garside seems a little snappish, pay no attention. He was rather put out at the inspector having asked me along without consulting him, and more so when I admitted to having left a note for you to join me."

We advanced to the excavation, an area some thirty feet along each of its sides, dug to greater depth than the rest of the workings. A pungent reek of freshly scattered lime invaded my nostrils, even through my handkerchief, and the general atmosphere was far from agreeable. I had read of the miasma given off by some excavated burials, and of horrible infection being transmitted after many years. There was evidently little such danger here, however, for three men, one elderly and two young, in shirtsleeves and bareheaded, were down there, wading among the very bones. They seemed to be sorting through them in the way that a team of ragpickers might go through the latest consignment. Their only concession to the effluvium was handkerchiefs bound over their nostrils and mouths.

The bones lay, jumbled and broken, where the dismembered corpses had been cast contemptuously in the good old days of two centuries past. Time and pressure had tangled them together. Apart from skulls and rib cages there was little at first glance to distinguish the remains as human. It was an appalling spectacle.

"Ah, Mr. Holmes. This will be the eminent Dr. Watson?"

The greeting came from the oldest of the men in the pit itself. He was so pale and thin that he resembled a bundle of bones himself, albeit one which had somehow been ignited at the top into a red glow. He had dragged the protective cover from his face, to hang down upon the full red beard reaching to his breast. Burning bushes of side-whiskers hid his ears, but his high-domed head was only sparsely vegetated with straggling wisps. What little face showed through the underbrush was earnest and peering, with intense eyes magnified by thick lenses.

"Dr. Garside, of the British Museum," introduced Holmes.

"Dr. Watson, Lord Belmont," introduced the scholar in turn, bowing toward another man, in frock coat and top hat, who was leaning on his cane at one side of the pit, looking down into it with a thoughtful expression. His face was thin, with sardonic dark features. I could tell that he was above average height, in his early forties, making allowance for the aging effect of a thick black moustache, curled upward at its ends. He nodded silent and unsmiling acknowledgement of my bow.

Dr. Garside reclaimed my attention.

"I am your devoted reader, Dr. Watson," said he, though with noticeable absence of the warmth that goes with sincere compliments.

"I'm flattered to hear it, Doctor," said I. "You are here in your capacity as an anthropologist?"

He shook his narrow head. "Historian. The history of London is my field. Someday, depend upon it, this great city shall

have a museum of its own, devoted solely to it, and long over-
due. If only the authorities would make over one fraction of
the funds which they squander every year on useless pageantry
and passing show, here one day, gone the next, our people
would have greater cause to thank the example of more enlightened spirits, such as my patron, Lord Belmont."

He bowed to his lordship, and I followed suit again. He
did not respond. His whole attention was upon the workers
among the bones.

Dr. Garside continued; his manner was as brittle as his
appearance.

"His lordship has come forward with a munificent offer to
inaugurate the foundation of the great museum which I envisage. It has not yet been announced publicly, you understand. I
must request you not to write of it, Dr. Watson."

"No, no," promised I, secretly gratified to be considered a
journalist of influence.

"It is to be hoped that his lordship's gesture will stir up
support in high places," he added, as if providing me with a
printable quote for later use. "Though what one can expect,
with a monarch preoccupied with horses and women . . . ! A
fine inspiration to national pride, indeed . . . ! But that is outside the record, of course."

"Is there to be a coroner's inquest on these remains?" I
asked the inspector, by way of deflecting a potentially embarrassing topic.

"No need, sir. They are here in consequence of due legal
processes. There is nothing mysterious to be inquired into."

"But a nice little historical mystery, for all that, eh,
Doctor?" Holmes addressed Garside, whose eyes gleamed
knowingly.

"Ah yes, Mr. Holmes—such an opportunity to solve it!"

"My friend Watson is the soul of discretion," said Holmes.
"While some results of his publishings may prove unfortunate

—I refer to this present absurd outcry about phantom hounds at Hampstead . . . "

Inspector Arkwright chuckled. The historian's blank look showed him to be one of those beings whose souls do not loiter in the wilds of sensational journalism.

" . . . Nevertheless," Holmes continued, "he is noted for his ability to turn a Nelsonian eye to details which were better left unreported."

"Holmes," I demanded, "what exactly is that supposed to mean?"

"Merely, my dear Watson, that your scrupulosity and good taste would not allow you to include in your narratives anything which you might, with good reason, be requested to leave out."

"I hope I can recognize the difference between the public interest and sensationalism for its own sake."

"You see?" Holmes turned again to Garside. "Although, as Dr. Johnson said of Goldsmith, 'that which he sets out to write as Natural History he inevitably transforms into a Persian tale.' Watson is fully to be trusted with the real reason for your present quest."

"Please come down, then," invited Garside, seeming satisfied that I was not proposing to go hotfoot to the *Daily Mail*. He reached up to give me a hand into the pit. Holmes followed. The brooding nobleman and the policeman remained at their separate places outside. I did not blame them, and pressed my handkerchief to my face.

Dr. Garside addressed me in muffled tone, gesturing with his arms.

"The gibbet itself was a three-sided structure, an equilateral triangle of beams, twelve feet from the ground, each with space to hang eight. After being hanged, they were all left suspended until space was needed for more. Traitors, however, were cut down alive, disembowelled and finally hacked into

five parts—head and four quarters. The heads and other por-
tions were displayed on poles on London Bridge and other
places where most people would see them and remember their
place under the crown."

"You don't say that women were treated in this awful way,
too?" exclaimed I.

"Even some children," he answered to my horror. "A certain ghoulish decorum prevailed in the case of the gentler sex.
They were burned alive."

"Great Heavens!"

"At least some effort was usually made to strangle them to
death before the flames reached them. You can distinguish the
female remains from the rest by the charring."

I glanced around, and recognized what he meant. A chill
seemed to pervade the place, in spite of the summer heat on
the tarpaulin roof. The swirling traffic's din was transformed
into the roaring of a mob as bloodthirsty as any that made the
Paris guillotine a notorious emblem of mass hysteria in less-
distant years. Even as a medical man who had witnessed
slaughter in Afghanistan, I could not remain dispassionate
toward these victims of judicial execution, whatever their
crimes had been. I would have liked to leave the place, but for
curiosity over Holmes's banter about some historical secret
which I might just be trusted to share.

"Is there anything especially interesting to study here?" I
asked Garside.

"History, Watson. History," murmured Holmes senten-
tiously. He went wandering off, deep among the bones, to
where the younger men appeared to be studying them closely.
Ths historian glanced up at Lord Belmont, who still appeared
to be paying us no attention, before returning a tactful reply.

"Of course, Doctor, you recall the story of Oliver Cromwell and his generals?" Seeing me hesitate, he went on.

"Cromwell died in 1658—as you know. After his embalmed body had lain in state at Somerset House for a month, he was given a most lavish funeral in Westminster Abbey."

"I remember now!" said I, recalling a passage read long ago. "That was the one which John Evelyn said was 'the joyfullest funeral that ever I saw, for there were none that cried but dogs.' I don't mind saying," I added, "it is hardly surprising. Cromwell was a killjoy humbug and a menace to the British way of life."

Garside returned me the disapproving look of an academic man who is not given to generalizations.

"We-ll, I suppose that was the way some looked at it. As a race, the English have never been strong for rectitude."

"Especially not for having it rammed down our gullets," said I. "Nor for having our cathedrals and churches pillaged, property confiscated, the theatres all closed down; not to mention our crowned monarchs executed."

"Whatever their failings," Dr. Garside amended. "Good heavens, though! I'm forgetting myself. Time is precious!"

With what I took to be an apologetic glance up toward his patron he hurried away, as best a man can hurry through thickets of human bones.

"Now do you remember, Watson?" asked Holmes, who had come up on the other side of me.

"Remember what, Holmes?"

"Dear me! I have always understood you to have undergone a satisfactory, if not remarkable, education."

"What, exactly, is the point you are making so elaborately?"

"One of the very few things which every schoolboy is said to know is what happened to Oliver Cromwell after the monarchy was restored in 1660."

"I'm sorry if you consider me lacking in elementary knowledge, Holmes," I answered. "You yourself surprised me once by expressing disinterest in the workings of the Solar

System, because it was of no practical value in your profession. I, for my part, have conducted a full and fairly active life without being aware of any disadvantage from not knowing what happened to Oliver Cromwell. By the way, considering that he died a couple of years *before* the monarchy was restored, what did happen to him?"

"Why," replied Holmes simply, "they dug him up and hanged him—here at Tyburn."

As soon as Holmes reminded me of Oliver Cromwell's posthumous fate, I recalled learning it as a boy. My flesh had crept upon picturing that unrelenting revenge which Charles II had taken upon all who had been associated in any way with his father's execution in 1649. Men and women were imprisoned, dispossessed of money and estates, banished, sent to the block or gibbet. Even the carpenters who had made the scaffold on which Charles I had been beheaded were hunted down to pay the penalty. The most grisly retribution of all was that performed upon Oliver Cromwell, Henry Ireton, his principal general and one of the signatories of Charles I's death warrant, and John Bradshaw, who, as president of the High Court of Justice, had pronounced the old King's death sentence.

All had died from natural causes in the years between. In January 1661, Cromwell's and Ireton's graves in Westminster Abbey were reopened for a mock lying-in-state. Huge crowds were encouraged to file past, paying sixpence each to spit and jeer. After two days, the shrouded corpses were taken to the Red Lion Inn at Holborn, where they were joined by that of Bradshaw, brought in a cart from St. Peter's, Westminster.

The macabre final act was played on January 30, the anniversary of Charles I's execution day. The three bodies were drawn on sleds to Tyburn and hanged in green waxed shrouds, one from each of the gibbet's three angles.

"Great Heavens!" I remembered. "They beheaded them as well!"

Holmes nodded. "After sundown, when they were cut down. Then the heads were impaled on the roof of Westminster Hall. They were left there throughout the rest of Charles's reign. What ultimately became of them has been a mystery ever since."

The realization that we were standing at the very scene of the beheadings added nothing to my comfort.

"Is that what Garside is after? He can't hope to identify three skulls in a charnel house such as this."

"Not the skulls. They are almost certainly not here. The headless skeletons, though, are recorded as having been thrown into the common pit under the gibbet."

"Ugh! Does it matter to anyone?"

"An historian must feel it satisfying to discover tangible evidence of that which he has only been able to study from documents. Look at it this way, my dear Watson. The world has only your word for it that those events on Dartmoor concerning the Hound of the Baskervilles really occurred. You alone are the recorder of Stapleton's villainous use of it, and his own drowning in the Grimpen Mire. Suppose you had been less positive in presenting the facts, and had given an incomplete description of his end?"

I smiled. "The newspapers would not only be speculating about that poor hound's spirit taking some sort of revenge; they would be saying that Stapleton is behind it!!"

"Precisely. See what a burden of responsibility you have taken upon yourself? Had Dr. John H. Watson had his notebook upon the scene of the disposal of the little princes in the

Tower, the guilt or innocence of Richard III would have been beyond question. Yet, as with the Hound, there will always be fresh generations of Garsides and his kind, for whom the word of the chroniclers is not enough."

"Well, if he doesn't find what he is looking for by tomorrow morning it seems he will have to put up with his uncertainties. I don't see the authorities leaving Marble Arch in chaos for the sake of the late Oliver Cromwell."

We gazed about that vast tangle of ribs, limbs and skulls.

"Not," I added, "that it should be difficult to distinguish Cromwell and his companions from the rest."

Holmes turned to me sharply.

"How do you mean, Watson?"

"Unless it was common practice to behead corpses that had been several years dead already . . . "

"To my knowledge, this was the only instance."

"Then there will be three skeletons differing from all the rest."

"Because they're headless? My dear Watson, see for yourself how many are in that incomplete state."

"Only because their skulls have become detached with the passage of time. When those three were cut down and beheaded in that disgusting fashion, I very much doubt that the headsman was any more a professional than the degraded wretch who had hanged them."

"The same man, in all probability."

"Exactly, Holmes; and no doubt he used any axe or sword that happened to be handy. Blunt, most likely. He was probably half drunk into the bargain. From what you and Garside say, the crowd probably encouraged him to make a thoroughly ghoulish spectacle of it. That, and the dryness of the old bones, which would make them splinter under his hacking, would certainly show in the condition of the skeletons."

Something like respect gleamed in Sherlock Holmes's keen eyes.

"My dear chap, I have had occasion once or twice in the past to remark that your limits are beyond my grasp. I can only add that they remain so. Come along!"

Following his eager example, I began to search among the bones. It was a grotesque and nauseating task, made more so by the presence of decayed rags of clothing, withered leather belts, buttons and other valueless relics that survived. Bones in themselves were nothing out of the way to me as a medical man, although the sheer quantity of them boggled my mind. It was the pathetic remnants of dress which reminded me more potently that these had once been living people. Many of their misdeeds would have been far less drastically punished in more enlightened times. Some had no doubt been innocent of any crime at all.

We had no time for niceties, however. We worked with growing haste, carelessly tossing aside rib cages and limbs and vertebrae in our efforts to get at others beneath them.

The three-quarters had just sounded from distant Big Ben when I saw with a thrill that a headless trunk I had just uncovered bore jagged indentations in clavicle and sternum. They were split and cracked. At my cry, Holmes moved swiftly to join me, calling out to the others. Dr. Garside and his two assistants hastened to us. Inspector Arkwright lowered himself with dignity into the pit.

"Could it be!" exclaimed the historian, when I pointed out the evidence of inexpert decapitation. "If the two others are near it your point would seem to be proved, Doctor."

The younger men impatiently rummaged among the adjacent bones. A movement above caught my eye, I saw that the hitherto taciturn Lord Belmont had come round to the side of the pit where I had made the discovery. He made no move to enter it, but craned down to look, supporting his hands on his black-trousered thighs.

"Do you intend taking them away?" I asked Dr. Garside, as we watched the assistants excitedly picking up bones.

He shook his head. "It had been made clear that it would not be permitted. It is not what the Museum would desire, in any case. If only my own museum were already in being."

An excited exclamation told us that another find had been made.

"Quickly!" urged Garside. He turned to the inspector. "Perhaps an extra half hour, in the circumstances . . . "

Arkwright shook his head. "I'm sorry, sir. My orders are strict. To get the road done overnight the workmen must have free access to the whole site."

"I thought there was to be a final viewing tomorrow morning?" said I.

"For one hour only, sir. Just a few high-ups. The Home Secretary may be looking in, and perhaps the Archbishop. If they'd been able to get along this evening, that would have been the end of it. As it is, this lot will have to be boarded over pro tem."

"The old story," Garside lamented. "History must defer to progress. One might wish that, after more than two centuries, a few little hours could be spared. Ah! This appears to be something!"

The men had been unashamedly hurling bones aside to make the most of their last minutes of searching time. A further mutilated trunk was coming to light. It was dragged to the surface.

"Well, sir, that seems to be two of 'em for you," said the inspector consolingly. "I don't suppose the third one would be all that much different to look at."

"Perhaps not," murmured the historian, now on his knees to peer at the bones and run his fingers along the jagged clavicle and sternum. "It would at least be something to have seen all three together, though. I believe that scholars would accept it as proof positive."

"If I am not mistaken, you are about to be granted your wish," said Holmes over his shoulder.

His tone proclaimed his own excitement. The assistants were prising out a third skeleton. It was headless, too, and the upper bones showed that same disfigurement.

"*Eureka!*" cried Dr. Garside. His helpers grinned with mighty pleasure. A thin pattering sound proved to be Lord Belmont clapping politely. He went so far as to raise his hat.

Garside beamed around at us all. "My lord," he declared, "gentlemen, we are the first men for more than two hundred and forty years to set eyes on the remains of one of the most significant figures in British history! I, personally, find the privilege deeply stirring."

"I beg pardon, sir." It was Inspector Arkwright who interrupted him. "Which one of them might be which?"

Garside peered at him, then blinked, as though needing to pluck himself back to reality from a centuries-long flight of fancy.

"As I said," apologized the policeman, "they are much of a muchness."

Whether my perceptions had been whetted lately by that reinvigoration which romance can bring I do not know, but it seemed to be my rare day for surpassing Sherlock Holmes at his own game. I indicated the last of the skeletons to have been retrieved. I felt all eyes upon me as I stepped forward and knelt where those particular bones had lain, a few feet apart from the other two sets.

"This was Oliver Cromwell," said I.

Something had caught my eye which my companions, in their preoccupation with the headless skeletons, had not noticed. It looked like a narrow strip of wood or metal. Seen from closer to, it was undoubtedly the latter. I saw another like it lying nearby. The difference between them was that while the first of them was slightly curved and came to a point at one end, the second terminated in the hilt and pommel of a sword.

I picked up the two pieces and held them end to end for the others to see. They were the two rusted halves of an old-fashioned cavalry sabre. The hilt had a rag of faded cloth still hanging from it.

"Bravo, Watson!" exulted Holmes.

Dr. Garside uttered an excited chortle as I passed the heavy remnants into his hands.

"Not a doubt of it!" cried he. "We know that Cromwell's sword was buried with him in his coffin in the Abbey. What became of it after his exhumation and posthumous 'execution' is nowhere recorded. It was presumed carried off as a trophy and lost to all knowledge."

Holmes, who had been looking over the historian's shoulder at the pieces, pointed out where they had been joined originally in one piece.

"It has been filed across. The indications are quite plain."

"What does that tell us, Mr. Holmes?" asked the police inspector.

"The blade was weakened beforehand. Remember Dreyfus?"

Although more than seven years had passed since those events in Paris in 1895, they were familiar to us all. The firing squad itself could not have given a worse ordeal to the French officer convicted of espionage than that public humiliation: the contemptuous square of five thousand soldiers; the ministers and diplomatists and their fashionably dressed wives; the jeering public beyond the War College parade ground walls; the sudden rolling of drums which prefaced the march of the prisoner and escort; the general officer's chilling proclamation, "Alfred Dreyfus, in the name of the people of France, we degrade you!"; and then the ripping away of Dreyfus's uniform insignia by a gigantic sergeant of the Republican Guard, who also took his sword from him and snapped its blade like a twig across an upraised thigh.*

I had wondered how this latter could be managed by even the strongest of men without damaging himself more than the blade, until I read that it would have been weakened in readiness by filing. Obviously, there was ancient precedent for such an insulting gesture. Someone had gone to the trouble of making it part of the gruesome degradation of the remains of the Lord Protector of England.

Dr. Garside looked up at the intent Lord Belmont, as if appealing to him to intervene. There came no flicker of response. Garside turned anxiously to the inspector instead.

"Surely the Museum may have this, at least? Cromwell's sword of state is preserved already, but this is something quite special. It is undoubtedly his fighting sword."

What was left of my boyhood's blood thrilled upon hearing this. I took back the two parts of the blade from him and examined them keenly. Although I abominated the memory of Oliver Cromwell as dictator over the British people and despoiler of much of our ancient national heritage as self-appointed representative of the Almighty, I had to respect him as soldier, creator of the New Model Army and brave fighting general. Holding his shattered sword, perhaps the very one he had wielded at the head of that downhill charge upon Prince Rupert of the Rhine at Marston Moor, I became oblivious to the conversation around me. My ears filled with the thunder of hooves, the scream of trumpets, shouts of command, clash of sword upon sword, bursts of artillery and musket fire, the

---

* The reader who is curious for the details of the part that Holmes and I played in this sensational case will find them in the published account entitled *Prisoner of the Devil*. —J.H.W.

frantic neighing of plunging horses, the shrieks of men in fury and pain . . .

"Ahem, Watson!"

I was jerked to consciousness by Holmes's cough. I blinked my eyes, and was in 1902 again.

"Arkwright reminds me that it is time we were taking ourselves off."

"I'm afraid so, Doctor," confirmed the inspector. "Just be kind enough, please, to lay the sword back where you picked it up from."

"It's not going to the Museum, then?"

"I shall be making a strong plea for it," Dr. Garside answered for him. "I hope to persuade the Home Secretary in the morning. Meanwhile, it and the remains must be replaced exactly as they were."

With great reluctance I put back the two halves of Cromwell's sword beneath the skeleton where I had found them—a skeleton that must certainly have been his. I had been privileged to discover the historic relic and hold it for a few moments. Tomorrow it would be reburied, perhaps for ever.

"Do you suppose they will let Garside have it?" I asked Holmes, as we made our way back to Baker Street by hansom cab.

"If they have any sense at all, they certainly will not," he answered, to my surprise.

"What makes you say that?"

"Relics possessing emotive powers, like certain fabled jewels, are dangerous things to dangle before the public gaze. Passions of one kind or another are likely to be roused."

"Passions in the British Museum!"

"There, or the Tower of London, or anywhere else. You recall the Countess of Morcar's stolen blue carbuncle, in the little investigation involving the Christmas goose?"

"How could I forget it? I wrote it up under that very title
—*The Blue Carbuncle*."

"Then you recollect my term for treasures of that kind:
'the devil's pet baits; a nucleus and focus of crime.' Greed,
Watson, envy, covetousness, acquisitiveness. If a mere bauble
can stir such base instincts, what must be the power of an
object associated intimately with a man who once usurped the
rulership of this nation? The man who executed a King of
England and overthrew the royal house of Stuart?"

"That was over two centuries ago. What sort of passions
would Oliver Cromwell's remains rouse in 1902?"

"Revolutionary ones, perhaps?" suggested he mildly.

I glanced out of the cab window. We were entering Baker
Street from Portman Square. Respectable-looking couples were
strolling arm-in-arm on their way to the park to listen to the
band, or perhaps as far as the Serpentine, to join the line for a
boat. A housemaid in her trim black and white was walking an
immaculately clipped little dog. Down a side road, an Italian
ice-cream-seller's cart was surrounded by bareheaded children,
cheerfully waiting their turn. One of his compatriots was playing a barrel organ nearby. His scarlet-uniformed monkey was
parading on top of the instrument like a midget soldier, holding out his tin can for pennies. Children gathered about, laughing and clapping, and two little girls twirled together in a dance
to the jangling music.

We had had a glimpse or two during the South African
war of the British populace in its rare state of frenzy. I could
recognize no portents of trouble now.

"You sense something?" inquired Holmes, reading my
mind.

"I can't say I do, Holmes. A few poor folk were put out
over missing their Coronation dinners, if you count that. They
will have them soon enough and have to look for something
else to grumble about. It is a British trait."

"Then you would rule incipient revolution quite out of the question?"

What I took to be a mock-serious expression made me chuckle. Such a notion could only be a joke.

The Coronation was at the forefront of all our minds. It seemed to mark our handing on from the protection of the good but remote mother into what felt like coequal partnership with her pleasure-loving son. The disappointment of the departed foreign dignitaries can have been nothing compared to ours at the sudden news that it was all off.

Although nearing his sixtieth year when he attained the throne, Edward was a bluff, hearty man of the world. He got on with commoners and foreigners to a degree unmatched by haughty statesmen and ministers. One could well imagine their hoping that he might not begin to meddle in national affairs, but remain the playboy that he had always been. At the same time, there were prim folk who deplored his frivolity and morals. Some of his best friends were sportsmen, theatricals (chiefly female) and business magnates, whose great wealth and sophistication lent them a sinister mystery in ordinary people's eyes.

Of the rest of us, few but the stuffiest grudged the King his idiosyncratic friendships and his indulgences in the spheres of the dining room, the turf and the boudoir. We rather envied him. We trusted him like some favourite though slightly outrageous uncle, who would know what to do should anything serious come up and would see us safely through it.

As I have previously described, Edward's appendicitis proved too chronic for his courage. He was operated upon in Buckingham Palace and began to recover at once. He went on smoking his cigars and resumed his gargantuan eating, with a leeway of six inches off his Falstaffian girth. Revolution, I innocently presumed, was the furthest subject from his mind.

Meanwhile, the eminent visitors had left our shores, bearing with them yet another cause to resent the perfidious British, some of whom benefited unexpectedly. The royal kitchens, presided over by the royal chef, had prepared huge quantities of dishes for the official banquets. These could no longer take place. The food had to be cooked or wasted. The former was ordered, and the classic dishes, fragrant with delicate sauces, were taken to London's East End slums for distribution to the poor.

"Cor, Charlie," I could imagine the Cockney exclaim to his neighbour, "I don't 'arf go fer this *Poularde aux perles du Périgord!*"

"Nah, Bert. Too bland. You oughter cop a dollop o' the *Côtelettes de bécassines à la Souvaroff*. Beats boiled beef and carrots any day."

Throughout the land, thousands of arrangements had to be unarranged, at huge inconvenience and cost. There was anger in some places. Poor people, whose highest expectation had been of a free dinner and a mug of ale, saw parish officials selling off the victuals to those who could better afford them. There were rebellious protests. In one place there was stone-throwing, window-smashing and attempted looting, causing a battle with police. It made disturbing reading, being quite against our national temperament, and reminded me of Holmes's conjecture on the subject of revolution.

It was the end of the topic for the time being. We soon reached 221B and thankfully cleansed ourselves of the blended effluvia of lime, calcium and decay. Established in our sitting-room, Holmes fell as avidly as I upon the Geisenhemer '84 that I took from the wine cooler beneath our sideboard and animated in our glasses with a splash of seltzer. We sipped and sprawled in silence, awaiting our dinner hour in shirtsleeves and slippers, with the latest editions of the evening newspapers to occupy us before going to our rooms to change, as our ritual of respect for Mrs. Hudson's cooking.

The hound rumours were still flying, I read. There were unconfirmed reports of fresh sightings in the other Northern Heights village of Highgate. One leading article asked fiercely what the police proposed to do about the peril to local residents.

The finding of bones on the site of Tyburn was touched upon in all the papers, but only briefly. There was an official statement that they were not on public view and would be covered over in the course of the night's work. There was no mention of Oliver Cromwell.

The better to enjoy our meal, I had managed to put the thrilling yet still distasteful experience out of my mind. It kept returning afterward, though, as we took our post-prandial ease. In one of his unpredictable gestures, Holmes had produced a bottle of Hunt Roope's fine '85 vintage port, which he must have decanted clandestinely early in the day. We had exchanged shoes for slippers again, and sat with our feet upon the fender, extended toward our low fire, sipping the wine and smoking Juan López Reina Victorias. Holmes had favoured his purple dressing gown as a change from the mouse-coloured one. I had on my maroon smoking jacket with the black lapels, which made lighter summer wearing than the quilted one with velvet facings. The scene could not have contrasted more with that at the site of Tyburn, or with any notion of unrest, national or otherwise. Yet my thoughts amid our slippered tranquillity would stray back to what Holmes had said in the cab.

"Holmes," I found myself forced to say at length, "you were pulling my leg, weren't you? About some sort of revolution, I mean."

"I'm afraid I was not," replied he, quite seriously.

"*Here*? In *England*?"

Admittedly, I had spent the past several weeks largely sightseeing and squiring ladies. Perhaps I had not been paying attention to the greater issues of the day. Still, if there had been any talk of national upheaval, in the newspapers or elsewhere, I must have noticed something.

"I do not believe I exaggerate," answered Holmes, "if I say that the country is probably closer to open revolution than it has been since the time of the men whose bones we examined this afternoon. It might require no more than an incident to spark off a train of consequences like a fuse leading to a gunpowder keg."

"Not a postponed Coronation bunfight or two!"

Holmes shook his head. "Of course not. But those little disorders are symptomatic of a graver one. They are warnings that people are not prepared to wait much longer. To change the metaphor, they show us the impatient audience pelting the curtain."

" 'The British Revolution'? It sounds half theatrical itself. Whoever could be involved in such a production?"

"We all are in some way. We are not playing Victorians now. Our role is Edwardian. We have moved on from the nineteenth century to the twentieth. That old truce that we observed while Victoria still lived is ended. The lines of battle are re-manned."

"Truce? Lines of battle? We are into a military scene now, are we? I confess you have quite lost me, Holmes."

"I refer to the unspoken agreement between our dear old Queen's loyal subjects to do nothing that would tarnish the record of her glorious reign. The resumed battle is that same class war that provided motives for Cromwell, Pym, Hampden and their kind, and won half the nation to their support."

"And a great deal of good it did them!"

"I respect your royalist sympathies, Watson. They are part of your essential nature. All the same, the unhappy fate of Charles I was of his own causing. It was the culmination of years of indecision and disregard for the misery and hopes of ordinary folk. So was the French Revolution. It needed only

the running-over of a child by an aristocrat's carriage to make despair change into rebellion and violence."

"Thank heaven we have not the temperament of the French! Any British nobleman would have stopped his carriage and got down to tend the child."

"Or told his coachman to get down. There is a deal of difference. There is a new swell of feeling against everything that divides those who give orders and those who have to obey them."

"Then the remedy lies in Parliament. I suppose that is one thing to Cromwell's credit. He made it possible for any Tom and Dick to get a hearing."

"Quite right, Watson. Today's Tom and Dick are a new breed, though. While the old political antagonists conduct their conventional warfare from entrenched positions, it is the new ones who scheme to take the citadel by the back door."

"Hell-bent on wrecking and plundering!" said I. "It's easy enough for someone to destroy old values and convince people that everything they have been brought up to is a bad mistake. The question is, what takes its place?"

"Come, Watson, you must admit that there is much needing changing. You are a doctor. How many thousands must die of cholera and typhoid, not to mention hunger and sheer misery, before something is done for them?"

"Of course I admit it, Holmes. I agree with you wholeheartedly on that."

I needed no convincing. Fellow medical men who had served on recruiting boards during the war had told me what proportion of men examined for the volunteers were totally unfit to serve.

"Fifty percent," one doctor had said, shaking his head. "Malnutrition and associated disease. If this is our young manhood, Heaven help us!"

"All the same, Holmes," I added, "with the best will in the world, things cannot be changed overnight."

"Revolution could change them," he reminded me, "or so its proponents would lead people to believe."

"And you think that there are people, at this very moment, working to stir one up?"

"I am positive of it," replied he. "For good reasons and for wicked ones. It is not so unimaginable, is it? There need be no bloodshed. A swift coup, without violence; one of those firm but polite gestures that suit our national personality so admirably. We should be reunited in a twinkling into a single nation. Our potential enemies would see us united and resolute once more, and would think no longer of attacking us. You can see the appeal of it, Watson."

The South African war had exposed the inadequacies of our Army. The Royal Navy was still the greatest that the world had ever seen, but it could not sail upon land. Everyone blamed everyone else for our state of affairs. Talk of invasion by Germany, France or Russia was commonplace. Foreigners were regarded as potential spies, no matter how many years they had lived among us. There had been disgraceful outrages against long-established tradespeople who had not been ashamed of their alien-sounding names on shopfronts. Jealousy of their industry and comparative prosperity was too easily cloaked in patriotic fervour.

The so-called Yellow Peril was poisoning our thoughts, too. The patient Chinese community was swelling with an influx of low-paid workers. They were being imported to do work which was not to our taste. Their clannish way of life made them easy subjects for spreaders of rumour. They were becoming increasingly suspected of massing their numbers, ready for the signal to slit enough throats to make us beg for mercy.

Many earnest people were working to improve things for our millions of poor and needy. There were others, though, who were more interested in revolution for its own sake, or, rather, for their own. I suppose that, like many of my compatriots, I had become complacent. Our Empire was still the richest and most powerful in the world. We felt entitled to enjoy our privileges, as our King was entitled to his.

We were unconsciously aware that he had come to the throne an old man. He had been trained for nothing that mattered. He was past his physical prime, gross, overindulgent of his appetites and pastimes. He could not have many years ahead of him. We felt that we should all enjoy his inevitably short reign with him, and put off troubling about what would follow it.

"I can see the delusion of it all, Holmes," I answered, meaning only revolution.

He sighed. "Alas, my dear fellow, it is not only women in this world who by nature tend to the short-term response. Men who are being dragged under by frustration and despair will clutch at anything that might save them, if only to face another drowning at some later date."

"Do not discount women lightly," I admonished him with mock severity, recharging our glasses with the vintage wine. "They say that the reason no one dares give them the vote is because they would take over completely. Now, *there* would be a revolution to shake the world!"

"Heaven forbid!" groaned Sherlock Holmes.

T he following morning was again warm. I awoke feeling idle and luxurious with being in love, so I decided to start for Lausanne by the second boat train, an hour after the one I had told Holmes I should take.

When I had completed my packing, which did not take long, for old army methods remained my habit, I went down to breakfast. Holmes had evidently just sat down at table. He was in a dressing gown over shirtsleeves and a neat black cravat, and was already shaved. As usual, a newspaper was propped against the big silver-plated coffeepot. He was on the point of opening a boiled egg in his abstracted, unenthusiastic way. At my greeting he glanced up at me, then at the clock, with seeming surprise.

I put down my small portmanteau near the door and turned to the sideboard, where the row of plated dishes on spirit heaters offered the ingredients for a hearty repast.

"You are early today, Holmes," said I, ladling my porridge. "Ah, I had forgotten your appointment with the newspaper people on the Heath. What time did you arrange?"

His reply was a kind of snarl: "It is not my business to satisfy the sensational appetites of the press."

"Like it or not, you have been producing sensational results for them for years," I reminded him as I took my seat.

"Public notoriety has never been of my own seeking. Simply because I have allowed you to supplement your wound pension by chronicling some of my more easily explained investigations does not imply any hankering for acclaim."

I let his jibe pass. He looked at me sharply.

"I thought you would be off to Lausanne by now. You have not changed your mind?"

He spoke almost impatiently and I thought that his pale cheeks bore a slight unaccustomed flush. I told him of my decision to take the later train.

"Anything new about the hound?" I added, as I got up to assemble a mixed grill. I added a little extra from each dish, on the seasoned traveller's principle of providing against the uncertainty of the next mealtime.

"Nothing that is not downright rumour, speculation and invention. I have no desire to have my name bandied about in connection with it. I blame you, Watson, for letting it be believed that I would be drawn in. I have given Mrs. Hudson strictest orders . . ."

Our street bell rang at that instant. Holmes winced.

" . . . I have instructed her to admit no one this morning. I propose to go to ground until your return from Switzerland, or until this ridiculous matter blows over, whichever is the sooner."

I had not been mistaken in thinking that I heard steps ascending the staircase to our apartment. Mrs. Hudson entered placidly.

"*No one!*" roared Holmes, before she could speak. "Not the King himself!"

"But I *am* the King," came a bland voice from out of sight on our landing. "That is to say, I am here on His Majesty's business, which is much the same thing. Thank you, Mrs. Hudson, that will be all."

She made way for the burly figure of my friend's elder

brother, Mycroft Holmes. He lumbered past her, his corpulent bulk almost filling the door space. Under his ample cover, our landlady was able to make a good retreat from her tenant's ungrateful glare.

In spite of the warmth of the day, Mycroft Holmes was dressed in strictly formal clothes, with a velvet-collared overcoat buttoned over a frock coat, a tall wing collar and a black tie. He had removed his top hat, revealing his balding dome cascading with perspiration.

I thought he was surprised to see me. If so, he recovered quickly enough.

"Such heat," he groaned. "And only just turned July. Good day, Dr. Watson. Sherlock, why *did* you do it?"

"You're surely not here to blame me for the weather, Mycroft?" returned Holmes, who had not risen to greet him.

"You know perfectly well why I am here," answered his brother, scowling at him as I took his hat and ebony silver-topped cane, and helped him struggle free of an enormous weight of overcoat. He sank with a groan onto our sofa and began patting his head with a handkerchief and fanning himself with the nearest newspaper to hand. "You had no right, Sherlock. No right at all!"

"On the contrary," replied Holmes calmly but firmly, "I have every right. The right of any ordinary subject."

"Nonsense! You are not an 'ordinary subject.' " He turned his perspiring face toward me. "Dr. Watson, I have always respected you as the staunchest of patriots. I should never have imagined you condoning such an outrage."

"Watson had nothing to do with it, Mycroft," intervened Holmes, before I could overcome my astonishment enough to protest that I had not the faintest idea what was meant. "In any case, he has abrogated all interest in my welfare. He is a spent force. He is courting again."

Mycroft Holmes regarded me with interest.

"Hardly a spent force, then," he commented. "*Again?* But, surely, that would make it—"

"The third time," I completed for him testily. "Eccentric as it might seem to a pair of bachelors, I *do* intend to remarry. I have had the misfortune to lose two wives in painful circumstances. A certain lady has been gracious enough to accept my proposal, and I am damned if I am going to be called to account for it!"

Mycroft Holmes raised a fat palm. "My dear fellow, I congratulate you with all my heart. I myself have contemplated matrimony in my time . . ."

"But couldn't face up to the energetic demands," scoffed his younger brother, rising from the table to get one of the pipes from the mantelpiece.

"At least it was not from shirking the responsibility," came the sharp retort, and they glared at each other, this physically disparate pair, seven years separated in age and wholly contrasting in vitality, yet so matched in intellectual and deductive brilliance.

Mycroft Holmes was lying back on the sofa, his heavy legs splayed and his frock coat straining at its buttons over his broad chest and stomach. I knew him too well, however, to be deceived by his almost uncouth grossness into imagining him anything but my friend's equal in intellect and perspicacity. Holmes had assured me that, had his brother possessed energy and ambition to go with his brains, he might have made an even better consulting detective than himself. Mycroft's only regular exertion of a physical kind was the short walk between his lodging in Pall Mall and the club for unclubbables, the Diogenes, in that same dignified thoroughfare. His office in Whitehall being some few hundred yards away from either, he invariably went there and back by cab.

To the best of my knowledge he had been a civil servant all his adult life. He had risen from some kind of auditing to a position so influential and central that he was consulted upon all State business of consequence. Many secrets were locked inside his massive head, and it was my impression that many of them had been of his concocting in the first place.

It was usually a pleasure to me to be in the presence of both brothers, listening to them score points of deduction off one another, alternating humor with mockery. This morning my soul felt too light for intellectual banter.

"You must excuse me if I finish my breakfast," said I, addressing Mycroft Holmes. "I must be off. I have a train to catch. On business for Holmes," I added, in case he pictured me hastening to some suburban tryst.

"While you are here, Doctor," he requested, "between us, Sherlock simply *must* be made to see reason."

Holmes ejaculated angrily and went on lighting his pipe from a blazing twist of the *Sun,* his favourite paper for the purpose.

"About what?" I asked his brother. His reply astonished me into laying down my fork and knife.

"His knighthood, of course!"

"You have been offered a *knighthood,* Holmes!"

Mycroft slapped one of his vast thighs.

"Now you will tell me he has said nothing of it to you! Sherlock, this is too bad."

Holmes shrugged. "I see so little of Watson nowadays. He is too preoccupied for light gossip."

"Take no notice of him," I told his brother. "He is thoroughly put out at my flying the nest again. Holmes, it is my turn to express congratulations. No one deserves an honour more."

He only went on puffing out smoke and tamping down the tobacco with a forefinger. It was his brother who responded.

"That's the very point, Doctor. He *does* deserve it—none more so; but he *won't have it!*"

"You haven't refused, Holmes!"

"Yes, Watson; and my decision is final."

"But why on earth . . .?"

"Mycroft can tell you."

"No, I can't! Oh, I could repeat to you the reason he has given in a letter to the Lord Chancellor—which, fortunately, has been brought to my notice before being laid before His Majesty. There is some hocus-pocus about not seeking personal honours, and the work being its own reward; you, more than anyone, Doctor, are familiar with that line of his."

I knew well enough what Mycroft alluded to, and I knew that it was unfair of him to term it "hocus-pocus." Holmes accepted payment for his services, it was true, and sometimes in princely sums. He did not adhere to that declaration of his, made once only: "My professional charges are upon a fixed scale. I do not vary them, save when I remit them altogether." He had said that to the gold magnate, J. Neil Gibson, whose wife's suspicious death at their estate at Thor Bridge, Hampshire, we were investigating. The exaggeration had surprised me at the time, until I realized that it had been Holmes's proud protest at being told to name his own figure by a man vulgar enough to boast of having money enough to burn.

There was nothing false in Holmes's claim that he played the game for the game's sake. Time and again I have seen him at the conclusion of a case step back to let the credit go to the official policemen whom he had outshone because they would not take his advice. He had guided them toward results, implored them to follow his leads, pushed them if they still would not go. He often derided the Scotland Yarders for their slow wits and cumbrous methods. He would tell them so to their faces; yet I never knew him to lose sight of the fact that the majority were honest, hard-working, underpaid labourers in that field in which he was able to adventure as and when he chose. Holmes suffered discomforts voluntarily, undertook long hours of intellectual and physical toil and sometimes placed himself in personal danger. It all satisfied his need to be busy. Lestrade and his kind endured such things in order to earn their daily bread. No one recognized that more than did Sherlock Holmes.

"Holmes," said I, "won't you allow yourself, this once, to accept credit where it is due? There is not an inspector or constable at Scotland Yard who would begrudge you."

"My dear Watson," he replied seriously, "do not think that I have been insensible all these years to your determination, through your writings, to do me a justice that I deny myself. If I have sometimes rebuked you for overembellishing my exploits, it has been chiefly due to my fear that your readers might imagine superhuman qualities in me. I am no superbeing, Watson. I am an ordinary fellow who happened, long ago, to find within himself a gift that might be developed into an unique form of occupation, ideally suited to my personality and inclinations. As I have told you, Mycroft might have shone far more brightly than I, had he had the zeal to apply himself. That he preferred to insert himself into the government service and machinate behind the scenes of Whitehall was in keeping with the lack of vitality upon which he has come to pride himself. It has meant his moving among men who need honours to prove to themselves and to others that they have served well."

"The State expects it," his brother interrupted. "Titles and orders show the taxpayer what high quality of servants his money is paying for."

"Besides which," corrected Holmes, "an honour is cheaper than a higher pension. Mycroft's case," he returned to me, "is somewhat different. His work tends to be of an inscrutable, not to say clandestine, nature, which it might be difficult to acknowledge publicly without raising awkward questions. It is a pity. I picture him in the House of Lords—"

"Oh, come, come, Sherlock—" protested his brother, shaking with laughter.

"—spreading himself upon the cross-benches in the attitude in which he at present honours our humble settee . . ."

"Do stop being so Oriental! You are right, though, Sherlock; titles do not come automatically to people such as you, because you have never allowed yourself to be made part of the established order. You live as you please, and cut the most bohemian capers. You behave abominably to statesmen and even to royalty. In spite of it, you have been singled out as one of the first men to be honoured by a new sovereign. And what is your loyal response? You propose to throw it back in his face!"

I had never seen Mycroft Holmes so animated. Our sofa creaked as his massive weight rocked from side to side. Holmes faced him, standing with his back to the fireplace, legs straddled.

"You have expressed my very reason, Mycroft. It is why I do not wish to surrender any part of my independence. I will not be a hostage to society, which accepting a title would make me. I will not become 'genteel.' For a quarter of a century I have cultivated privacy. By remaining behind the scenes of criminal London I have been able to act with stealth and discretion. My name and reputation are known everywhere, but, beyond a shadowy notion of my profile and a few misconceptions which I have encouraged my friend here to spread for his amusement and profit, I am the odd man out. You, Mycroft, should know how much I should stand to lose by going public."

I drained my coffee cup, folded and rolled my napkin, placed it in its silver ring and got to my feet.

"I am sorry, Holmes," said I, "that you regard my humble literary endeavours as conveying misleading trivia concerning you. Fortunately, I have grown immune to your insults. I only hope that when His Majesty hears of your refusal he will over-look that insult, too."

Snatching up my coat, hat and cane, I made for my portmanteau. Silence reigned at my back. I turned at the door to make my bow to Mycroft Holmes. He was sitting up on the sofa, staring at me. Holmes was staring, too. My spontaneous parting volley had hit, left and right.

I turned back to the door and opened it. On the landing, facing me, with his knuckled fist upraised to knock, stood Inspector Lestrade.

"Might have given you one in the eye, Doctor," he said, grinning. "Why, Mr. Mycroft Holmes! We don't often see you about, sir. How are we doing these days?"

"*We* are *doing* tolerably well, Inspector—all things considered."

"That's the ticket, sir. Keep looking on the bright side. Well, I'm sorry to interrupt your little *teet-ah-teet,* but I've an item that I think will tickle Mr. Sherlock Holmes. You, too, Doctor, if you have a moment to spare."

I closed the door again. To my surprise, Lestrade began to chuckle quietly. He started to tremble, and then to shake with mirth.

"Oh dear, oh me!" he sobbed. "I'm sorry, gents . . . Oh, lor'!"

"What is it, Lestrade?" Holmes snapped. "We are busy men."

" . . . I'm sorry, Mr. Holmes. You can't help seeing the droll side of it, though. That hound—" He broke down into giggling again.

"What about the confounded thing?"

"Why, sir . . . just that . . . someone must have taken pity on it, running about on the Heath there, hungry for a bite to eat. . . . Oh me!"

"For heaven's sake, pull yourself together!"

Lestrade straightened up.

"You know those bones they've been turning up? At Marble Arch, where Tyburn Tree used to be?"

"We had the privilege of viewing them yesterday evening," said I. "They will have been covered over again by now."

"That was the idea, Doctor. Only . . ."

Lestrade seemed likely to dissolve again, but managed to master himself.

"Somebody's got there first."

"Got there first?"

"Took them—in the night."

"Stole the *bones?*"

"Some of them, anyway. Dog-fancier, eh, Doctor? Took it some bones, to keep its mind off tramps for a while."

Laughter doubled him up finally. I picked up my bag and made my escape, leaving the combined brains of Whitehall and Baker Street to make what they might of the Tyburn Bones, the Hound of Hampstead Heath, and the Laughing Policeman.

If it should appear to Sherlock Holmes's devout admirers that my account of his behaviour toward me at this time is less than flattering, so be it. A chronicler's duty is to set down the details honestly.

It had never been his habit to treat me as the simpleton that some of his enthusiasts have made me out to be. That I dwelt in his shadow, I admit readily. In matters of the intellect he was far my superior, and neither of us pretended otherwise. All the same, he generally gave me my due, took any opportunity to praise me and sweetened those jibes which he could not resist making by coating them with good humour. They were accompanied by a certain grimace, or look, which I knew of old. A stranger might be misled by his words or tone to believe that he was being condescending or even scornful. I knew differently and accepted his reproofs without more than a show of objection. Nothing delighted him more than when I took my chance to score off him.

"Watson has some remarkable characteristics of his own," he is upon record as having said, adding: "A confederate to whom each development comes as a perpetual surprise, and to whom the future is always a closed book, is, indeed, an ideal helpmate." I find nothing offensive in that. Ours was anything

85

but the master-and-dog relationship which some have made it seem. Yet on rare occasions, and especially when his comfort or convenience seemed in any way threatened by my behaviour, he could be petulant to the point of insult. His attitude toward my engagement to Coral, threatening as it did his domestic security, provoked some of the worst in him. I could sense his unspoken hope that it would fall through. Thinking over the situation in the course of my journey to Lausanne, I determined that, having found the mislaid Lady Frances Carfax, I should start looking for a new home without delay. I should move into it alone and start up in medical practice again, in preparation for marriage. Holmes must accept that he would have to fend for himself, whether at Baker Street or in his unlikely retirement.

My decision was justified during the following few days. I have described in my published account of the case* how I found myself upon a fruitless trail. It led me from Switzerland to Germany and thence to France, and nearly ended in a beating at the fists of a villainous-looking ruffian upon the same quest. Admittedly, Holmes saved me in person, popping up in the nick of time disguised as a French workingman; but I might have felt more grateful if he had not proceeded to mock me for having made what he charmingly termed a "very pretty hash" of my entire investigation.

"It is quite obvious," said I bitterly, as we sat in the train carrying us homeward from southern France, "that you have been using me as your pawn yet again."

"Scout, Watson, would be a happier way of denoting your role."

"Call it what you will. I object strongly."

"How often have I told you, my dear fellow, that it has been through your shortcomings that I am led sometimes to the truth?"

---

* This matter is covered in detail in *The Disappearance of Lady Frances Carfax.*

"I notice, Holmes, that you were able to get away from London when it suited you. I take it that 'Old Abrahams,' on whose account you felt unable to undertake this wild goose chase for yourself, was one of your inventions?"

Holmes's lips twitched in a sharp little smile. He turned to gaze out of the window of the compartment in which we were travelling alone.

"I might have known!" said I. "You could have taken me into your confidence and told me that I was merely your decoy."

He shook his head.

"Then you would not have carried out your instructions in so straightforward and artless a manner. Your Machiavellian cunning would have led you into some complex and quite inappropriate course of action. Do smoke one of these little Swiss things. They are not at all bad, considering that it is virtually impossible to find a good Continental cigar.

"By the by," he resumed, when we had lit up the slender Vevey Fins, "it might interest you to know that the hound drama has continued to run unrelentingly in your absence. There have been several more reports of sightings. At least two howlings have been attested to by sober residents."

"Have there been any further attacks?"

"None. But how could there be? There is no one for it to attack. The people living near the Heath venture out only into the busiest streets by day, and not at all after dark. There is mounting consternation among the local licensed victualling trade."

"You are teasing me, Holmes."

"Do I ever, my dear Watson?"

Whatever the truth of that, he had good-humouredly deflected my protests against him. There was no resisting his wiles.

"Any news of those stolen bones?" I asked. "I made a point

of looking in the Continental editions of the London papers, but saw no mention of them."

"That would be because there was none. The theft was reported to Dr. Garside when he arrived at the site early in the morning after our visit. The distinguished visitors were due. Rather than risk charges of lack of vigilance, he ordered his staff to keep silent about those particular bones having been exhumed."

"Then *they* were the ones taken!"

"Those and no others, so far as he can tell. Three headless skeletons, and that broken sword to which you were attracted. Don't tell me you were responsible, Watson! You didn't sneak out of the house by night and fetch them back? Will that old campaign chest of yours stand a search?"

"Do be serious for a moment, Holmes! How could anyone have taken them? The place was swarming."

"Precisely. Workmen everywhere. No one would be likely to ask questions about a wheelbarrow draped in sacking."

"Weren't the bones guarded?"

"I fancy not. Arkwright's bobbies had their hands full with the traffic hold-ups. It would have been left to the Museum people to mount a guard. I expect they preferred the comfort of their beds."

"The question arises, then, were they taken on the spur of the moment, or did someone go after them deliberately?"

"Two questions, Watson, to which the evidence available so far provides not a single answer. But here, I perceive, is the port of Dieppe. We must prepare to deliver ourselves into the railway servant's tender care and the rigours of the buffet."

The next hour was occupied with transferring to the Channel steamer. It was crowded with excursionists—men, women and children and their baggage. We had a struggle to get aboard, and were lucky to commandeer a pair of canvas chairs upon the open upper deck. It was not until we were some way from Dieppe, heading for that invisible halfway mark past which the Frenchman would become a foreigner and the Briton's sense of proprietorship would reassert itself, that we resumed our topic.

It was late afternoon. People were coming and going about us as we sat placidly isolated with our pipes, watching the seagulls floating clear of the two funnels' smoke, which streamed at an angle astern.

"I have been thinking, Holmes. Who knew the bones were there to steal?"

"Garside maintains there were only the few of us who knew their significance."

"A workman could have found out about them. Some antiquarian would pay decently for them, no doubt?"

Holmes nodded.

"Possibly. Frankly, though, I don't much care, any more than I do about Lestrade's wild dog on Hampstead Heath. Tell me, Watson, what is your up-to-date opinion of our monarch? Should you say that history will pronounce favourably upon King Edward the Seventh?"

Accustomed though I was to his firing questions out of the blue, I was taken by surprise. He was not given to initiating small gossip, however.

"I have wondered," I replied. "I am sure he has many strong qualities, if only people will trust him and he can live down his reputation."

"I should have thought that the British people, with their sporting preoccupations, would not be too disapproving of him."

"You asked about history's verdict, Holmes, not the British people's. Anyway, I suppose he will have to change his ways completely, once he is crowned and has his part to play in full."

Withdrawing his pipe from his mouth, and fixing his gaze

out across the sea again, Holmes astonished me further, this time with a quotation:

> *"So, when this loose behaviour I throw off*
> *And pay the debt I never promised, . . .*
> *My reformation, glitt'ring o'er my fault,*
> *Shall show more goodly and attract more eyes*
> *Than that which hath no foil to set it off."*

"Good heavens, Holmes! I don't believe I have ever heard you quote Shakespeare."

"*Henry IV*, Part One. You are at liberty to remark that you never get my depths."

"We did it at school, I remember," said I, still amazed. "I played Bardolph."

"Hm! Worked as a tapster, and was hanged. There is nothing further to comment, Watson."

"For more than twenty years I have heard you profess ignorance of literature," I accused him. "I never believed you, and I was right."

"Do not infer too much from trifles. There happened to be a fragment of Prince Hal's speech lying in my brain attic. It seemed so appropriate that I read it up again, directly upon my return from the Palace."

"The . . . ? Your . . . !"

Holmes gave me his cat-with-the-cream smile.

"Ah! I *knew* there was something I had omitted to tell you."

"Holmes! Are you giving me to understand that you have been to the *Palace? The* Palace?"

"Buckingham, yes. A brief visit only. His Majesty is making an excellent recovery, but he tells me that his doctors are severe with him. They insist on his conserving his strength. He will be off by now, convalescing aboard the royal yacht."

All at once, I realized the truth.

"Your brother Mycroft! So *that* is why he was wearing formal rig on that hot day. He had come to take you to Buckingham Palace! The King had sent for you over your knighthood, to persuade you personally! You had to relent!"

Holmes shook his head slowly. "I regret to disappoint you, my dear Watson. It is not *Sir* Sherlock Holmes who sits beside you. The subject was not even discussed."

"Then, do you propose telling me what other reason took you to him? Or are you making this up to pass the time?"

He lay back in his deck chair, gazing distantly across the water.

"Picture," said he, with the air of doing so himself, "a large sitting room, wholly masculine in character. Photographs of racehorses with their jockeys up and their owners at their heads are prominent upon the walls. In silver frames, on various surfaces, are smaller photographs, whose subjects are chiefly human and female.

"His Majesty reclines upon a daybed, with one leg up and the other foot upon the floor. He is wearing pumps and a flannel suit. He is exactly as you know him from his portraits: stout, bearded and pleasantly gruff, with a shrewd, direct stare. Upon what might be termed his lap lies a white fox-terrier dog. When he addresses it, in a voice whose heavy timbre matches his stature, he calls it Caesar."

"Is it true that he has a German accent?" I could not forbear to interrupt.

"A distinct legacy from his father," confirmed Holmes. "His eyes are his mother's legacy; protuberant, very blue, and remarkably thick-lidded. His beard is whiter, seen close, than we have hitherto imagined. The air is thick with fragrant smoke. From its density, you might agree with me that he is on his third or fourth Corona y Corona of the morning."

"That is sufficient scene-setting, Holmes. What did he say?"

"He confided something which, if I repeat it to you, I beg you will not pass on."

"When did I ever let out a secret of yours?"

"Never, my dear Watson. Circumstances, however, have become a little changed."

"If you are referring to Coral—to Miss Atkins—I hope you do not suggest I have taken to relating your confidential business to her!"

"How often have I remarked that women are never to be entirely trusted—*not even the best of them*? Besides, she is, I understand, American."

"What of that?"

"Were the matter solely a British one I should not imagine her being too curious about it. Since it happens to concern her own country . . ."

"Holmes," said I, "before you cause me to lose my temper with you, you had better complete your tale."

He sighed.

"Very well, my dear Watson. Since your persuasion is so winning I will tell you what passed between King and commoner upon that morning in Buckingham Palace."

"The pleasantries were concluded," went on Sherlock Holmes, "and the equerry who had conducted us to the royal presence took his leave. I was placed in a chair closest to the King. Mycroft sat a little apart, wearing his most complacent air. On our way to the Palace he had refused me the least hint as to the purpose of the summons. I was convinced that it had to do with the title question. I resented being placed in a position of having to accede mildly or repeat my refusal to His Majesty's face."

"That would have been an unsporting trick by your own brother," said I.

"The ethics of sport are wholly inapplicable to Mycroft. His position as *éminence grise* to the Government was attained through artful skill and unscrupulousness. I noticed, by the way, that he seemed wholly at ease with the King. I was sure that he was no stranger to the Palace.

"It turned out to be an agreeably informal interview. We were not exactly offered cigars, but there was none of that speak-only-when-spoken-to protocol.

" 'Mr. Holmes,' said His Majesty to me, 'your brother will have told you that an important change in the Government is imminent?'

" 'Mycroft tells me nothing, sir.'

" 'Then it is left to me. Lord Salisbury has been to see me. He is stepping down as Prime Minister. He is seventy-two. He has been in poor health for some time. It is a great pity. What the nation needs is stability: the security of familiarity and continuity. Her late Majesty personified it for over sixty years. For a long time so has Salisbury. Within a few days he will be gone, too.'

" 'Might one ask, sir, who is to replace his lordship?'

" 'It is to be Mr. Arthur Balfour.'

" 'His nephew!'

" 'I read your mind, Mr. Holmes. It is not nepotism, though. Lord Salisbury's recommendation of Mr. Balfour will be endorsed widely. Even so, it means a change at a time when change is least desirable. The eyes of the world are upon us. Germany, Russia, France—all are watching us for signs of weakness. Any symptoms will be read like omens in a teacup. At this very moment the war rooms of Europe are busy with long-standing plans being brought up to date, as your brother will confirm.'

" 'Quite true, sir,' said Mycroft. 'Our intelligence reports are full of it.' He addressed me. 'They are jealous of the Empire, of our wealth, our trade, our influence. Our embarrassments in the Boer War have given them bold ideas, though not yet quite bold enough. Each hopes that one of the others will fire the first shot. Then the rest would come tumbling in for a share of the spoils.'

" 'Even more disturbing, in their way,' His Majesty added, 'are the reports about our internal security. We should all hope that my *dear* nephew, the Kaiser, doesn't find out how serious things are. It is a relief that he has gone back to Germany for the moment, although there are plenty of his people still here, eager to report every new case of civil unrest.'

" 'There are growing signs that it is becoming organized,' Mycroft informed me. 'The extreme anarchist groups and rabble-rousers generally are recruiting and discussing combining together. For the moment, they are bickering among themselves about who should have the biggest say. One of these days, though, they will reconcile their differences. That will be the dangerous moment.'

"At this point a twinge of discomfort showed in the King's face. He pushed the dog Caesar off him and used both hands to move his leg. Mycroft made no attempt to assist, so I sat still. We waited in silence until the dog was restored to his place and the King spoke on.

" 'I have tried to keep up with affairs of state since I was a boy. The Prince Consort, my father, discouraged it. After his death, my mother still refused me any responsibilities. I was allowed uniforms, colonelcies, ceremonial roles, parts to play and lines to speak, but nothing that would give me a chance to do something worthwhile for my country. However, Mr. Holmes, I believe my hour of destiny is come at last. I propose to be the first reigning British monarch ever to visit the United States of America.'

"Before I could think how to respond, the King's laugh told me that he had been observing my expression.

" 'You are wondering if I am not being hasty and rash? Your brother has put that to me more than once, haven't you?'

" 'Half a dozen assassinations in as many years,' responded Mycroft. 'President Carnot of France. Premier Cánovas of Spain. Stambolov, the Bulgarian Premier. The Austrian Empress Elizabeth. King Umberto of Italy.'

" 'I have looked down a pistol barrel myself, in my time,' His Majesty reminded us. 'As my cousin, Alfonso of Spain, put it, though: "Being a king may be dangerous, but it is devilish well paid." '

"He laughed until the twinges it caused made him leave off.

"I ventured to interject at this point, addressing Mycroft.

" 'You have left out the most significant of them all—the shooting of President McKinley, at Buffalo last September.'

"It was the King himself who took me up on it.

" 'Significant in more ways than perhaps you realize, Mr. Holmes. I have especial sentiments toward America and the Americans. In 1860, when I was eighteen, I was allowed to tour Canada and the States: Detroit, Chicago, St. Louis, Cincinnati, Pittsburgh, Baltimore, Philadelphia, New York, Boston. It was welcome and excitement and goodwill all the way.' He held up his right hand. 'This hand was disabled from so much shaking. I was black and blue all over. The New York girls who couldn't get a dance with me jostled me and pinched me instead. Mark my word, gentlemen, someday this country will wake up to the public value of its royal family. They will win more goodwill abroad than all the diplomatists.'

"The King drew out another thick Corona from his case and prepared it as he spoke on.

" 'I intend more than a goodwill gesture this time. My chief purpose will be to talk to McKinley's successor, President Roosevelt. My message will be that the peace and prosperity of our countries, and of the world, have everything to gain from a formal alliance between the United States and Great Britain.

" 'I know that your feelings upon the subject match mine, Mr. Holmes. Mycroft has shown me accounts of one or two of your cases, written up by your friend—Wilson, isn't that his name?'

" 'Watson, sir. Dr. Watson.'

" 'Hm. *The Noble Bachelor,* would the piece be called? He reports you as remarking how you are among those who regret the folly of a monarch and the blundering of a minister in far-gone years which severed the two nations. That is my feeling, Mr. Holmes. It was our high-handedness, and hotheaded dudgeon on their part. It is the greatest pity that we didn't shake hands afterward and throw in our lots together. We have so much to share and offer one another.'

"While he lit his fresh cigar I took my chance again.

" 'From all I have read, sir, Theodore Roosevelt and his journalist friends are among the loudest voices against us.'

" 'Not now, Sherlock,' Mycroft put in. 'Now that he is President he seems to have changed. He wants to be the man of peace, at home and abroad. He seems set upon stamping out strife and lawlessness. He talks of a new morality in America. His new objects of dislike are the financial combines and corrupt local administrations. He sees them as oppressors of the small man. It's a strong platform, and Roosevelt is the sort to make the most of it.'

" 'Quite so,' the King agreed. 'We are on the threshold of change, too. A new century, a new reign, a new Premier soon: I am convinced there could not be a better time to open an initiative with a new President.'

"My face must have shown my feelings again, Watson, for he said, 'Never fear, Mr. Holmes. I'm not about to ask you to come as my bodyguard. I have another request, more in line with those special capabilities of yours about which I've read.'

"He paused to examine his cigar keenly, as though it were

not drawing well. I saw him glance at Mycroft, who sat as impassive as a toad upon a water lily. The King cleared his throat and went on.

" 'A sovereign's, ah, personal life, Mr. Holmes, is to a large extent public property. One's associations are subject to scrutiny from every point of view. You understand me?'

" 'I have acted for royalty of several countries, sir.'

" 'Then, to put it briefly, in a nutshell, man to man, and so forth . . . an, ah, association with a certain *lady* is giving me some cause for anxiety. It is nothing extravagant or improper. It is not even public knowledge. The very devil of it, though, Mr. Holmes, is that if it were to *become* known it might be interpreted wrongly. There are people who will believe anything about me, and newspapers only too prepared to print it. When I was heir to the throne a certain licence was allowed. I have enjoyed many a good laugh at some of the things they have published about me. My situation is different now—and when we come to the President of the United States we are beyond laughing matters. Do you get my drift?'

" 'Completely, sir,' said I. 'If it were to reach the President's ears it could put paid to Your Majesty's mission to America.'

" 'You understand the problem completely, Mr. Holmes.'

" 'Americans expect an impossibly high example of rectitude from us, sir. It is a legacy from the Pilgrim Fathers. In some ways, it might have been better if they had missed their boat.'

"The King laughed briefly, but his expression became serious again.

" 'It would be in the interests of certain foreign powers to ensure that the President and I do not make friends. The bullet and the bomb are not the assassin's only weapons. You take my meaning still, Mr. Holmes?'

"I replied that I took it completely. As you, my dear Watson, do too, I am sure."

"Blackmail, Holmes!"

"Undoubtedly, Watson."

The movement and increased chatter about us on the ferry steamer's deck told me that the white cliffs of Sussex must be in sight. It would not be very long before we docked at New-haven. Then we should take the boat train to London. I was agog to hear more from Holmes before having to share a railway compartment with others.

"He said there was nothing improper," I pointed out.

"My dear Watson, I know how little you share my distrust of women. You exhibit a positively dog-like faith in female high-mindedness."

"Be that as it may, Holmes, what is the danger?"

"You surely do not need me to spell out the menace of used notepaper."

"There are letters!"

"A single letter, but that is enough. His Majesty has no copy of it, and I thought him rather studiedly vague about it. That was probably Mycroft's advice. I formed the impression that it might be nothing more than an extravagant chimera. A flight of fancy. The sort of thing which I am sure your own ready way with the opposite sex renders quite unnecessary."

"Holmes, this is no joking matter! Notes of that sort can convey an impression of something that went deeper than it did. Does he know that it is still in existence?"

"What woman would destroy an affectionate note from a future king?"

"But if she hasn't attempted to make use of it before, why now?"

"Mycroft, who seems to have started this hare running, has had a tip that there are agents actively seeking anything at all which might be used to discredit the King."

"Why not simply ask her to return it, or destroy it?"

"To echo your own question—why not have asked that of her before now? It was written two years ago. They have not met since, and there is no certainty what the lady's attitude might have become. Besides, it is not desirable to draw attention to it on the eve of the very enterprise which its publication would certainly spoil."

"A two-year-old note!"

"Any new name or circumstance linked sensationally with the King would be seriously damaging at this time. The name of Glanvill would be especially unfortunate in the context."

"Glanvill? I don't know it."

"That is perhaps because your modest income debars you from the sphere of international finance. Mr. Hubert Glanvill is one of the rising stars in that firmament."

"Her husband?"

"As you must know, all His Majesty's ladies have been married ones, with husbands prepared to turn a blind eye. Hubert Glanvill, it seems, is the exception. Mycroft tells me his self-esteem is too well developed to let him play the *mari complaisant*. He is what they call a self-made tycoon. He has thrown in his lot with the Americans. Pierpont Morgan and Rockefeller have taken a shine to him. He is only in his forties, and that is on his side."

"Bully for him, then! The Americans admire men with grand designs."

"So they do, but it is one of the things President Roosevelt is set upon altering. He sees such men as public enemies, tramplers upon workers' rights, exploiters of labour for their own gain. He would regard our aspiring Mr. Glanvill in that same dim light."

"Well, Holmes, if Glanvill would have objected to an association between his wife and the King two years ago, and there has been no attempt to revive it, I can't see what harm an old note can do."

"What the King did not see fit to tell me, Watson, but

which Mycroft added afterward, is that it contains some skittish reference to the writer's determination, at his first opportunity, to elevate the lady to the place which she would 'so decoratively fill' in the ranks of the aristocracy. That could only be read to imply that he intended a peerage for her husband as soon as he should have power to give him one. With the Coronation, you can see, that time has come."

"There's nothing binding in that, surely, Holmes? He was only Prince of Wales when he wrote it."

"The foreign press might not draw that nice distinction. Neither might Mrs. Glanvill herself."

"You think she'll try to hold him to it?"

"There is no knowing. Nor is there any knowing what her husband's own aspirations are. He was sounded out for a knighthood some little time ago, but declined it."

"Two of you! They will be advertising for takers next."

"You know my reasons," replied Holmes tartly. "Mycroft's opinion is that Glanvill is holding out for a peerage."

"A knighthood would do to be going on with."

"It does not follow. Further elevation tends to come later than sooner. A change of government might strand him on his knighthood for years. Besides, 'Lord Glanvill' would ring more impressively than mere 'Sir Hubert' to American ears."

"It's simple, then. Give the fellow his peerage. Everyone will be happy."

"Except the President of the United States. The King's anxiety is that if he is perceived by the President to be honouring the very type of man whom Roosevelt is currently deploring, it will mean farewell to the goodwill mission upon which he has set his heart."

"I give up, Holmes," said I impatiently. "It all sounds to me like a storm in a teacup, and I can't begin to think what it should have to do with you."

"Unfortunately," he replied gloomily, "for a man who is

said to read almost nothing except the racing forms and the studbooks, His Majesty is surprisingly *au fait* with the chronicles of one 'Wilson,' as he will persist in calling you. He knows how we tried to recover that compromising photograph of the King of Bohemia and Irene Adler, of blessed memory. He is aware that I acted on his late mother's behalf in the Dreyfus business, and that I have been of service in my time to other monarchs, premiers, cabinet ministers and an assortment of the nobility and aristocracy."

"Don't tell me, Holmes, that you are expected to get that note out of this wretched woman!"

"My dear fellow, how could you have guessed?"

I was spared having to answer. Our discussion was brought to an abrupt and dramatic end by a man's voice, somewhere at the stern of the ship, crying urgently, *"Man overboard!"*

T he alarm was taken up at once by the stentorian voice of a deckhand near us. He broke into a run. A whistle shrilled. The double ring of the engine-room telegraph sounded from the bridge. The ship's gruff whistle gave its deafening double blast. The paddle wheels churned and thundered. Within a matter of seconds more, the vessel had lost her forward way. Her paddles brought her awkwardly about, canting steeply to port. Women and children screamed. There was a stampede of scrambling feet as passengers sought either safety or vantage points from which to look down into the foaming sea.

Holmes and I had leaped to our feet and taken positions at the rail. We were scanning the sea when the cry went up from many voices.

"There he is!"

"Fetch a lifebelt!"

"He's waving. He's all right."

"No! He's going under!"

"Oh, be quick, someone!"

They were being quick, in the exemplary fashion of well-trained seamen. In response to more rings from the telegraph, the ship was heaving to, well short of the hapless figure whose head could be seen bobbing between the swells. Deckhands were throwing out lines with lifebuoys attached. The man in the sea made no move toward them.

"Chinese steward," remarked a male passenger. "That waiter who fetched us tea."

"Can't swim," observed a know-all. "Sailors can't. Spend their lives at sea, and never learn."

This was immediately given the lie, as a seaman dived semiclad from the starboard rail. Another followed. Cheers arose from the passengers as the men surfaced, shook their heads like wet dogs and struck out strongly. Cheers and unheard shouted directions urged them on.

A third member of the crew jumped into the sea feet first. He gathered one of the bobbing lifebelts under one arm, and with his other paddled forward, dragging it on its line. It took only moments for the first two swimmers to reach and support the steward. Joined by the third, they got the lifebelt over his head and hooked his arms over its sides. From the drooping way in which they hung, and the way the head sagged forward, it was plain that he was unconscious.

"Work for you, Watson," said Holmes.

I hurried to the bows in the wake of his purposeful stride. Everyone else's attention was seaward, the deck listing under their weight, as the gallant rescuers were cheered and exhorted. The incident had added welcome zest to the last stages of an uneventful Channel crossing.

We pushed our way through the growing crowd. A young deck officer had taken charge, having already cleared himself for action by removing his tunic and hat. A section of bow rail had been dismantled to make a gap. Men on the lifebelt lines were waiting there for a signal from another, leaning out over the side.

"Keep back, gentlemen, if you please," requested the burly, fair-haired officer.

"I am a doctor," said I.

He nodded acknowledgement. He was pale under his tan, but he answered confidently, "Respiration ought to be enough, sir."

"Ready below!" signalled the man keeping watch at the side.

"Haul away!" the officer ordered. "Steady as you go."

The linesmen took the strain and began to pull together. The passengers' cheers and rallying shouts died away. Hushed murmurs of concern formed the only accompaniment as the victim was drawn up. There was respectful applause as he was brought inboard. He was hanging inertly in the lifebelt, supported by one of his dripping rescuers. Other hands eased him from the belt and laid him face downward on the deck.

He was in early middle age, with a shaven head of black stubble. He was wiry and very short. I had noticed him during the crossing, moving about the deck in his white cutaway jacket and black trousers, carrying trays of tea.

He sprawled motionless in a spreading pool of seawater. The young officer quickly knelt astride him to begin artificial respiration. One of the seamen had turned the steward's head to one side and groped in his mouth to ensure that his tongue was free. They knew their business, and I made no move to interfere.

The officer began the rhythmic pressure that would force the water from the lungs. I noticed him hesitate, though, and knelt beside him. A glance was enough to show me what was troubling him. There was blood, diluted with seawater, on the palm of his right hand.

Holmes got down to join us. I heard his hiss of surprise as he, too, saw the bloody area of shirt above the unconscious man's waist at the right side. Motioning the officer to go on working, I felt for a pulse. At the same time, by crouching low and bending my head in an upside-down posture, I was able without interrupting him to see the place from which the blood had got on his hand. Most of it had been washed away by the sea, but there was no mistaking the presence of a wound. No more blood was issuing from it.

"This man has been stabbed," I said quietly.

"You're sure of that, sir?" asked the young man, pausing to stare at me.

"Almost certainly. Go on pumping, though I'm afraid it will be no use."

Holmes had shifted his position rapidly, in order, I realized, to screen the prone man from the watchers.

"Is a stretcher coming?" I asked the officer.

"On the way, sir."

"I suggest it would be best not to upset the women and children with the sight of blood," I said. "Keep working on him, while I go on trying for a pulse. When the stretcher comes we must get him onto it in a way that hides the wound. Is there somewhere completely private to take him?"

"The captain's cabin, sir."

"Very good. Let them think he's only unconscious. We can decide what to do afterward."

I looked to Holmes for agreement, but found that he had got to his feet and was addressing himself to the onlookers.

"Ladies and gentlemen," he called out, "the poor fellow is in a doctor's hands. It will be better if we all stand well clear."

The watchers clearly resented this attempt to deprive them of their spectacle. They murmured, and only a few obeyed. Holmes held up a coin from his pocket.

"I propose a collection for the benefit of the gallant rescuers. I'll start it off with a sovereign."

This drew a more willing response. A young man volunteered his boater for a collecting box, and a small cheer went up when Holmes tossed his coin into it. Scrutineers appointed themselves, and the collector turned to move among the people, who chattered excitedly as they delved into pockets and purses. The ship's whistle resounded. We were already under way again and heading for the white cliffs of Sussex as sedately as before.

Holmes returned to kneel beside us.

"Well, Doctor?" he asked, and I recognized his signal to me to avoid speaking his name.

"Gone, I'm afraid," I replied, taking care not to shake my head for the passengers to notice.

The young officer showed himself to be intelligent as well as resourceful. He needed no instructing to keep on applying the artificial respiration, and did not question my medical authority. When the stretcher came, he helped me roll the victim onto it in the manner that I had suggested, keeping the wounded side and the blood hidden even from the bearers. He took his hat and tunic from Holmes, who had retrieved them for him from the deck, then led the way briskly to the captain's cabin. The sympathetic inquiries that reached our ears as we passed along were successfully fended off with noncommittal grunts.

The stretcher was set down on the narrow bunk and its bearers dismissed, none the wiser. Our officer friend hurried off, struggling into his jacket as he went, to report to the captain, who had not left the bridge throughout the drama.

"Now, Watson," said Holmes, and I began at once to remove enough of the victim's clothing to gain access to the wound. It was quite clean and neat, and had undoubtedly been caused by a knife thrust.

"Not a seaman's knife," I pronounced after close examination.

Holmes nodded agreement. "A slender, sharp-pointed blade. A stiletto, perhaps?"

"Certainly slid in, rather than rammed home," I confirmed. "The absence of bruising points to that."

"Therefore a swift, unanticipated attack, rather than a struggle?"

"Definitely."

"Well, his cutaway jacket would expose an expanse of shirt above the waistband of his trousers when he stooped or stretched. An ideal target for an opportunist, shouldn't you say?"

"Except that I can't imagine someone thrusting a stiletto into a tempting target just because one presents itself."

"I'm inclined to agree." Holmes nodded. "What else, then? Small change in the trouser pocket. Tips, no doubt. Petty robbery was not the motive. There could scarcely have been a fight without commotion."

"The officer would have mentioned anything extraordinary, wouldn't he?" said I.

Holmes looked doubtful, though. "To him, we are merely a couple of passengers, one of whom happens to be a doctor. Anything he has to report he will tell to his skipper first."

"He's taking long enough over that," I pointed out, but Holmes held up a hand.

"Here, I think, comes the worthy master at last. Let us find out what he has to say about things."

The cabin door opened violently and the captain came stumping in. He was middle-aged, thickset and gray-bearded. He exuded a faded air, with none of the autocratic aura of his counterpart, the oceangoing master, but soon showed himself more than conscious of his supreme authority over his ferry and all who sailed in her.

"Who said he could be fetched into my cabin?" he was demanding of someone following him in. It was our young officer. "Get off my bunk, blast you!" he bellowed at the corpse.

"I fear that is beyond the poor fellow's capacity," answered Holmes.

"What's that? Who the devil are you?"

"My name is Sherlock Holmes. This is my associate, Dr. Watson."

He gave us a hard, suspicious stare. The younger man did not hide his awe upon hearing our names. He straightened his back and clasped his hands behind it, to stand stiffly like a soldier on parade.

"Sherlock Holmes," the captain echoed. "To do with the coppers, ain't you? What are you up to in my ship?"

"Making our way home from an all-too-brief vacation. I assure you, this affair has nothing whatever to do with me."

"It had better not. What goes on in my ship, concerning my people, is *my* business, and the company's."

"Not entirely, if it happens to be criminal," replied Holmes crisply. He moved aside, revealing the exposed area of flesh and the wound.

"This poor chap has been stabbed," said I. "He is dead."

Captain Bassett, as we discovered his name to be, gaped, stepped closer and gaped again, then turned angrily on his subordinate.

"You didn't tell me this, mister. You led me to think he'd been taken up safe."

Holmes came to the young man's rescue. "My fault, Captain. I asked the officer to say nothing to anyone."

"*Anyone? Anyone!* I'm captain of this ship! One of my crew gets himself stuck, and I'm not to be told?"

"The officer erred on the side of prudence," replied Holmes. "At the time when he left us to report to you, we were not yet in a position to confirm that murder had been done."

"His life may have been finished off by drowning, but that was incidental," I explained to the dumbstruck master. "This was a mortal wound."

Before he could recover himself, and probably inform us that no one could be murdered aboard his ship without his and the company's authority, Holmes had forestalled him.

"With your permission, Captain, I should like to ask Mr. . . .?"

"Anderson, sir," supplied the young officer.

"I should like to ask Mr. Anderson if he can throw any light upon what has occurred?"

The young man licked his lips, but answered without waiting for the permission to be refused.

"In what way, sir?"

"You were upon the scene before my friend and I came up. Had you been in the vicinity when the alarm was given?"

"Oh, yes. As close as anyone, I should think."

"Pray, tell me anything you particularly remember."

"There's not much, sir. I noticed this fellow go behind one of the lifeboats, collecting up tea-things. That was just before it happened."

"You didn't see him emerge again?"

"No, sir. I don't think he could have done in the time before someone shouted 'Man overboard!,' and I ran to the rail. He was in the sea and already astern of us."

"It was not you who raised the alarm, then?"

"No, sir. It was some other man I didn't see."

"Someone already behind the boat?"

"There was no one there when I arrived."

"But the tea-things he was collecting?"

"There had been a whole party, but they'd gone for'ard to look at the land a few minutes before."

"Men and women?"

"Several couples. Quite a jolly crowd."

"You would know them again?"

"Some of them, certainly."

"See here, Mr. Sherlock Holmes . . . !" interposed the captain loudly. Holmes turned to him with a little bow.

"I was about to ask Mr. Anderson if it would be possible for anyone to fall over the ship's rail. I beg your pardon. Of course, the question should be addressed to yourself."

"I should think it ought!"

"Then, *is* it possible?"

"Fall over a four-foot rail!"

"It would be necessary to climb up and jump?"

"Or be bundled over helplessly," said I.

"Of course, Watson!" cried Holmes. "To the heart of the matter as always! The victim is stabbed and bundled over. Then he who did both deeds cries 'Man overboard!' thereby attracting an excited crowd with which he quietly mingles."

"He or *she*," I reminded him, warming to the work. "A woman could easily have stabbed him as he stooped unawares. As for throwing him overboard, see how small he is. A child could have hoisted him over."

"Oh, we're down to nippers now, are we?" the captain broke in with heavy irony. "Now, this has gone far enough. I'm master of this ship, and I say what goes. What I say is, that this is a matter for the coppers. Detective or whatever you are, Mr. Sherlock Holmes, if there's any question that John Sweh's been done in, I'll thank you to leave the investigating to them. The company will expect to have a director present, as well."

Holmes shrugged. "As you say, Captain. I take it you'll be informing them immediately after we dock?"

"I was just coming to that. Mr. Anderson . . ."

"Sir?"

"Soon as we touch, hotfoot it into the company's office. Tell 'em to get a director down here smartly. Any one of 'em will do, only don't say what it's about. They won't want word getting all round."

"Aye, aye, sir."

"Then catch hold of the first bobby you see and tell him an inspector's wanted on board. Nothing less, mind. No one else is to set foot ashore meanwhiles. Not crew nor passengers. That goes for you, too, Mr. Sherlock Holmes—*and* for your 'associate,' " the captain concluded triumphantly.

Holmes stared at him, aghast. "Dear me! That will be most inconvenient."

"Ah! You should have thought of that before you begun meddling. You'll just have to lump it with the rest."

"My dear Captain, I was not referring to any inconvenience to my friend and myself. I meant to you."

"Me?"

"You; your crew; your passengers. Your *company,* even."

"Here! How do you mean?"

"I am not exactly aware of the resources maintained by the Sussex Constabulary at Newhaven, but I fancy they are limited. An inspector, no doubt. A few sergeants. A number of constables."

"The inspector will be enough."

"Ah, but will he be available? Suppose he is away, or off duty?"

"Well—perhaps a sergeant would do. A good senior man, though, mister."

"Aye, aye, sir."

"Even there, you limit yourself severely, Captain," said Holmes. "If I might advise it, Mr. Anderson should request the assistance of every available man."

"What for?"

"Why, to search for the weapon."

"Go on! They'd have to look under the Channel."

"I fear they will insist upon going through the ship, nonetheless. They are particularly thorough in Sussex. As for questioning every passenger and member of your crew . . ."

"Every . . . !"

"Men, women and children. Perhaps with the exception of infants. Believe me, Captain, I know their painstaking Sussex ways."

Although we were in the proximity of a foully murdered man it was all I could do not to smile. The captain's expression was the very picture of comic dismay as he contemplated the hours of plodding procedure, the irate protests of several hundred passengers, the tears of women and sobbing of babes, the sullen animosity of the crew, the holding-up of the boat train, the delay in making the vessel ready for its next outward sailing.

"The company will go crazy!" he moaned.

I thought I glimpsed a fleeting smile on young Anderson's face as he continued to stand stiffly at ease behind his skipper. A ring on the nearby bridge telegraph and a change in the vibration of engines and paddle wheels brought us back to recollection that we were nearing port.

"Mister," the master addressed him heavily, "belay them orders for now. Go on to the bridge and tell Mr. Poole, my compliments, and to stand off till I come up."

"Aye, aye, sir."

"And don't go answering any questions," the captain added, as Anderson made what seemed to me a hesitant departure. "Look lively!"

The young man went, closing the door. The master turned at once to Holmes.

"Look, mister . . ." he began, but Holmes silenced him with a swift gesture. With his finger still to his lips, he went quietly to the door and, after listening closely at it for some moments, jerked it open. No one was there. He closed it again quietly.

"Captain, we have very little time. I urge you to agree to do exactly as I advise. Believe me, it is imperative, unless you wish to have a full-scale police investigation upon your hands. I assure you I did not exaggerate the inconvenience it will cause you; besides which, it is unnecessary."

The captain looked toward the corpse.

"You reckon somebody did him in," he said. "Whoever he is will have ditched his knife, but he's still aboard himself."

"Precisely," agreed Holmes. "But trying to identify *him* would be like looking for a pin in a field. It is a task far beyond the capacity of the Newhaven police. They would need reinforcements from headquarters at Lewes, which would cause more delay. Even then they would not find him. There are no clues, and there is no pointer to a motive, unless perhaps you know of any hostility toward him."

"Never a murmur. John Sweh, which is how he was always called, has worked in this ship, off and on, for as long as I've been master, coming up three years. Good as stewards come. Quiet. Keeps—kept to himself. Always went off by himself on shore, and never got into bother."

"Thank you. All you have just said confirms that I am right in dissuading you from alerting the police."

"Holmes!" I protested. "Commuting a felony is one thing, but this is murder. You can't hush it up."

"It is hushed up already," said he, beginning to speak urgently. "No one aboard this ship, other than ourselves and Mr. Anderson, knows that murder has been done."

"The murderer does," I reminded him.

"Yes, but he can scarcely proclaim it without giving himself away. All that anyone else knows is that a member of the crew had the misfortune to fall overboard. They have not even been told that he is dead. My advice, Captain, is that you berth your ship as though nothing were amiss. If any departing passenger has the solicitude or curiosity to inquire after the man overboard, the simple and truthful answer should be that he is in medical hands."

"But . . . but once they're let ashore, this murderer you speak of has got away with it!"

"Precisely as he had hoped to do."

"Then?"

"I shall make it my urgent business to have a confidential chat with the police. Not the Newhaven branch. I shall go over to Lewes. Remember Mr. White Mason, from our Birlstone Manor case, Watson?"

"Indeed!"

"If he is no longer head of the Sussex detective branch, I am sure that someone equally excellent will have replaced him. He will understand the situation at once."

"I'm blowed if *I* do!" responded the captain; and had it not been for twenty years' experience of Sherlock Holmes, his methods and his enigmatic manner of applying them, I might have agreed with him.

"But you will do as I suggest, Captain?" urged Holmes.

The master shot me a helpless glance. I nodded to him.

"My work's sailing ships," he responded to Holmes's question. "Yours is solving crimes. I reckon you know more than me about dealing with coppers."

"I flatter myself I do," said Holmes. "By the way, when Mr. Anderson comes back, not a word to him about what we have just been discussing. As any good conspirator will confirm, it is an admirable principle to limit the number of those who know everything. For the time being, let there be just us three."

There was, of course, a fourth in the room. But if he had ever conspired about anything in this life, he was in no position to do so ever again.

Holmes's low numerical estimate of the
police establishment at the port of Newhaven proved to be
overgenerous. A cheerful young sergeant was in charge of the
small station for purely local purposes, anything of a substantial nature being dealt with from headquarters at Lewes, the
county town of East Sussex, eight miles away inland.

The sergeant, who was visibly impressed at finding himself
face to face with Sherlock Holmes, confirmed that the excellent
White Mason was still in office there, now holding the well-
deserved rank of superintendent. Holmes, who politely declined to discuss his business with the sergeant, was able to
telephone to Lewes and request an immediate interview. White
Mason himself came on the line to speak to him. Holmes again
refused to name the nature of his business, and was not pressed
to do so. He also rejected the offer of a police carriage. Urgency
would be served better by engaging a cab from the Newhaven
dockside rank.

Thus it came about that instead of taking places in a busy
first-class compartment in the London train, we had the pri-
vacy of a neat four-wheeler that carried us at a brisk trot up the
Lewes Road, through the picturesque valley along which the
River Ouse winds below the grand undulations of the South
Downs.

117

Captain Bassett had fallen in with Holmes's tactics, to which he had had little alternative. On his return from the bridge, young Anderson had received his orders to say nothing of the death or even the stabbing. He was informed emphatically by his skipper that the matter was no longer any of his concern, until required to give evidence at an inquest.

From his name and extremely light colouring, I guessed Anderson to be of Scandinavian seafaring stock. Like many other members of the crew he lived in the London docklands. The custom was for the crew to disembark after the passengers, and for the Londoners among them to take the same boat train. A fresh crew was waiting to begin preparing for the next day's outward crossing. Captain Bassett remained in command, and stayed aboard from choice. He explained that he was a widower and kept a home with his sister at Croydon. During the busy summer season he found it convenient to live in this fashion for much of the time. The tiny cabin could not have been designed for prolonged occupation, but it seemed to suit his simple needs.

It could not have been intended for a mortuary, either, but that had become its temporary function. Rather than risk exposing the corpse to anyone's chance view by moving it elsewhere, Holmes had counselled locking it in where it was. The captain moved himself into nearby passenger accommodation, where he could keep watch on his own door while awaiting police developments arising from our visit to headquarters.

I was thankful for the diversion to Lewes. It gave me that time alone with Holmes which I had not anticipated in the train. There were so many things I wished to hear from him that I lost no time in making an opening, hoping to forestall one of his introspective silences.

"You must admit," said I, "that there is no lack of incident these days. Even you can't complain that there are no crimes and no criminals any more."

He stared up at the Downs, on which sheep stood out in the mellow evening light. There was no sign of human presence. I feared he was not going to answer.

"The Carfax case," I persisted. "The hound. The disappearance of Cromwell's bones. Now this murder. Not to mention such incidentals as your concern about invasions, revolution, the 'Yellow Peril' and being commanded to act for the King."

"Requested, Watson. His Majesty made it clear that I was under no obligation to act for him."

"It amounts to the same thing, doesn't it? You didn't decline?"

When he made no answer, but only went on looking out of the window, I took the opportunity to add, "He is my King as well as yours. You would not have begun to confide in me if you didn't mean to go on."

"Very true, my dear fellow. In any case, it is one of those matters in which I am certainly going to need your inestimable help."

"Aha! That means you are not about to retire after all!"

"*Proposing* to retire and being 'about to,' Watson, are entirely different things. To a large extent my decision rests with you."

"Come, Holmes! You're not making me responsible. And what was that about needing my help?"

He surveyed me for some moments with his lofty stare, as if puzzling why any man, free to live independently, should volunteer instead for the fetters of matrimony. Then he sighed heavily and looked away once more to the hills.

"The South Downs, Watson. These primeval, mystic, haunted masses. Their grandeur is softer than Dartmoor's. Their empty slopes are subtly misleading. They are peopled by an invisible host: the Roman, the Saxon, the Norman; the English yeoman; the signallers who watched for Napoleon Bonaparte's fleet, and their forefathers who lit the beacons to tell of the Armada's coming. Generations of ghosts, mingling with elementals of every known and unguessed kind.

"What man of solitary and contemplative tendency such as mine, and with a substantial portion of his expected span still before him, could waste it redressing the putrid, petty follies of mortals who persist in wasting theirs? Why should I continue to place myself at the disposal of knaves and fools, assuring 'Business as Usual' to all comers? Why endure city filth and noise, when I could nestle undisturbed in a fold of these hills?

"You are quite right to prefer your American lady and a pleasant home of your own. I wish you all joy, my dear chap. You have done me a greater service than any of those with which your record is illuminated already. You have brought me to the realization that it is time for me to break free.

"What else is there? I devised my own career, to my own unique specifications. I have proved, to my complete satisfaction and to that of many others, that my methods are soundly based and almost always effectual. I have led in ways where many now follow. The scientist and the laboratory worker are taking over my role.

"My studies of blood, of bruising after death, of dust and stains in the clothing, of the ashes of tobaccos, of footprints, of wheel tracks, of cyphers and other secret writings: all these have been formulized into a science that is poised to overtake me and leave me redundant in its wake. The day when the individual's trade and personal habits could be read by observing his dress, the callosities on his hands, his fingernails, the way he has shaved his chin and laced his boots—yes, Watson, that, too—that day is fast waning. Those better conditions of life and work for which I hold out hope will bring with them even more sweeping changes than the reformers foresee. The old trades will disappear, along with the old deprivations. The slums will give way to a fresh environment, based upon notions of equality of the ways of life, as well as of health, and welfare and opportunity. When all men dress similarly, eat similarly, work cheek by jowl at occupations that have ceased to mark them with their telltale imprint, what will remain that the microscope and chemical test cannot discover more easily?

"Inductive reasoning, based upon the observation of trifles and idiosyncracies, held up for comparison against the countless other examples stored in my archives and memory, has been the basis of my method. Depend upon it, there will soon be such a levelling that people will sigh for the 'good old days.' They will think back to a time when, as they seem to remember it, all were not near-duplicates of one another. I refer not only to dress and manners, but to character, habits, attitudes, living style, differences of behaviour and morals, and those other details upon which my singular profession has relied for its results.

"So you see, my dear Watson, why I must go, and why I apologize for any recent display of petulance toward you on my part. I really am most grateful."

Naturally, I was pleased to have our difference healed, and I realized what depth of brooding went on behind that inscrutable façade of his. At the same time, I was disappointed that he had used up so much of our journey with his rationalizing. I did not think that he had done it in order to evade answering my question. Yet he had not answered it, and now we were within sight of Lewes Castle, on its individual hill among the many which surround it, and I knew that I should have to wait again.

Superintendent White Mason received us cordially. The *Vally of Fear* case, in '88, had done his career a deal of good, even though the popular credit for solving it had gone to the more glamorous personage of Inspector MacDonald, of Scotland Yard. Considering that Holmes had achieved it entirely alone, in the face of their obduracy, both had cause to be grateful to him. He held them in genuine regard, however, which was not always the case with policemen whom he helped from behind the scenes.

White Mason was immediately recognizable, some fourteen years on from that case: white-haired but still ruddy and stoutish as a farmer or retired gamekeeper, though perhaps now of a more prosperous specimen of either. He was close to retirement, he told us, and had never expected to renew our professional acquaintance. He asked eagerly whether Holmes had been consulted about the Hampstead Hound, and showed disappointment upon getting a negative reply that was almost curt.

His bucolic features drew into more serious aspect, however, when Holmes unfolded his reason for coming to see him. By the time the recital was at an end the detective chief was pacing his office carpet, uttering dismayed noises.

"I don't know what to say, Mr. Holmes," said he. "I really don't. I shouldn't like to think that one of the last acts of my career would be to prefer formal charges against you, of all people; but I might have no alternative. At the very least it's hampering the course of justice. But letting a murderer go scot-free, on a whim of your own . . . I don't know what heading that would come under."

Holmes's habit of keeping his motives to himself until he chose to explain them in retrospect was familiar enough to me. He revelled in the dramatic effect of elucidating, point by point, to a bedazzled audience, the stages through which his solution of a case had been reached. I was also aware that on this, as on many another occasion, everything he had seen and heard had been shared by me, on equal terms. The difference was that he had used his observations to uncover a murderer, whom he had then seen fit to let go unchallenged. I was as much in the dark as if I had not even been present.

"My dear Superintendent." He laughed. "You don't suppose that I should have let the guilty party go free if I had not known who he is, and where we may find him at our convenience?"

"You know *that*?" exclaimed Mason, abruptly resuming his desk chair and leaning across to stare hard at the lounging figure opposite.

"Oh, yes. No doubt my friend Watson can oblige you with his identity."

"No doubt he can *not*!" I retorted. "I haven't the faintest conception."

"You are saying there *was* somebody behind that lifeboat, after all?" said the officer. "One of that party who'd lingered there."

Holmes shook his head.

"No one had lingered, but there was someone there. The steward was gathering up crockery when he was *joined* by someone: someone who had seen a chance for which he had been watching and waiting. Naturally, I refer to the officer, Anderson."

"*Anderson!*" cried I. "But he . . . It was he who . . . He told us . . . "

I surrendered with a groan.

"Who else?" said Holmes, arching his eyebrows in feigned surprise. "He had stationed himself on the afterdeck, anticipating that time when, as passengers invariably do, they would rush forward to gaze upon our welcoming white cliffs. The steward on duty there would begin immediately to clear up after them. Anderson knew precisely what he was going to do, and he did it swiftly and cleanly—well, not entirely cleanly—without his victim hearing him approach, let alone seeing him. He needed only a few seconds to drive home his blade, and, almost with the same lunge, to hoist the little man over the rail. Perhaps the knife was still in him as he fell to the sea, and became dislodged later. At all events, that is where it was consigned."

"Why did he kill him?" White Mason inquired. "Some

quarrel between them? The steward had something on this Anderson, and threatened to blackmail him over it?"

"It has always been a maxim of mine that it is a mistake to theorize without facts," said Holmes. "This is an instance where the motive may be left undefined for the time being. Sufficient unto the day is the evil thereof."

"You asked Anderson if it was he who shouted 'Man overboard!' " I reminded him. "He said he hadn't."

"Of course he would not have done. He would have preferred his victim to drown without trace. If he were picked up, the fact that he had been stabbed would be discovered. As it happened, no sooner had the steward gone into the water than some other passenger saw him there and gave the alarm. Our friend Anderson struck us as a resourceful chap, the way he superintended the rescue and himself attempted artificial respiration. His resource extended further than either of us realized at the time."

"In what way, Holmes?"

"When he heard the alarm given, he knew that his natural place, as a ship's officer, would be at the rail, scanning the sea for the man overboard. To have *left* the rail, just as excited passengers were running *to* it, would have been remarked as curious afterward. Besides, there was the bloodstain."

"Bloodstain?"

"Tut, Watson, I don't need to remind you that one cannot expect to stab a living person without provoking some effusion of gore! The victim had bled only briefly before going overboard—Anderson had foreseen that he should throw him as quickly as possible, to preclude too obvious a stain on the deck. In keeping his head, and staying by the rail, he also had the admirable common sense to hide the blood by standing on it, which, of course, accounts for some of its having got onto the soles of his shoes."

"You mean to say you saw it there?"

"You mean to say you did not? There is always some water slopping about in the scuppers beneath the rail, and he had taken the precaution of dabbling his feet in it to wash off the worst staining. It was there, nevertheless, when he was squatting over his victim, trying to revive him."

"Revive a man he'd just attempted to kill!" exclaimed the superintendent. "Why on earth should he do that?"

"He had to. Having suffered the unanticipated setback of his victim's being recovered from the sea so swiftly, he had to put the best face on it. He was able to do that by showing himself the person most actively concerned in trying to restore him. Remember, I said that his victim had not seen him about to attack. That was an assumption, but a safe one. Had there been any possibility of the steward's identifying his assailant, Anderson would have been done for. He knew that he must try to restore him, because he had you, Watson, a medical man, as witness to his attempts. He knew, anyway, that he was safe from being exposed by his victim or by you; and, as a bonus to him, the victim died."

"What put you on to him, then, Mr. Holmes?" asked the policeman wonderingly.

"Chiefly, the bloodstained soles of his shoes. He showed us the blood on his hand. He had to, because the wound, which he had to touch in giving artificial respiration, would have been found anyway. Almost simultaneously I noticed his feet. Then, of course, followed the confirmation provided by his jacket."

"What about his jacket?" asked I. Holmes treated me to his pitying look.

"The blood on its sleeve, of course."

"I didn't see any!"

"You were not meant to. Neither was I. At our first encounter with Mr. Anderson, he had already shed his tunic and hat and placed them upon the deck. You would agree that the same gush of blood that stained the deck must to some extent also have marked the hand and forearm of the wielder of the knife?"

"Inevitably."

"As, of course, it had done. No one saw him with blood on his tunic, which he had taken off quickly and folded up. It was after seeing blood on his shoes that I was curious enough to take a peep at his jacket. I was able to do so without arousing his suspicion by taking it up from the deck and handing it to him still folded."

White Mason was beginning to chuckle.

"You've given me my retirement gift in advance, Mr. Holmes," said he. "I shall recollect this demonstration of your powers for the rest of my days. Not but," he added, straightening his features again, "that you've still got some explaining to do."

"You certainly have!" I seconded him. "Anderson put on his tunic when he went to fetch the captain."

"Not entirely true," corrected Holmes. "He *started* to put it on as he hurried away. We did not see him wearing it."

"The captain would have spotted a bloody sleeve."

"No doubt. Only he was not given that opportunity. You will remember remarking how long he was taking to fetch the skipper to us?"

"That's correct."

"The reason was that he did not go directly to the bridge. He went somewhere else first—his own berth, most likely—to sponge the blood from his sleeve and anywhere else on his tunic that it happened to have splashed. The captain would see nothing remarkable about a wet sleeve. I noticed it at once, when they came in together. It, and one further detail, confirmed my suspicions finally."

"What other was that?" asked the superintendent eagerly.

"Anderson's reaction upon hearing my name for the first time," came the answer. "He appeared quite awestruck."

"Plenty of people would, Mr. Holmes. I can understand how he felt."

"Thank you, Mr. Mason. It was not so much how he looked as what he did. Remember how he stood during the interview, Watson?"

"In the Army we call it 'at ease.' I must say I was impressed by his smart bearing. A free-and-easy lot, on the whole, sailors."

"He assumed that attitude only upon hearing my name. Up till then he had been standing in the nautical officer's habitual stance, that is, with his hands clasped *in front* of him. They wear their rank, like their hearts, upon their sleeves," Holmes explained to White Mason, a countryman landlubber in appearance if ever there was one. "Study any photograph of ship's officers in a group and you will see it. It is partly for identification, partly vanity. Anderson had assumed that stance automatically. It gave me ample time to observe his damp sleeve. When I spoke my name he whipped his hands behind his back and kept them there."

"He sounds like a cool 'un," remarked the superintendent.

Holmes nodded. "Until that point, he had had no reason to suppose that the two men assisting him were any but ordinary passengers. He took natural precautions but not meticulous ones. Dampness does not show much on navy blue serge. Ordinary eyes would not have noticed it or thought it odd. Suddenly, he was thrown upon the alert, and responded accordingly."

"But you didn't let on, so as he wouldn't see you were wise to him! Very good, Mr. Holmes. And you, too, Dr. Watson."

There was little response I could make. I saw White Mason's perception cloud again.

"But why?" he asked of Holmes. "Why not take him there and then?"

"For reasons which I have told you. So as not to inconvenience Captain Bassett and several hundred people, not to mention your good self and your Force."

"Come on, Mr. Holmes. I know you better than that."

"Well, then, it was in order to give Anderson a run for us to follow. To let him feel that he has got away with something, and from beneath the very nose of someone whose reputation is clearly well known to him. To bolster up his confidence in himself and satisfy him that his luck, so far, is in."

"A run where to?"

"Initially, to his home in the East End of London. He lives alone in Burdett Road. His captain gave me the address. See, Watson, how safe it is to let a registered mercantile officer roam free? One can always trace him, because his career depends upon his availability to respond to the company's telegraphic summons. In any case, Mr. Peter Anderson is regularly on the ferry run. There will be no difficulty getting hold of him, metaphorically or literally."

"You still haven't answered," White Mason reminded him, tapping a rigid forefinger upon his desk top. For all his jolly farmer exterior and his deference to Holmes, he had been chief of his county's detective force these twenty years.

"The incident puzzles me," Holmes answered, quietly and with respect. "The very absence of any apparent motive is a mystery. Young Anderson seems to me a well-raised, well-spoken type. He has worked conscientiously to gain his mate's ticket. He has no vices—at least, none that are obvious enough to be known to Captain Bassett, who claims to be perceptive of such things—and has never been in any trouble. There is not the slightest apparent connection between him and his victim.

"And yet, I will stake my reputation on the certainty that he alone can have killed that steward. Take him, Mr. Mason, and you will have in your hands a purported killer whom no jury would convict for lack of evidence, lack of a weapon, lack of any apparent motive. Let him remain free, confident that he is unwatched and unsuspected, and through some action or association he will lead us to those hard answers that prosecuting counsel would need to take with them into court against him."

"It's a tall order, Mr. Holmes," exclaimed the detective chief. "I wish you'd consulted me first."

"We were within minutes of docking. I came to you as quickly as I was able. If I'd left him in his captain's custody while we are sitting here debating, my whole game would have been given away."

White Mason looked helplessly toward me, but I had no words for his reassurance.

Holmes resumed. "Instead, he is congratulating himself on having had a lucky escape. He believes that I have dismissed any connection between the murder and himself, or I should have acted. All the same, the future sound of my name, or sight of me, will be enough to make him watch out for himself. The responsibility, should he kill again, falls squarely upon myself. I can but hope to find out enough about him and his motives in time to prevent its happening."

"You're not convinced that this was an isolated killing?"

"Not certain enough to rule it out."

White Mason jumped up to pace his office floor again.

"In other words," said he measuredly, "you're asking me to let you follow up this case yourself. You want me to square it with Captain Bassett that this steward of his is put down in the log as dying of accidental drowning, and make no report of what you've been telling me. You're quite sure that's *all* you want of me, Mr. Sherlock Holmes? I mean, if there are any other irregularities and breaches of the rules that you'd like tossed in as well, you only have to name 'em!"

"*Thank you,* my dear Mason," replied Holmes, smiling at the other's sarcasm. "I fancy that with both our careers drawing to their close we are mutually well placed for a gamble. Watson will correct me if I am wrong, but I think it is true that of the countless murder investigations in which I have been involved I have never before been on the spot when the crime was done. It offers a challenge that might enable me to end my career in unique style."

"End your career! That's me, not you, Mr. Holmes. You've got many a year still to go, hasn't he, Dr. Watson?"

That was a question I preferred to leave Holmes to deal with himself. He chose to let it pass.

"Very well." White Mason sighed, letting his arms fall limply to his sides. "I'll slip over to Newhaven and have a quiet talk with that captain myself. Come if you like, but you could as easily take your London train from here."

"Thank you, I think we will do that," said Holmes. "There are one or two little concerns awaiting our attention at Baker Street."

He shook hands with our old friend, and stalked to the door.

"Aha!" said the chief of detectives to me. "Then, for all his talk of retiring, this isn't positively his final appearance?"

"You know Holmes," I responded confidentially. "He likes to keep one guessing."

"Well, Doctor," said White Mason, "do what you can to ensure that he guesses right, will you? I wouldn't like my retirement gift from the Chief Constable to be my own head mounted on a plaque!"

"**H**ad you not been so preoccupied
with softer matters lately, Watson, leaving me to keep our
invaluable reference library up to date alone, you would have
found it necessary to add no less than four newspaper items
under the letter Y."

"For 'Yellow Peril,' Holmes?"

"Precisely."

"Ah! I half wondered if that was in your mind."

We were in an empty first-class compartment of the London, Brighton & South Coast Railway train that was bearing
us homeward from Lewes. Our diverted journey had brought
the advantage of travelling in a quieter train than would have
been the case from Newhaven docks, and we could converse
freely.

Holmes's successful application to Superintendent Mason
to let him follow Peter Anderson's trail in his own way had left
him buoyed up and willingly communicative. I was not going
to miss my chance, and determined to stay deaf to any jibes he
might toss in about "softer matters" and the like.

" 'Yellow Peril' is a despicable term," said I. "Any Oriental
would feel insulted."

"Which I am sure was meant. Look who coined it."

"The Kaiser. Enough said!"

A little over two years before the time of which I write, the name Baron von Ketteler had been added to the mounting list of assassinations of people in high places. He had been Germany's minister in China. He was shot in a Peking street in broad daylight. His murderers were Chinese soldiers under orders to escort him to safety from that wave of violence against all foreigners upon Chinese soil which became known as the Boxer Rebellion. Other foreigners were massacred, and an international army was despatched from Europe to rescue survivors, of several nationalities, trapped in Peking.

Kaiser Wilhelm II made a public vow of terrible retribution. Many of us thought him half mad, even though his mother, the Princess Victoria, had been our own new King's elder sister.

He exhorted the German contingent sailing for China to spare no lives and take no prisoners: "A thousand years ago, Attila's Huns made terror their name. You will live up to that, and make sure that no Chinese ever again dares so much as look a German in the eye."

The outburst was deplored throughout Europe, and by many Germans. Nevertheless, the Germans as a people became tarred with the Kaiser's brush. They were automatically "Huns" to us. Those of them who had made their homes in England, working as shopkeepers, barbers, waiters, musicians and in other everyday pursuits, were now viewed darkly by neighbours who had been customers and friends for years. We had several ugly incidents of attacks upon them and their property. There will always be people whose patriotism takes immoderate forms, and no shortage of common louts of the kind who seize any excuse to persecute innocent minorities.

I had not missed reading some of those reports to which Holmes alluded. Three or four cases had occurred in the past few weeks of apparently innocent Chinese being beaten in dark alleys in Limehouse. It could be assumed that their attackers had not been detected, nor would be. No one outside the Chinese community knows much of what goes on in that small yet teeming territory within the heart of the London dockland. Few who do not belong there ever visit it, except in search of illicit Oriental pleasures, and then at the risk of dire consequences. The police keep aloof. Flagrant breaches of the peace are rare, for discretion is everything among the Limehouse populace of shopkeepers, lodging-house proprietors, and passing sailormen of varying nationalities.

No one doubted that the recent attacks upon Chinese had been influenced by the Kaiser's irresponsible words. The very term "Yellow Peril" had been used in his diatribe. It had sounded menacing to a Western world, wondering fearfully what radical changes to old orders the new century was going to bring. The crimes were quite obvious demonstrations of that fear. I reminded Holmes of this in relation to the stabbing of the ship's steward.

"If it had been a 'Yellow Peril' murder, surely the killer would have wanted his deed widely known? Such crimes are meant as warnings to the Chinese not to try to rise above themselves."

Holmes nodded. "That, and to protest to the government about allowing any further influx. Remember Seacliff last year? He made no bones about having shot that laundryman in order to test the immigration laws."

Seacliff's case had been an exceptional one. After killing an old Chinese in cold blood in a Limehouse street, he had gone straight to a police station to hand over his revolver and give himself up. He showed no compunction. The deed was so blatant that he was pronounced paranoid and put away for life, instead of receiving the death sentence.

"Are you suggesting that Anderson is a paranoiac, too?" I asked Holmes.

"No, although you will concede that he shows similarities to Seacliff, who was to all appearances normal. He was well-bred, educated, and had been an Army officer. Yet, according to those who understand such things, he had passed into that ultimate stage of his disease where the sufferer takes it upon himself to act in a way he believes the authorities are shunning."

"Well, if that is what motivated Anderson, he certainly wasn't owning up to it."

"That is in itself interesting. I asked myself whether he felt he had bungled his killing by doing it too secretly. He had an unexpected chance to redress that when the body was brought back on board the ship. Some such dramatic gesture as: 'Ladies and gentlemen, you believe this man to be a victim of accidental drowning. See this wound in his side! It is my work. I could have concealed it from you, but I choose to proclaim my deed as an act of sacrifice through which to draw my fellowmen's attention to the Yellow Peril that dwells among us.' It is a regrettable possibility that he might have got a round of applause."

"But he said no such thing."

"Not even later, when I identified myself to him. He recognized my name without a doubt. It was his opportunity to surrender himself to no less a captor than Sherlock Holmes, and thereby ensure a maximum of attention from the press and at his trial. Even then, he would very probably be acquitted. There would undoubtedly be petitions got up on his behalf. Yet he said nothing and watched us let him get away with it. Why, do you suppose?"

"I can think of several reasons. One is that he didn't do it."

"You had better let me hear the others," remarked Holmes loftily.

"He did it with a fit of his madness on him. The deed was enough to exhaust it, temporarily at least."

"Impossible. We saw him within seconds of its happening. He was not even dazed or confused, let alone deranged. He was in complete control of his faculties, even to acting to conceal the bloodstains."

"Quite simply, then, he didn't think he was suspected, and he had no intention of volunteering his guilt. It wasn't a 'Yellow Peril' killing at all. What about blackmail? The steward could have had something over him."

Holmes lapsed into thought for some minutes. Our train was clattering through the crowded acreage of sooty brick, greasy glass, smoking chimneys and narrow, mean streets that encircles the heart of an Empire boasting some of earth's fairest sights. Our long day's travelling would soon carry us into the terminus named after the late Queen. A cab would whisk us thence to 221B Baker Street, the welcome of our armchairs and slippers and something delectable from Mrs. Hudson's cornucopian larder.

Evening was not far advanced, but lowering cloud had been thickening as we travelled farther from the coast. A change of wind had carried it from the east, to pile it over the metropolis, where it merged with the oily smoke from thousands of factory chimneys. Premature darkness and a spattering of rain greeted our return to London.

"Blackmail or whatever," said Holmes at length, "it was no impulsive killing. It was timed so meticulously and executed so skilfully, so coolly covered up in the face of setback, that I can only see it as premeditated. If the 'Yellow Peril' is excluded, what remains, however improbable, must be the truth. The solution could never be got by the policeman's frontal attack, the blunt arrest in the belief that anyone so cool as Anderson would crumble and confess all. I am convinced that it lies too deep for any counsel to prise it from him in court. Hence my appeal to Mason to let me deal with it in my own way."

"Have you anything in mind?" I asked dubiously. "To begin with, you have no time for chasing after random murderers. You have the King's business awaiting your attention. Great heavens, consider the risks! Whether Anderson really is a cunning schemer, up to some deep game, or merely a madman who can kill without motive, he might claim another victim before you can stop him. Think of the consequences for you when it becomes known that you let him go!"

"Not to mention the consequences for his victim," added Holmes dryly. "There is one other consideration that you have not mentioned, Watson."

"What is it?"

"My long-held insistence, which I have often expressed to you, that a client is to me a mere unit, a factor in a problem. Rank, position, wealth, emotion: none weighs heavier in the balance than common humanity. Therefore, it behooves me better to use such powers as I possess on behalf of a humble, anonymous Chinese ship's servant than upon clearing up one of those superficial difficulties for which our artificial state of society is responsible."

"Very worthy, Holmes, if it weren't for the political implications."

"There is that side of it to consider, of course. It is comforting to have so ready a volunteer to assist me at such a busy time, my dear fellow. You haven't anything too pressing to preoccupy you just now?"

"Nothing," said I caustically, "apart from a certain domestic matter, which I'm sure you won't count. There is this Lady Frances Carfax business, of course."

"That can wait. Nothing immediate is likely to happen. Capital, then! It's settled. Since my hands are going to be particularly full of this new matter, you will be able to take over from me in His Majesty's interest."

Before I could answer, our train jerked and squeaked to a halt. We had arrived in Victoria Station, and the locomotive's steamy hiss sounded like a great gasp of exhausted effort. Carriage doors were clashing open, porters being hailed, trolleys trundled, items tossed down. It was not a very full train, but the concentrated noise under the high-arched, glass-and-iron roof was considerable.

As we got down, I seemed to sense an unusual bustle and a distinctly excited atmosphere. My glance at Holmes's surprised face confirmed that he noticed it, too.

The dramatic reason was soon apparent. I heard a porter dumbfound a passenger whom he was assisting with the news that the "poor old King" had lost his head!

Common courtesy prevented our interrupting the man to question him. The ticket collector at the barrier was preoccupied with trying to dissuade a party of sailors from swarming onto the platform until the departing passengers had gone through.

My stomach was hollow with apprehension as we hurried across the station hall. I scanned the newspaper placards. There were many, but none relating to the King. No one was crying "Special!"

A more noteworthy feature was the absence of policemen from the hall. Generally, they loomed conspicuous, deterring roisterers and keeping keen watch for pickpockets and luggage thieves.

Holmes strode through the archway leading to the forecourt, where the cabs waited. There were plenty free, but not all the cabbies were huddled on their perches in the drizzling rain. A commotion from across the cobbled space attracted our attention to a crowd, among and above which the helmets of the absent police constables showed.

I heard Holmes's high bark of a laugh.

"*That* king!" he chortled, and I joined my laugh with his.

Even before we had crossed the greasy expanse to join the

crowd we could make out clearly the centre of its attention. The stone statue of Charles II, in swaggering pose, had been decapitated.

In its perfect state it had been an undistinguished nineteenth-century representation, in no way comparable with the earlier one at Chelsea Hospital reputed to be the work of Grinling Gibbons. The Victoria one was no older than the station itself. It had been placed there during the construction, for no reason that I had ever heard explained. It was part of no statuary pattern, and bore no logical association to the neighbourhood. From time to time, letters to one newspaper or another called for its removal, but nothing had been done. One of its critics had evidently begun the desired demolition himself by chopping off its head.

The severed neck stood out starkly white against the figure's overall griminess. That and the clean cut were evidence of cheap, soft stone. All the same, it must have taken a good deal of strength to strike off the head at what appeared to have been a single blow.

The little crowd was making way for two of the constables to return to their duty on the station. Their expressions showed that they did not regard what had happened with any gravity.

"When did this happen, officer?" asked Holmes, accosting them.

"Half-hour ago," was the offhand reply.

"Some crackpot, no doubt?"

" 'Spect so."

"Strong fellow," I remarked.

"Must have quite an arm on him," conceded the constable.

"No arrest, then?" asked Holmes

I was surprised by the sharpness of his tone. So, clearly, was the officer's colleague, who leaned forward slightly to see better the questioner's features. He showed no recognition of Holmes, though. He peered at me in turn.

"You gents know anythin' about this?" he demanded.

"Not a thing, officer," answered I. "We have just come off the train."

They both subjected us to the policeman's slow head-to-foot scrutiny. With our hats pulled firmly on and our collars up against the rain, no doubt we could have been suspects. Had we shown ourselves the worse for drink, or been in possession of axes or other tools of demolition, that would have settled it. Their respective hands would have been on our respective collars. Seeing that we were not swaying on our feet, nor carrying anything more capable of causing damage than small valises, they grunted in unison and walked on.

"It is starting to pour," I pointed out. "Let's get our cab, Holmes."

"A moment, Watson," he surprised me by replying.

He turned and easily shouldered a way for us to the statue, which looked even more ridiculous than usual. The spectators were dispersing with the onset of the heavier rain, but two other constables were pulling on their waterproof capes, with the obvious intention of remaining by the statue.

The stone head lay beside the shallow plinth. Holmes crouched down to look at it.

"No touching, sir, if you please," one of the officers admonished him.

Holmes looked up, registering surprise.

"That's evidence," explained the other constable.

"Oh? Of what?" asked Holmes.

"Aha!" was all the reply he received. The speaker tapped the side of his nose with a finger.

"Scotland Yard evidence," supplied his companion portentously.

"I should have thought . . . " began I. I was interrupted by a touch on my shoulder. I turned, anticipating another uniform and those chilling words of arrest. Instead, I recognized the tall

form and wan features of Chief Inspector Tobias Gregson, of
Scotland Yard. He had on a mackintosh overcoat and a soft felt
hat. Under the hat's brim I could see the straggling ends of the
hair which, once flaxen but now a faded gray, he wore as long
as I recalled it from earlier days, when Holmes and I had
worked with him on such cases as *The Greek Interpreter, The
Red Circle,* and *Wisteria Lodge.* Indeed, it had been Gregson
and Lestrade together who had personified Scotland Yard for
me when Holmes had taken me with him on an investigation
for the first time, as long ago as 1881. My subsequent account
of it, under the title *A Study in Scarlet,* became the very first
chronicle of my friend's great career ever to appear before the
public.

Holmes had described Gregson to me then as the smartest
member of Scotland Yard, although he spoilt the compliment
be adding facetiously that he was "normally out of his depth"
and that he and Lestrade were "the pick of a bad lot." In fact,
they were neither better nor worse than the average official
detective of twenty years ago. They were also great rivals: "as
jealous as a pair of professional beauties," as Holmes put it.

We had seen more of Lestrade than of Gregson since,
largely because the latter's duties had carried him out of
Holmes's sphere of purely criminal detection. In the mid-1880s
the dynamiting campaign against London targets by the Fenian
Brotherhood, campaigning for home rule for Ireland, reached
its peak. Casualties and damage were caused by attacks on the
Houses of Parliament, the Tower, several mainline and Underground stations, and other targets. There were attempts against
Nelson's Column and even Scotland Yard itself. The worst consequences were widespread fear and panic, committing large
numbers of police wholly to protection work.

A specifically anti-terrorist wing, the Special Irish Branch,
had been set up to combat the dynamiters. After the brutal
campaign had been successfully brought to an end, the squad
was kept in being, known simply as the Special Branch. Its new

and broader task was to deal with anything seeming likely to jeopardize national security.

We had heard from Lestrade some years ago that his old rival had transferred to Special Branch. He had subsequently risen to the rank of Chief Inspector. Here he was now, a hand on each of our shoulders, telling us of his unexpected pleasure at running into us at so unlikely a site.

Holmes shook his hand warmly.

"A pleasure to see you again, Gregson, and on such a night. But what fetches you from your eyrie, pray?"

"Duty, Mr. Holmes. Duty."

"I see! Special Branch's protective service extends to royal statues."

"You have missed out this time, Gregson," said I, shaking hands also. "The assassination was successful."

Gregson smiled. "So they told me. I thought I had better step across all the same and have a look for myself. Might have been a crack in the stone. I can see it wasn't, though."

He nodded toward the headless trunk, down which the rain streamed. Further evidence was forthcoming at that same moment by yet another constable coming up, wet and massive in his waterproof.

"Beg pardon, Mr. Gregson, sir," said he. "I found this haxe."

From beneath his glistening folds he produced a long-handled axe. Gregson snatched it from him ungratefully.

"You've had your great paws all over it!" he accused. "Haven't you heard of fingerprints?"

"I'm sorry, sir, I'm sure. These newfangled ways take some remembering about."

"Where was it?"

"A little way up on Victoria Street, sir. In the gutter. Sergeant sent me to search that way, while he and Charlie—I mean, No. 423, sir—they took the other roads."

Holmes had contrived to turn the axe blade so that the

nearest lamplight shone along its cutting edge. I could see that it was jagged with damage. Gregson gave it a glance.

"You can call them back," he told the man brusquely. "This is it, all right."

The constable saluted and turned away, to exercise his lungs into his whistle. Gregson turned the axe despondently between his hands.

"Fingerprints, microscopes, chemicals," he intoned gloomily. "We didn't need them in the old days. We got our results just the same, didn't we?"

"You did indeed," Holmes assured him diplomatically.

"What difference are they going to make if the bobby on the beat is half-baked!"

"Patience, my dear Gregson. The tradition has been all eyes and brawn from the Bow Street Runners till now. A sharp new Commissioner or two cannot change that overnight. The bobby will adapt to his times."

"He'll need to, or the villain will be first in the chase. I'm forgetting, though, you've always been a microscope and chemicals man, Mr. Holmes."

"I have found them useful occasionally," responded Holmes. "But tell me if you will, Gregson, why Special Branch should take any interest in the defacement of a mere statue, especially one as undistinguished as this."

"Still don't miss much, eh, Mr. Holmes?" Gregson rested the head of the axe on the cobblestones, and leaned on the end of the handle. "The fact is, we had a tip-off."

"From the perpetrator himself?" said I.

"Almost certain. Anonymous note to the Commissioner."

"Saying he was going to do this!"

"No, Doctor. More like the real thing. The King himself."

"Good heavens! But you get a good many threats of that sort, I imagine?"

"Cartloads. They all get sent in to the Branch, and we can't afford not to try to take them seriously."

" 'Try'?" echoed Holmes.

"You can tell some are barmy at a glance," Gregson explained. "Making out the Archbishop of Canterbury's in a plot to have a bomb planted in the crown. You can laugh, Dr. Watson! We still have to go through the motions."

"I'm sorry, Gregson. Was this another crank one?"

"Fairly. Raving on about the King not being fit to sit on the throne, and then that bit of old nursery rhyme: 'Here comes a chopper to chop off his head.' It's obvious enough what it meant. Daft, but a plain threat, all the same. With the Coronation coming we can't be too careful."

"Tell me, though," intervened Holmes, "how came you to connect that particular warning with this particular statue?"

"There have been orders out since the Coronation was first arranged," explained Gregson smugly. "Anything in the nature of a demonstration against royalty has to be reported to us at the Branch. It's up to us to inform all divisions. It's the way we do things in the Branch."

"And someone down here was smart enough to see significance in this occurrence."

"Clegge, the Sergeant, is a deal brighter than some of his men. Chopper. Head. King. Statue of King Charles."

"It wasn't Charles the Second who lost his head," I pointed out.

"His dad did," countered Gregson.

"Well, congratulations to you, Gregson," said Holmes. "A pity you have no witness to crown your enterprise in deserved glory."

Gregson grinned slyly. "I don't think that need bother us, Mr. Holmes. I'd give you a bet we won't be long putting our hand on the collar of the chap we want."

"You think you know him?" said I.

"If he's the one we have in mind, he was sounding off at Speakers' Corner only last Sunday. Pity the crowd chased him out of the Park before the bobby on duty could give him a talking-to. Anything passes at Speakers' Corner, short of improper, and quite right, with freedom of speech. But there are some things the British man in the street won't abide, and I must say, between ourselves, I agree. It isn't our place, at the Branch, to lay down what a man may or may not speak up for in public. Even so, with His Majesty coming near to dying, and lying on his sickbed still, 'Down with the King, and three cheers for Saint Oliver Cromwell!' goes over the limit."

A sharp nudge from Holmes's elbow forbade my response. He spoke instead, in his most matter-of-fact way.

"No indeed, Gregson. And long may the impartiality of the British bobby hold out against the influence of microscopes."

"Eh? Oh, I see, Mr. Holmes. You've still got your sense of humour, too."

"Where should one be otherwise?" sighed Holmes. "Well, Watson, here we stand, getting soaked, and Mrs. Hudson will be concerned about her gravy. We trust you will make up for your wetting by nailing your man, Gregson. He sounds just the sort who needs taking off the streets until the Coronation is over."

Gresgon pulled his rainproof more snugly about him.

"When you see in the papers that a Matt Spurrier's been nabbed," said he, "that'll be him. By the way, Doctor, speaking of the papers, is it true about you inventing this Hampstead Hound?"

"It is nothing of the sort, Chief Inspector!"

"Just one joke for another, sir," Gregson guffawed. "It's got old Lestrade fairly on the hop, anyway. We've had a proper chuckle over him down at the office. He would go poking his nose in where the local lads could have handled things perfectly well, and now he's stuck with it."

"You don't say it's *still* going on?" said I.

"Not after tomorrow, he hopes. You won't have heard, perhaps? They're so sick and tired, out North London way, not knowing whether it's safe to be out and about, that some local bigwig threatened to get up a shoot, beaters and all. The Commissioner couldn't allow that, of course, so he told Lestrade to arrange an official sweep."

Gregson held up a palm for the rain to splash on it.

"They're starting off at dawn. Good luck to 'em, I say," he said finally, with a smirk, and, touching his hat brim to us, splashed off to greet the returning sergeant.

A number of messages awaited our return to our rooms, where closed curtains, lit lamps, and a well-stoked fire with our slippers airing inside the fender soon dispelled the memory of the dank gloom without. Although Holmes's cable to Mrs. Hudson had bespoken dinner for seven-thirty, that good lady was characteristically unflustered at our lateness. Compared with some of Holmes's lapses it was trivial.

She served us a hearty meal, unseasonable but perfectly suited to the climate's aberration. It comprised thick vegetable soup, steak-and-kidney pie with new potatoes, runner beans, peas and carrots, and blackberry-and-apple pie, with sardines on toast for savoury. I was glad of every morsel. Holmes, as usual, picked and pecked among the dishes, paying less attention to good victuals than to the slips of paper beside his place. He kept up a disjointed flow of exclamations and comments.

My mind was only half upon what he was saying. I had been disappointed to find nothing for me from Coral among the messages. While Holmes had been washing his hands before the meal I telephoned to the house in Russell Square, only to learn from the maid that Mrs. and Miss Atkins were not expected back home until late in the evening.

One of Holmes's messages was from Dr. Garside, of the

147

British Museum, reporting that there was still no trace of the missing Tyburn bones. He had been in touch with the few big collectors known to have ossiferous interests. The principal auction salerooms had had no approaches from furtive vendors. No monetary demands had been received.

Another note was more terse and to the point: "MY PLACE THURSDAY AFTER 5"

"Whose is that one?" I asked, when Mrs. Hudson had cleared our dinner plates, with much clucking of her tongue over Holmes's leavings.

"Shinwell," replied he. "I asked him to find Chapman and fetch him back."

"Chapman? That vagrant from Hampstead Heath? I didn't know you had any interest in him."

Holmes kept me waiting while he lit his briar pipe, crammed with preserved dottles from earlier smokings. His reply, when it came, surprised me further.

"I thought it might be useful to have another word with the fellow."

"How would Shinwell know where to find him?"

"He has his methods, as I have mine."

"Suppose Chapman has no wish to come back."

"Shinwell's persuasive powers are irresistible."

Shinwell Johnson, known less formally to his underworld peers as "Porky," was a recent recruit to that mercenary force of Holmes's which included, among others, the Baker Street Irregulars, the squad of urchin boys who brought him information from unlikely places. Shinwell's particular manor encompassed the night clubs, gambling dens and doss houses of both East End and West, where he could see everything and overhear anyone. Such surroundings seemed to me unlikely, though, for a tramp who had so recently been sleeping rough on Hampstead Heath.

"What do you want with Chapman, Holmes?" asked I.

"Have you started taking an interest in the hound mystery after all? You seemed inclined to dismiss it as some sort of unreality."

"It was real enough," he answered. "Real, and serious. That poor fellow might have lost his life."

"Well," said I, "I am relieved to hear you giving it credence at last. Hampstead and Highgate are like deserted villages, by all accounts. No one dares venture upon the Heath any more. Press speculation is rife, and the police are to make this sweep tomorrow. What else has happened to change your attitude?"

"Nothing has happened," replied he, "except that I have been doing some belated thinking. The dramatic event during our little sea passage today set me pondering."

"I don't see any connection between a murder on a Channel ferry and an attack by a hound upon Hampstead Heath. *Is* there one?"

"You know how deeply I am intrigued by seemingly motiveless crime. Here we have two examples. I have pledged my energies and perhaps even my reputation to getting to the bottom of one of them. Why, then, dismiss the other, whose possibilities are quite as extensive?"

"Why indeed, Holmes," I agreed. "I admire your humane reasoning that an unknown Chinese steward should merit priority over the King. I suppose the same goes for a tramp. The only thing I'd remind you is that while man bites dog would be crime, dog bites man isn't."

"Bravo, Watson! We shall make a dialectician of you yet. Only, if your reasoning is based on an assumption that what occurred on the Heath that night was no crime, you are bound to fail."

"What? You're saying that someone set a hound on him *deliberately*!"

"Something of that nature. Whatever occurred, it was criminally inspired."

"Well, well, Holmes!" I exclaimed, amazed. "Here's a change, and no mistake!"

He shook his head, turning down his lip.

"Mistake there was, I regret to say, and it was I who made it. I had leaped to an entirely erroneous conclusion. It shows yet again how dangerous it is to reason from insufficient data; worse still, to refuse to reason at all, merely because one happens to be impatient and out of humour. Detection is, or should be, a wholly objective science."

I forebore to say that I had known he had been sulking, and why. I asked him instead, "What are you now saying happened? One of Chapman's fellow tramps set a dog on him for some reason? You need hardly punish your conscience over that."

"If it were so simple, Watson, I should agree with you and leave it to Lestrade. It would be on about the intellectual level of someone capable of equating a stray dog with stolen bones. We are into something much deeper, however."

"I hope you are going to enlighten me."

By way of reply Holmes leaped purposefully to his feet.

"Fetch your waterproof," he ordered, going to the window to peer through the curtains. "The rain seems to have eased, but it will be damp enough. Wellingtons would be advisable, too."

An awful possibility occurred to me.

"You're not proposing that we turn out and traipse up to Hampstead!"

"An explanation is no more than your due. Pragmatist that you are, you would surely wish to see the evidence for yourself?"

"Your word has always been good enough for me, Holmes." The prospect of the cold, wet alternative to our fireside snugness was appalling.

"No, no. I insist," said he. "We have busy days ahead of us

and there might be no other opportunity. The police will be trampling all over the place tomorrow. Between them and the weather, the traces are almost certain to be destroyed."

"But I've *seen* the traces."

"Seen, but not observed. Besides, I fancy that when you come to write up the case for your annals you will be grateful to have absorbed all the atmosphere."

This was a more cogent proposition. His recent cases had furnished me with nothing that was worthy of comparison with earlier ones.

"You really see this turning into an important matter?"

"Unless I am much mistaken, it promises to be as strange a mystery as any we have encountered. I need hardly remind you of the singular clue that gave me the solution to our *Silver Blaze* case.

"The dog that did nothing in the nighttime? It draws more comment than almost any other feature of my entire chronicles."

"You will rejoice, then, to learn that it is singular no longer. It has become plural. Now, hurry up, my dear chap. Ring for our Wellington boots and let us be upon our way."

With renewed spirits I went to the bell.

"Oh, and Watson . . . "

"Yes, Holmes?"

"These are deep waters. Better bring your service revolver."

He hastened from the room with the signs of mercurial impatience that demonstrated he was in complete earnest. Some forty minutes later we stood once more upon Hampstead Heath.

The carriage we had engaged in Baker Street had set us down at the precise spot where the police vehicle had brought us on that earlier night. When told our destination, the cabby had demurred. It had taken Holmes's firmest persuasion, and the sight of gold, to get him to bring us to this unfavoured place. He refused Holmes's order to wait to take us back again.

"It ain't me, guv'," he explained. "It's the nags. You might not think they listens to talk, but it's all round the stables about this 'ound, and they knows—they knows!"

"Tell them they are to get an extra guinea's worth of feed," said Holmes, handing up the coin. "Drive on to Jack Straw's and take something nourishing yourself. Show them what a brave fellow you are. Only, be back here forty-five minutes from now, or you'll find yourself in the Carriage Office tomorrow, handing in your licence for refusing a fare."

It was an earlier hour than that of our last visit—not yet ten o'clock—but the fleeting rain clouds had made it quite dark. Although it was not actually raining, every bush we brushed past showered us with its accumulated droplets. The distant whirr of London was the only sound besides the squelch of our progress onto the Heath, which was lit dimly by the thin yellow beam of Holmes's patent folding lantern. I used my left hand for my cane. My right stayed in my mackintosh pocket, and in its palm rested the butt and trigger guard of my trusty Webley No. 2. Needless to remark, no vagrants sheltered under the trees and shrubs. The revolver was my reassurance against anybody—or any*thing*—we might encounter there.

We were soon at the clearing where Chapman had been savaged. Holmes shone his lantern about, then turned to stand facing me, leaning on his cane.

"First, to set the scene," said he. "You remember, it was a fine, warm night, late enough for darkness to have fallen. The evening's strollers had taken themselves away, save, no doubt, for a few young couples whose preoccupations admitted no thought of footpad or garrotter. That pathetic company of tramps and other down-and-outs which makes its bivouac here had settled down for the night. Chapman lay over here."

He took my arm and led me to the dim spot where the constable had indicated the cocoon-like grass hollow.

"Just lie down there, my dear chap," he commanded mildly.

"Lie down!" I protested, though instinctively keeping my voice low. "It's sopping wet!"

"Not so," Holmes corrected. "It is a bed sited and made by an expert."

"Must I really, Holmes?"

"Our reconstruction must be as realistic as we can make it."

"Oh, very well."

I groped my way down into the shadowed space, overhung with sheltering branches. Holmes was right. It was awkward, lying down in my coat, with the heavy revolver in my pocket, but I managed. Holmes sank to one knee beside me.

"Shut your eyes," he ordered. I did so, holding my tweed hat firmly upon my head.

"You are asleep," came his low tone. "One of those luckier ones to whom slumber comes easily, to obliterate for a few blissful hours the cares and fears of the wretched state into which you have fallen. You dream of happpier days, with your regiment and your mates . . . "

"Never mind what I'm dreaming, Holmes. Just get on, please."

"You sleep soundly," he droned on. "Your ears do not catch that odd, chilling cry from out across the Heath. Those others not yet asleep hear it, though. They stir uneasily. There it is again! What might it be? Beast or man? Hist! Again! Can it be nearer this time? Yes! Once more it comes moaning through the darkness—*and it is coming this way! Listen!*"

In spite of myself, I found that I was straining my ears. I moved to sit up, but Holmes gently pushed me down.

"You are asleep," he reiterated, "and hear nothing of this. Even as it draws ever closer, that high-pitched cry, now distinctly an animal's howling, you hear nothing of it. Nearer! *Nearer!* You do not fear its rapid onrush as those around you do. They are scrambling to their feet already, seizing hold of sticks or any other weapons. Some are bundling their things under their arms and starting to run, for there is that in the howling which conveys deadly purpose . . .

"Suddenly, bellowing out of the night, a great hellhound springs! Its jaws are agape. Its eyes blaze. Its howls are earsplitting as it scatters all before it. The other men run as one, defence abandoned. Only you remain, stirring now in your dream. And then . . . !"

A terrible grip seized my throat. The back of my head was pressed violently into the ground. My hands came up instinctively, to scrabble and clutch desperately. My suddenly opened eyes saw the pale blur of the face that was close to mine. Eyes glittering, mouth grimly set, Sherlock Holmes bore down upon me with his throttling hands.

"Holmes . . . !" I tried to cry, but could barely articulate. "Leave . . . off . . . ! For heaven's . . . !"

"Fight, man!" he raged at me. "Get up, and fight for your life!"

I wriggled and struggled, trying to throw him off. He was too strong for me in that prone position. My elbows thrust into the ground, seeking purchase to heave myself up, but I was pinioned.

"Life or death!" he cried into my face. "Fight!"

My last thought—for that was what, in my extremis, I thought it to be—was that Holmes had gone mad. My defection had preyed on his mind, to the extent of turning it. He had lured me to this spot, upon this excuse, intent on doing away with me. When my body was discovered it would be accounted to the hound.

All at once the fearful pressure eased. The grip left my throat. I sensed Holmes standing up erect and brushing at his trouser knee.

"You see?" said he. "Utterly impossible. The thing was stage-managed from start to finish."

My head spun and there were red flashes before my eyes. They were dispelled by his lantern's beam.

"Watson?" said he, in a tone almost of curiosity. "Do get up. It may not be wet there, but it is certainly damp."

I was aware of him stooping and extending a hand to me. I grasped it and let him pull me to my feet.

"Dear me, you are puffing like a grampus," he observed. "You are dreadfully out of condition, my dear fellow."

"You . . . you nearly killed me!" croaked I.

"Killed? What nonsense. A small experiment, with precisely the result I anticipated. No man, especially an underfed, emaciated vagrant, could have survived the attack he described. He would have been finished before he knew what was happening. Fought his way to his feet, indeed! Wrestled the beast right across the clearing! Even you found yourself powerless under my mild onslaught. As for the ludicrous circumstance which rescued him, can you really picture a savage hound struck with terror by the calm approach of the questioning lantern's beam, and the majestic tone of the London bobby's ' 'Ello, 'ello. Wot might all this be about?'?"

"Do give over, Holmes!" I spluttered, half winded still, half choking with laughter. A fit of coughing made my head swim even more. A match flared, and I saw him sucking upon his pipe as unruffled as if he were in his fireside chair.

"You see," he resumed, "not only is the story of an attack implausible on physical grounds. See the place where you were good enough to lie?" His beam picked it out as he spoke. "How rumpled and disarranged it has become as a result of your struggles. Yet, when we were shown it, only a hour or two after the incident, it was smooth and undisturbed. There had been no struggle there. Then there is the anomaly regarding the nature of dogs. . . . Do you note the points I am making, Watson?" he interrupted himself impatiently.

"Yes, Holmes," was all I had strength or inclination to say. " 'The nature of dogs . . . ' "

" . . . is not to attack sleeping prey. He would have had to be awake and stirring—rather a coincidence, just as the hound chanced to be passing by, wouldn't you agree?"

"Yes, Holmes."

"However, there is a far more obvious flaw in his tale. It concerns the wrestling match that our little experiment has proved could not have taken place. Come and see here."

I was thankful for the arm by which he propelled me again, this time to the base of the tree where we had seen the gigantic paw marks. The sheltering boughs had kept them intact from the rain.

"See?" Holmes stooped to point. "Excellent impressions, made by a large four-footed animal. *Four* feet, Watson, where there should have been only two."

"A two-legged hound!"

"Two on the ground, the other two on its victim's shoulders. That a large animal had been present at some stage is patently obvious—too obvious. It had merely ambled about on all fours, leaving the traces which we see. To go for Chapman's throat while he was standing erect, as he said it did, it would have reared up on to its hind legs alone. So great a weight upon them would have caused two most distinctive impressions, but there are none such to be seen."

"You are saying that this was a put-up job, Holmes?"

"From start to finish."

"The officer who found Chapman testified to a struggle."

"He got here after it was over. He saw no hound."

"He had heard the howls, though. So had the other policeman. We ourselves heard some distant ones. Hang it, *something* must have happened to make all those other men run off and stir up such panic."

"The howling is the most interesting aspect of all, Watson. It is the touch that lifts the drama from the banal to the spectral. The sight of a large animal running about the Heath would not itself be enough to drive off the entire vagrant population. A wild dog may be hunted down and shot. That is what is expected of Lestrade tomorrow morning. If he can furnish a plausible corpse, the North London streets and Hampstead Heath will be thronged again and 'Lestrade of the Yard' will figure in everyone's gossip. What will they make of it, though, if, the dog being dead, its howls persist?"

"What on earth are you talking about, Holmes?"

"I believe that the 'attack' on Chapman was prearranged. Some sort of hound was brought here to provide these paw marks, but it played no part in the mock struggle."

"Some prank, perhaps? Medical students!"

"I do not think so. The man was genuinely hurt and shocked, though by no means as much as he should have been, going by the story he was paid to tell."

"Paid!"

"Without doubt. I was able to verify as much the following day, while you were out playing squire to your lady. You recall Lestrade coming to tell us that Chapman had absconded from hospital?"

"You seemed to take no notice of him. You were incensed about that newspaper interview."

"I confess I was put out, but it was not for that reason. It was resentment at your personal news, with its unwelcome implications for my domesticity. I do not, as a rule, allow emotions to come between me and my work. On this one occasion I lapsed. Had I given this matter of the hound the consideration it merited, I should have had the answer before we even left the Heath."

"What *is* the answer, Holmes?"

"That the victim had lied to the policeman about the attack, therefore he was a willing actor in the charade. That he should have allowed himself to be injured, without being paid for his pains, is unthinkable. I should have challenged him over that when we had him at our mercy in his hospital cot. I should have inspected his injuries closely. Instead, I let him get away with only the questions he had expected. He slipped off from the hospital that night in order to evade deeper interrogation."

"You are overlooking something, Holmes. Tramps of Chapman's sort carry their wordly belongings with them everywhere. It is routine practice, when one of them finishes up in hospital or any other public institution, to list everything he has on him. It prevents him from claiming later than he had been robbed by the staff. If Chapman had had anything more than a few pence in his pocket, it would certainly have been mentioned to the police as suspicious."

"I know their dodges," Holmes confirmed. "Old soldiers are the most adept at them. It was, of course, obvious that Chapman had served in the Royal Mallows."

"I heard you mutter something at the time. Tattoo, I suppose?"

"On his right forearm. The regimental crest. Remember that case of ours at their depot at Aldershot? The strange death of Colonel Barclay? Their crest was inscribed everywhere."

"Be that as it may, Chapman can't have had money on him."

"He had not. He had hidden it here. Come, let me show you where. I came the next day, after hearing that he had disappeared. That, by the way, was enough to confirm my suspicion of him. A man of that type who can make out that he has suffered any public wrong invariably demands compensation. But this old soldier, who claims to have been attacked by a roaming animal on public land, does not linger to screw one halfpenny out of the authorities. Why? Because he wants no further questioning, and has money already. He wants only to retrieve it and get out of the neighbourhood."

Holmes stopped with the lantern again and once more shone it into the hollow where I had lain. He reached into it and scraped the grass floor aside, to show me where a wedge of earth had been removed.

"It does not need much space to contain any of those poor devils' worldly estate. They are only off guard when they sleep, so they bury what they have and lie upon it. It was only when I saw how the whole episode had been fabricated that I realized his money would be hidden here, in the traditional place. By the time that had dawned upon me, and I came to search, it was too late. Chapman had been and gone."

He straightened up.

"If that cabby has come back for us, he will be waiting now. We had better reclaim him before his horses talk him out of it."

We set off toward the road.

"Holmes," said I, as we went.

"Yes, Watson?"

"Are you going to continue being peeved about my getting married?"

There followed the slightest pause before he answered, "No more. In some odd way this evening's expedition seems to have purged my jealousy."

We walked in silence for some moments.

"If I could have got at my gun," said I, "I might have shot you."

"I might have throttled you first, my dear Watson," answered Sherlock Holmes.

"**I**t strikes me," I remarked to Holmes as we sat over our nightcaps following our return to Baker Street from this second excursion to Hampstead Heath, "that you are about to be busier than at any time for years. This new dog-that-did-nothing-in-the-nighttime mystery makes up four urgent matters, with the King's letter, the Channel steamer murder and Lady Frances Carfax. It wants only some sensational development over Cromwell's bones to make a fifth."

"That is one for leaving off our agenda." He smiled. "Those bones will have been locked away by some fanatic. They are like the stolen art masterpiece, too conspicuous for the open market. Anyway, they are no loss, except to museum-keepers such as Garside. As to Lady Carfax's case, that must be allowed to run its course and dictate its own timetable. We shall act as developments require."

"Well, it still leaves the King, the ship's steward and the hound. Have you any plan of campaign?"

Holmes tapped his cold pipe into the cooling grate, preparatory to retiring to bed.

"With your inestimable help, Watson."

"You're not going to send me creeping about the East End after Anderson," I warned him. "You may be able to disguise yourself as anything under the sun . . . "

"Except an Oriental," he corrected. "It is the one area of disguise from which Nature debars even me."

"Well, it certainly rules me out."

"I had already done so," he concurred. "In any case, there would be little to be gained by inquiring about the victim, John Sweh. You know how the Chinese community prefer to deal with their own affairs. It is one reason why I recommended letting Anderson run free. To have arrested him without hard evidence would be useless. No information would be forthcoming out of Limehouse. Police questions would be met with a silence as impenetrable as the Great Wall. Sweh's very existence would be disowned, while they conduct their own inquiries into his death. They will find out what happened either by investigation or inference. For his own sake, Anderson will do better to be taken by me before they can reach him. Their vengeance would be terrible."

"It may have been a random 'Yellow Peril' killing after all."

"We shall soon know. If there's nothing in tomorrow morning's papers it will mean that he had not sent them the customary anonymous letter calling attention to the foul deed. However, since he lives in Burdett Road, which is right on the border of Limehouse, I am afforded a rare chance to link East and West in one investigation. It is too intriguing to ignore. Some of my most valuable gossip shops are down that way, and Shinwell himself lives in Stepney. I am to visit him on the day after tomorrow in connection with Chapman. Clearly, my habitat for the next two days lies East Endward."

"What about the King? You can't go on doing nothing."

"You are right, Watson. It is why, with sincerest apologies for intruding upon your personal preoccupations, I see no alternative but to requisition your help."

"Holmes! No!"

"You have never failed me, Watson" he continued blandly, ignoring my dissent. "For all your faults, you are the one person to whom I have ever wholeheartedly entrusted my affairs. Just bring this trifling business to completion for me, and, should you wish it, I daresay Mycroft could contrive your own summons to Buckingham Palace—for services to literature, of course."

"The man is a fiend!" said I to Coral and her aunt next day. "He creates impossible situations for himself, knowing that he has only to appeal to me to help him out."

"I guess he appreciates your sweet nature, John," said Henry, cocking her blond head at me across our luncheon table at the Hotel Russell. "Look how we took to you at first meeting."

"It's not the same," I complained. "He has been exploiting me, off and on, for more than twenty years."

"You should be proud, dear," said Coral. She put her white-gloved hand briefly over the back of mine. "Just think, whenever anyone in years to come reads your stories of his great cases, how they'll envy you, having been in on them at the first floor."

"They might also read, in a final chapter, how I slipped cyanide into his tobacco," growled I. " 'Sherlock Holmes Victim In Own Greatest Unsolved Case.' "

The ladies laughed gaily, bringing glances of reproof from the stuffier lunchers.

I had told them as much as I felt able without violating my protestation to Holmes that I did not discuss his business behind his back. It was no consolation that I had as good as talked myself into it. By persisting in reminding him of his growing load, I had given him the opening to claim a favour which, he pointed out, might be the last he should ever ask of me.

"It will be nothing to you, Watson," he had urged. "There

is nothing to argue. All you have to do is show her this tactful little request, which has been prepared in His Majesty's own hand. I must remember to congratulate Mycroft on his latent abilities as a prosodist. She will hand over his note willingly."

"She might not view it as simply as you do," said I.

"Absurd! Besides, my dear fellow, the fair sex has always been your department. Your winning charms are certain to appeal to all that is best in her nature."

"That, Holmes, is not the most tasteful thing to suggest to a man who is engaged to be married!"

I left out this exchange from my account to the ladies. I omitted also the details of why I could not take them to the military band contest at the Albert Hall. They insisted sweetly that they would not feel deprived, and would enjoy a quiet dinner *à deux* at the Hotel Russell.

"Why don't you bring Mr. Holmes around with you one evening and make up a foursome?" suggested Henry. "We'd just love to hear him talk about his cases, wouldn't we, Coral darling?"

"*Would* he come?" asked Coral. She had heard more about him from me than had her aunt.

"No," said I emphatically.

I set off the next morning for Canterbury from Charing Cross Station. Holmes had made an appointment by telephone with Mrs. Glanvill. He told me that he had explained to her who he was, and that he had been entrusted by His Majesty the King to deliver a note into her hands alone. She had invited him to tea. Her house, Mickleden, was between Canterbury and Folkestone, in Kent, and he would be met off the train at Canterbury station.

"So you are going yourself, after all?" said I with relief.

"No, no. You will go, as arranged."

"But you just said . . . "

"I shall telephone her again tomorrow morning, when you

have left. I have been detained by an urgent case, but you are on your way instead. It will too late for her to think of cancelling."

"You are quite unscrupulous, Holmes!"

"She sounds as charming as she is said to be attractive, Watson." He positively beamed.

I came in to breakfast next morning to find at our table a disreputable seafaring type of man, grime-faced, greasy haired, with blackened fingernails. His checked shirt was stained with oil patches and his coarse trousers were stiff with the congealed grease and salt of years. A red-and-white spotted neckerchief was knotted round his throat. Over a chair he had flung his navy blue donkey jacket and a hard-peaked felt cap. The sour effluvium of "oil of sea rover" polluted the air.

"Ready for the fray, Watson?" Sherlock Holmes greeted me, already deeply enough into his assumed character to shove aside his plate, drain his coffee cup noisily, with a final smack of his lips, and wipe his mouth with the back of a filthy hand.

"I can see *you* are, Holmes," remarked I. "Shall you be back by the time I return this evening?"

"I doubt it. If I sleep anywhere tonight it will be a penny doss or the Salvation Army."

"Pity the poor blighters next to you. Are you off now?"

He was picking up the jacket and cap.

"Mrs. Hudson will sneak me out by the area door. I will telephone Mrs. Glanvill from Wigmore Street Post Office."

"Thank goodness I can have the window open before I start breakfast," said I fervently.

He bade me a coarse form of farewell and slouched off with the rolling gait of the sailor. I had seen him in dozens of disguises over the years, and never failed to wonder at the way he assumed not only the appearance, but the personality, mannerisms and idiom of whatever type he was portraying, from absent-minded clergyman, to artisan, to drink-sodden groom.

• • •

My outfit for my own expedition had exercised my mind upon waking. I did not wish to add to my task by approaching it with stiff formality, therefore rejected city black and a top hat. I settled for my new suit of blue serge, which Coral had admired at first sight, a tall, stiff collar, a spotted tie, and my best straw boater. The day was warm, though sultry, and I decided to leave off any overcoat and simply carry kid gloves and cane.

I took an early afternoon train and reached Canterbury punctually. I was approached on the platform by a smart young man in gray livery with one of the new military-style hats with a hard, shiny black peak. I had anticipated a dogcart or some other small carriage. He conducted me, to my surprise and pleasure, to a large Daimler automobile, whose coating of dust from the roads did not conceal the proud gleam of maroon and brass. He seemed to take it for granted that I would sit up in front beside him, and chattered cheerfully to me throughout a drive of some three or four miles under a lowering sky threatening more rain before nightfall.

We turned off at length into a driveway guarded by a half-timbered and stone lodge, well distanced from any other habitation. The broad entrance gave onto a well-kept, straight macadam drive, with the house beyond.

Mickleden, as it was called, was not the Tudor pile its gatehouse had led me to expect. There were medieval resemblances in its facings of stone, brick and timber, and steeply sloping tiled roofs, from which chimneys stood up half as high again. I saw that it was a planned illusion, an almost brand-new "Arts and Crafts" composition upon a sixteenth-century theme. The grounds were of a few acres only, compact and trim with carefully sited lawns, borders, shrubs and trees.

An unusually young butler, fair-haired and dressed informally in black alpaca jacket, pepper-and-salt trousers and soft shirt and black tie, greeted me from the steps and opened the car door for me.

He exhibited none of the studied pomposity of his calling as he apologized that Mrs. Glanvill had not yet returned from a luncheon engagement at Folkestone. This rather blatant unconventionality of not being present to receive an expected guest made me feel agreeably at ease. I tossed my gloves nonchalantly into my hat for the young butler to take away, and sauntered with my most casual air into the small washroom off the vestibule.

I was soon installed in what proved to be a spacious drawing room and hallway combined, left alone to wait on a long settle at right angles to a green-tiled fireplace with a polished copper canopy above a broad grate, filled with a vast spray of assorted dried flowers and reeds. As I glanced about me, I saw that these were certainly the most up-to-the-minute surroundings I had ever been in. Windows of varying size admitted light from three sides and afforded views of the park from different angles. The studied brightness was heightened by light, shiny paint, glazed tiling, light fabrics, coloured ornaments behind glass doors, screens with stained-glass panels, brilliant-toned pictures in engraved silvered and coppered frames and arrangements of flowers blossoming forth from capacious vases decorated with animals, birds, flowers and landscapes in the modern-medieval style. The house and its decoration and furnishings had been created together and blended with the latest "Artful and Crafty" notions of shape and contrast.

The room seemed perfectly reflective of a rich man's sophisticated wife, with refreshing taste and enthusiasm. My spirits rose higher. The fancy came to me that I had passed through a looking glass dividing the old and new centuries. The world at large showed little change as yet. Our cluttered Baker Street milieu had been allowed to become fixed in time, much as it had been when Holmes and I had first settled there more than twenty years ago. He preferred it to remain so, and I had come to take it for granted.

By contrast, I found this assertively twentieth-century room as exciting as a new theatrical set, revealed for the first time at curtain rise. My sensation was of belonging in it easily. It reminded me that I was due soon for a fresh start in life, in marrying a younger woman from a newer world embodying more future than past. I was glad that I had chosen the blue suit.

"The celebrated Dr. Watson!" cried a woman's voice, and she came sweeping into the room from outdoors, holding out a white-gloved hand to be shaken by me and wrenching off a small motoring hat with the other. She tossed hat and veil onto a low table, and peeled off her gloves as if glad to be rid of them. She shook dust from herself and flopped onto the settle from which I had stood up to greet her, patting its flowered cushion in invitation to me to sit again. "How do you do? *Such a pleasure!*"

Mrs. Lavinia Glanvill was truly beautiful in a distinctly English way. She was younger than I had imagined; she would be only a few years older than Coral, scarcely more than thirty. Her windswept appearance from motoring, with displaced wisps straying down from her piled-up chestnut hair, her long white neck and glowing cheeks, the smart gray suit, plain white blouse and dusty shoes, all combined to give her the look of an emancipated young schoolteacher, or even the Head Girl.

"You have seen some of my work, madam?" said I, surprised and gratified.

"Oh, yes. We take in the *Strand* regularly. Is Sherlock Holmes *really* as you paint him? What an *extraordinary* man! How *exciting* for you to be able to *help* him, as well as write about him. If I were a man I should *love* a life like that. Yes, William?"

The young butler had retrieved her discarded things and was waiting nearby.

"Shall I serve tea now, madam?" he asked.

"Yes, why not? Are you *starving,* Doctor? Plenty of sandwiches, William."

She sent him off with a smile, which he returned. His insouciant air made him seem almost capable of whistling as he went.

"William is *so* good," Mrs. Glanvill was telling me. "I prefer young staff, and he came so highly recommended. We have had him only a few weeks, but he has settled in wonderfully. Hubert leaves such things to me. He is in America, as usual. He goes there very often. He has dealings *all over* the place. He says that Americans will make this century their own property. Have you been over there much yourself?"

I replied that I had had a little experience of the United States. I was thankful that she did not press for a detailed account.*

"Do you like our house?" she was prattling on. "We got Voysey to run it up for us. He did Spade House, across at Sandgate, for H.G. Wells. It's not far from here. Do you know the Wellses? Old Mrs. Wells, H.G.'s mother, used to be a housekeeper, you know? At Uppark, in Sussex. He was brought up there, belowstairs, and vowed that when he was famous and rich he'd build her a house with every labour-saving feature, that would need hardly any servants. We asked Voysey to do something of the same sort for us. Rather charming, don't you think? And *so* easy to run. Just William, the butler; Hubert's man, who's off with him in the States; my maid and a couple of others; cook and her girls; Jack, the chauffeur who fetched you; a few gardeners and boys. We don't *believe* in a servant class. Do you?"

---

* The full particulars are in my autobiographical work, *The Private Life of Dr. Watson.*
—J.H.W.

It was a monologue, calling for a minimum of response. The longer it went on, and the further it rambled, the more I suspected that Mrs. Glanvill was putting on a performance for my benefit. As William and a maid served us tea where we sat, bringing forward a cedarwood-and-brass butler's table, I thought I detected a certain amusement in his expression.

When the servants had gone again, and tea was well under way, I knew my turn had come. Mrs. Glanvill proffered the plate of salmon-and-cucumber sandwiches yet again, and cut short her descripton of the benefits of having a private electrical generator, to ask: "But, tell me, Dr. Watson, about this 'confidential and personal' business."

She sat very still, watching my lips. I knew that nothing but a straight answer would suffice. I had made up my mind during the train journey what form that answer should take. Without any attempt at explanation or any sort of preamble, I took out the sealed note and handed it to her. I got to my feet and walked away, to stare unseeing through one of the windows while she opened and read it.

No storm of indignation erupted behind me. I did not hear her ring the bell for the butler to show me off the premises. She said quietly, "Please don't let your tea get cold."

I returned and sat down silently. Perhaps it is written somewhere in the rules of etiquette how a man should conduct himself, having just delivered a request to his newly acquainted hostess to hand over her keepsake of a royal suitor. I had no precedent to go upon. Even taking a sip of tea or eating another sandwich seemed somehow offensive. Mrs. Glanvill took my cup and saucer, poured off the cold remains, and gave me a refill.

"Another sandwich, Doctor—or some cake?" said she, indicating the plates. Her tone was still calm. "Do you know what this is about?"

"I have not seen the note, madam. I am only its bearer."

"But you do know something?"

I was sure that an evasion would not deceive those wide green eyes, as shrewd as they were lovely.

"A little,"

"Good." She smiled suddenly. "Then we can talk about it frankly. I should like a slice of the seedcake, if you'd care to do the honours."

I breathed again. I realized that she had given up her odd pretense of being an empty, prattling woman.

"The King asks me to return a note he wrote to me when he was still Prince of Wales. He is evidently afraid that, in the wrong hands, it might compromise him. Why should he think that?"

I repeated the story about foreign agents on the lookout for anything that might discredit the King in any way.

"So he engaged Sherlock Holmes to get it back."

"Holmes's brother has a high position in Whitehall," I explained lamely. "Holmes has acted for royalty before in discreet matters."

" 'Discreet matters'!" she flung back at me. "Is that what this is made out to be? What have they been telling you and Holmes about me?"

"I assure you, Mrs. Glanvill, that—"

"Wait a moment!" she cried. "I *knew* there was something familiar about this! You have played this game before, you and Sherlock Holmes. Some foreign king, wasn't it? Bohemia, that was the man. The King of Bohemia, who was afraid he had compromised himself with some actress in a photograph. What was her name again?"

"Adler," said I unhappily. "Irene Adler. An opera singer."

"*A Scandal in Bohemia!*" Mrs. Glanvill was recalling, sounding both indignant and victorious. "So, I am your latest Irene Adler, am I? Holmes got into her house by a ruse, to spy out where she kept the picture. Is that what you've been sent to do, Dr. Watson?"

"I assure you not, madam. I am here on a plain errand,

which I don't mind admitting is embarrassing me no end. I wish you would only give me what I have come for and tell me to go."

My appeal seemed to postpone her mounting wrath. She glowered at me, her beautiful face flushed and her lips pouting. I dared not flinch.

I was perhaps saved by the loud rapping on the front door, followed, as if on a second thought, by a prolonged ring of the electric bell. The butler appeared swiftly from the inner regions. Before he had time to tell the impatient new arrival that his mistress was engaged, someone was advancing into the room.

"Lavinia, my dear!" I heard a man's voice. "I saw you driving up the Folkestone Road and told Jackson to turn the horse's head round. It's been too many weeks since . . . Oh!"

He had seen me rising to my feet and turning toward him.

"I'm so sorry!" he was blurting out. "Seeing you out alone, it didn't occur to me that . . . But . . . surely this is Dr. Watson!"

"Lord Belmont!" I greeted him with equal surprise. "How do you do, sir?"

He was no longer the sombre figure who had kept his silent, watchful distance at the Tyburn excavation. He was in country uniform: shooting jacket, knickerbockers and gaiters, carrying a tweed hat and plain ash stick. He appeared younger and fresher, his tall frame more erect. Seeing him hatless for the first time I noticed the single silver streak in his thick black hair.

"You know each other?" said Mrs. Glanvill, as we shook hands.

"We picked a bone or two once," answered his lordship, who did not look like a man given to making quips. "I didn't know you moved in literary circles, Lavinia. I'm a regular reader of his, you know."

"So am I, James," she returned, and I noted her easy use of his Christian name.

"Well, well! Are you staying in the district, Dr. Watson?"

"Just a flying visit, Lord Belmont."

"Sherlock Holmes not with you?"

"Dr. Watson is a friend of a friend," Mrs. Glanvill helped me by answering.

"Really!"

"Do sit down and have some tea, James," she invited him. "We are only chatting."

I was relieved to see him shake his head.

"I beg both your pardons for interrupting. Another time, I hope, Dr. Watson. There are a hundred-and-one things I'd like to ask you. All kind of questions."

"I should be honoured, Lord Belmont," I replied foolishly. He seized the opening I had given him.

"Look here! Come across and take some dinner with me this evening. Quite informal. Lavinia, you'll let him bring you? Hubert's off as usual, I daresay?"

I began to protest. I thought Mrs. Glanvill showed reluctance, too. But Belmont looked so disappointed that I faltered and accepted. He was much less reserved than he had seemed before.

"Tell you what!" he declared inspirationally. "You'll stop the night with me. We can talk the hours away."

I demurred at this. I pointed out that I was expected back at Baker Street, and anyway, I had no overnight things.

"Nonsense! I can fit you up. Telephone to Baker Street, mayn't he, Lavinia?"

She was looking even more doubtful. I decided suddenly that I would accept. Coral and her aunt were out of town for the day and night, and I had no other engagement that evening or next morning. Besides, I could see that I needed more time with Mrs. Glanvill. I had not had much success with my mission so far, it seemed. She could scarcely throw me out to kick my heels until the agreed time of eight o'clock at Lord Belmont's house, Alkhamton, some miles away toward the coast.

"Settled, then!" said he, and strode off, appearing highly pleased with himself. Mrs. Glanvill stood for some moments looking silently and a little pensively into the fireplace. I could not help speculating about their relationship. Unconventional she might be, but he did not give that impression. Yet he had marched into her house uninvited and unannounced, seeming in no doubt that her husband would not be there.

"Do smoke your pipe, Dr. Watson," said she, when she had ordered a fresh pot of tea and we had moved to share a sofa farther along the drawing room. She had assumed a re-signed air, as if deciding to make the best of my company until the time for us to set forth in her motor car. I sensed something of a return to her earlier artificial manner. "I *love* your descrip-tions of yourself and Mr. Holmes at your little fireside with your pipes, and good Mrs. Hudson popping in and out."

I told her that I had no pipe with me.

"A cigar?" she suggested. "Hubert smokes only Coronas. Would you like one of those? Or will you join me in a ciga-rette? You don't mind my smoking? One isn't supposed to in company, but I hope you'll forgive it. You haven't a wife, have you? If you had, should you try to stop her smoking?"

It sounded like one of Holmes's own casual tests of per-sonality. I answered robustly that I had no objection at all to women smoking in private. I said I would join her with plea-sure, and I had the impression that I had done the right thing. She drew forward a large cigarette box in figured pewter and opened it. An exotic aroma was released.

"I smoke Egyptians. Alexandrias. But of *course*! *Alexan-drias*! They were what Sherlock Holmes smoked in that case of yours—what did you call it again?"

"*The Golden Pince-Nez.*"

"That's the one! When he had to chain-smoke so many to make an ash that would give him the clue. I thought that was *awfully* clever, didn't you? You must admire Mr. Holmes so *intensely.*"

I restrained myself from telling her exactly what I thought of both Holmes and his scheming brother for landing me in my shameful situation. Still, there were worse things to be doing on what had now become another wet evening than lighting up Alexandrias on a sofa with an attractive and liberal-minded woman, whose enigmatic background added mystery to her charisma.

She seemed to be making an effort to put me at my ease.

"Do tell me something of yourself, Doctor," she invited. "You are so modest in your tales. One can only read between the lines."

I sketched the outines of my life, adding my latest happy news.

"I'm very pleased for you, and for her," she surprised me by saying, letting the airy manner drop again. "Hubert is a good deal older than I—fifteen years, in fact. He treats me like a rather wayward naughty daughter sometimes, especially when I rattle on too much. I suppose it does get on his nerves a bit."

I could not imagine her being encouraged to chatter overmuch at her husband. I saw him as rather dour and un-attending, a man who would come and go, speak or listen to suit himself. I thought that this house was perhaps a form of plaything to keep her amused. She did not strike me as likely to be deeply passionate toward men, nor even very flirta-tious. If she had had an association with the former Prince of Wales, I did not imagine its having gone far.

"His business is his life," she was adding to her comments upon her husband. "He is mostly away. However, we're good chums. They call him a 'real tough nut' in the States. He's proud of that. I only hope that he won't become too like those tycoons of theirs."

"Shouldn't you like to be a millionaire's wife, Mrs. Glanvill?"

"I'd hate it. I detest society and show. There are much better uses for money."

"You mean for good works?"

"No. I think people deserve to have more, but would rather earn it than be given it. There is a dignity in poverty. Charity takes that away. I am sure that better-off people would gladly pay more taxes to help others."

I doubted the existence of any such altruism, but did not say so. I wondered whether her husband supported her view— if it were her view, and not another pose.

"I don't mean that rich people's money should be taken from them," she explained further. "James Belmont has the right idea. If other men of his class would do like him there would be no need for the government to enforce anything. It would only have to help set up schemes all over the country, and spend money on them instead of fighting pointless wars."

"What is Lord Belmont's idea, Mrs. Glanvill?"

"The nobility of work. Getting people to realize what a magnificent thing it is. Opening their eyes! But it isn't just an idea. He founded a crafts guild, to teach metalworking and printing and such things. James provides equipment and the craftsmen pay him back out of what they sell. It's quite astonishing how easily quite uneducated men, and women, can pick up some of the fine old skills that machines are driving out."

I had heard a little about John Ruskin, William Morris and one or two others. My instant vision of beards, sandals and poetry readings must have reflected itself in my expression.

She gestured around the room.

"Almost everything here has been handmade by modern craftsmen. Even the house itself. Don't you feel it's all so *alive?*

How James can continue to live in that place of his I can't think. It's like a museum that no one visits."

"But Lord Belmont is a museum enthusiast, isn't he?"

"You know about him, then?"

I assured her that I knew only what Holmes had told me when we had encountered him at Tyburn, and his friend Dr. Garside had told us of their hopes for a museum devoted to London.

"Don't speak to me of that man Garside!" she surprised me by responding. "James brought him here once. Ugh!"

"You didn't take to him?"

"He was so false and patronizing. He went about the house praising everything in sight and gushing about my good taste. I knew that he didn't mean any of it. He was just flattering me. He wanted to dip his hands into Hubert's money."

"For his museum?"

"Yes. James has given him a lot of backing, and they wanted Hubert to go in with them. Dr. Garside offered me a place on the committee if he would."

"But you refused?"

"Hubert did. He told them I could do as I liked in the matter, but they must not turn to him. You see, Dr. Watson, my husband is a very successful and ambitious man, but he started life with very little. He has worked hard and taken many risks. He's very proud of all he's achieved, and determined not to see it slip through his hands."

I could easily imagine the English tycoon looking forward to confronting America's so-called robber barons with a real barony to his name. Even more vividly I could picture his reaction when he learned that he was not to be Lord Glanvill after all.

What I wondered most, though, was what his wife's real feeling would be then—and what she and Lord Belmont might have to say together about it!

CHAPTER FOURTEEN

Mrs. Glanvill had told me that Lord Belmont was a bachelor. His house, Alkhamton, near the old coastal town of Deal, had belonged to his elder brother, who had inherited it and the estates and title from their late father some five years earlier. Then, a year ago, the brother, an amateur botanist, had been drowned in the lake in the grounds, evidently overreaching himself in pursuit of some specimen. James Belmont had come into everything. He had kept on only a few of the large staff and made no changes at all to the place, continuing to live in the one wing where he already had his apartment.

"Although he's only about Hubert's age they could not be more different," she told me in the hooded back of her Daimler, as the young chauffeur drove us through spitting rain. "James's passion is history. His craftspeople follow only medieval models. I don't think he can find anything much good to say for things nowadays. By the way, Dr. Watson . . ."

"Yes, Mrs. Glanvill?"

"Please try not to . . . provoke him."

"I am afraid I don't follow."

"Don't make him lose his temper. He does sometimes . . . rather suddenly . . ."

I refrained from assuring her that I did not go about provoking my hosts.

"Very well. I shall watch my step," I promised instead,
wishing increasingly that I had refused the invitation and was
back at Baker Street, with my slippers and pipe and Mrs. Hudson's homely cuisine.

Alkhamton House proved to be as sepulchral as my companion had intimated. No doubt it had a few bricks somewhere
in it dating from the sixteenth century, but they were well
hidden. It had been rebuilt by some early-nineteenth-century
dreamer in the Romantic, half-Eastern half-Gothic manner, involving a confusion of towers, domes, pinnacles, battlements
and a great deal of plain stucco, now largely smothered by ivy.
It looked resigned to soaking up the rain, which was falling
steadily by the time we arrived. The gloomy, ill-lit entrance
lobby smelled as though many earlier rains had permeated
stone and wood, and were stored in them in a state of perpetual
wetness.

Lord Belmont opened the door to us himself. He was wearing a drab green smoking jacket with darker quilted lapels and
cuffs, and an artist's flowing cravat at his neck. He shook hands
with me gravely. I noticed that he kissed Mrs. Glanvill's hand
and looked deeply into her eyes. I could not help wondering
whether any message concerning me might be passing between
them.

He conducted us into a shadowy room, too cavernous for
comfort. A log fire was smouldering in the huge stone fireplace.
The furniture was predominantly of uncomfortable-looking
oak. The board floor was strewn with loose mats, woven from
some natural fibre. I guessed that they were products of the
crafts guild, and thought how much more a factory made,
bright-hued carpet would do for the room's atmosphere. It was
not relieved by the narrow oil lamps or a sombre winter snow-
scape, in the dullest of tones, that hung over a mantelpiece
devoid of ornaments.

Following the customary ten minutes of general conversation about the weather, we were summoned to dinner by a
portly, red-faced butler, the first servant I had seen there. The
adjoining dining room was as cheerless as the sitting room. As
a further concession to informality, Lord Belmont seated Mrs.
Glanvill at the head of the long table, with me at her right hand
and himself opposite me. A pair of clumsy silver candelabra
were our illumination. The flickering flames gave at least an
impression that we were within a smaller, cosier space. The
light made Mrs. Glanvill's skin glow, and struck sparks from
her eyes as well as from her simply designed modern brooch
and necklace of gold and emeralds.

I had my first chance to study Lord Belmont closely. The
candlelight accentuated his facial bones, surmounted by a
broad, high temple. His cheeks were hollowed and shadowed,
like Holmes's. His mouth and jaw were strong and almost grim.
The silver streak shone from his dark hair. I could imagine his
brooding manner interesting some women, and wondered if
my fellow-guest were among them.

His dark eyes were restless. His fingers played constantly
with the knives and forks beside his place, aligning and realign-
ing them. I sensed an habitual impatience. He had seemed
eager enough to invite me, but I wondered whether he regretted the impulse.

I was glad of the sherry that accompanied the soup.
Holmes and I observed the nautical, military and colonial custom of a glass of something before dining. Our investigations
seldom took us into formal society, which he abhorred. When
we could not escape it, we went prepared with hip flasks, for
l'heure de l'apéritif was not yet an English institution. On this
expedition, confident of being back at Baker Street by dinner-
time, I had not put my flask into my pocket.

There was not much more wine forthcoming. The foot-
man poured a glass of Chablis with the fish and some claret
with the lukewarm roast mutton. He and the butler remained

chiefly in the shadows, silent and motionless beyond the candles' limited range. I seemed to be the only one drinking. Lord Belmont ignored his glass and only toyed with his food, using the cutlery more for his endless measuring and spacing. Lavinia Glanvill had lost her former ease. She left her glass untouched and kept darting nervous glaces at him, as if in anticipation of one of his outbursts. Her warning inhibited any conversation I might have had to offer. He said little, and she less. It was a glum occasion.

I volunteered an account of our Garrideb investigation. It did not appear to interest either of them much, and the few questions which were put to me did not confirm the enthusiasm Lord Belmont had expressed that afternoon. I determined to venture no more topics, and the bleak and tasteless meal dragged to its end.

When we returned to the sitting room afterward, I hoped that Mrs. Glanvill would make an opportunity to give me her decision about the letter. Instead, she seemed to avoid me. She took a fireside chair and drew from her skirt pocket a silver cigarette case.

It was only as the distinctive aroma of Egyptian tobacco arose that I realized that the same smell had been hanging upon the dank air when we had first entered the house. I had been too conscious of the prevalent odours of woodsmoke and damp to wonder about it. I doubt if I should have thought about it now, had she not reopened the case and extended it to me.

"Do have one, Dr. Watson. James doesn't smoke, so I'm your only source of supply."

I had observed during the meal that he ate very little and did not drink at all. Although he was served wine, he merely raised the glass occasionally and pretended to sip, in what I took to be a courteous gesture to make his guest feel that he was not imbibing alone. Now I had learned that he did not smoke, either; yet someone had smoked Egyptian cigarettes in that room not many hours before. Mrs. Glanvill's butler had told me that she had been at Folkestone, which was a good few miles along the coast. I found myself suspecting that she had been at this house, which would in turn give the lie to Lord Belmont's assertion that he had not seen her for weeks.

He poured me a glass of port from a decanter on a tripod table beside his chair. He did not offer Mrs. Glanvill any, and gave himself only a small amount, which again he did not drink. He contented himself with moving the glass to and fro by its base on the table top, in what proved to be a prelude to re-joining the conversation.

"Ridiculous, I suppose, Doctor, but one can't help thinking of you and Sherlock Holmes in constant harness. Odd, finding you down here alone."

"We do go our own ways for much of the time, Lord Belmont. Holmes has his interests, and I mine."

"Might one ask what yours are, Doctor?"

I told him my few occupations, which sounded tame and trivial compared with Holmes's intellectual array. I was more proud to add that I was soon to marry again. Lord Belmont nodded.

"Then does this mark the end of the famous partnership at last?" he asked.

"I don't know," I replied, not wishing to encourage this line of inquiry.

"Presumably there are a few cases still hanging over your heads," he persisted.

"Nothing in particular," said I. I turned to Mrs. Glanvill, hoping she might help. She had been smoking quietly without speaking, and still said nothing. I tried to deflect Lord Belmont's interest through triviality.

"There is a search going on for a lady missing on the Continent. Of course, you'll have read about the Hampstead Hound?"

"You don't tell me that the great Sherlock Holmes is concerned in that!" he ejaculated, his face a picture of amazement.

I told them briefly the circumstances of our involvement, although without revealing Holmes's theory of a hoax or fraud, or his newly aroused interest in the vagrant, Chapman.

"It quite beggars belief," Lord Belmont almost snorted. "Wasting his powers on such a triviality. I have said all along that it is another stunt in this disgraceful newpaper circulation war. However, every man has his price, no doubt."

"I don't quite follow, Lord Belmont,"

"Holmes has to live, like anyone else. While there are fools of editors eager to line his pockets I'm sure he's happy to let them."

"Holmes takes no money for such things," I told him firmly.

"You don't tell me! What? He receives nothing at all?"

"I do not say that, sir. Sometimes he is offered a fee and accepts it. At others, the question never arises. As a private consulting detective, Holmes may involve himself or not, as he sees fit. He judges each case on its merits."

"The better-placed the client, the greater the fee, eh?"

"Not at all, sir!"

"Come, Dr. Watson. You yourself have told us in your casebooks of him pocketing a princely sum or two in his time."

"James," I heard Mrs. Glanvill attempt to intervene, "I really think . . ."

He ignored her.

"I imagine that he who retains Sherlock Holmes in any dispute knows he must win it. The sight of that exalted name as expert witness must guarantee a favourable settlement out of court."

"He does not work like that at all!" I protested.

He winked, and made that offensive gesture of rubbing together a thumb and finger to signify grubby money dealings.

"*We* understand such things, Doctor." He smirked. "We are men of the world. And Lavinia." He turned to her. "All of us here know what oils the wheels of the big business machine. Money. Favours, Honours. Each plays its part."

"James . . . !"

"Lord Belmont, I assure you there are no such considerations at all in Sherlock Holmes's practice."

"Well, well, since you assure me! Tell me, who is he acting for in the matter of the bones? The ones at Tyburn. Who is the interested client in that?"

"Holmes himself. His interest is purely historical. He knows more of the annals of crime and punishment than anyone. Naturally, he had made a point of asking to be told if the bones were found."

"Who by?" he demanded sharply. "Who told him they had been found?"

I was sure he must have been told the answer to that already by his friend Dr. Garside.

"The local police inspector," I answered.

"Not Garside?"

"I am sure not."

"Holmes has not been retained in the matter of those bones which later went missing?"

I wondered momentarily how he knew of that, since it had not been reported, but supposed again that Garside would have told him.

"Not at all, Lord Belmont. As a matter of fact, Holmes thinks we are well rid of them."

I recounted the gist of what Holmes had said to me after we had paid our visit to the excavation.

"Personally," I added, "I think Dr. Garside is probably the only one who has lost anything. They would have made quite a prize attraction in one of his glass cases, no doubt. Morbid, perhaps, but harmless enough. So far as any harmful significance they might have for more impressionable folk, Homes himself put it perfectly once in some other connection: 'The world is big enough for us. No ghosts need apply.' "

I was surprised to see his pale complexion flush to crimson. His hands, always restless in his lap, had begun to writhe and clasp and unclasp. I recognized chronic nervous symptoms.

"So that is this writing of which the world has been deprived so far!" he sneered. "When he stops drawing his no doubt handsome retainer from Scotland Yard, and is no more in a position to mulct the wealthy and the influential for covering up their scandals, he can set himself up afresh as a lord among wits. 'Quotations for calendars supplied to order. A witticism to suit every occasion. Clichés cheaper by the bushel. Aphorisms fresh daily from the great Sherlock Holmes . . . !' "

A crash made him swing round in his chair. Mrs. Glanvill, leaping to her feet, had rushed toward the door. Seeming not to notice the tripod table in her path, she had run straight against it, sending it toppling and the decanter and glasses flying.

I found myself upon my feet also, hurrying to help her. She stood swaying and rubbing the knee that had collided with the table. I steadied her and she leaned against me, breathing heavily.

"I'm so sorry!" she gasped, pressing a hand into her side. "So clumsy."

"You are unwell, Mrs. Glanvill?"

She looked up with a wincing smile. "It's really nothing, Dr. Watson. A little trouble that my own doctor is treating. A hot bottle and a lie-down, you know?"

She turned to Lord Belmont, who had risen and was standing, swaying slightly, though he had had nothing to drink.

"James, do forgive me. I had better take myself straight home to bed."

"Allow me to escort you, Mrs. Glanvill," I offered, seizing at the hope of getting away from that uncomfortable place and its objectionable owner. She shook her head.

"There's really no need, thank you. These turns soon pass with rest. Besides, it is very late. Good night, Dr. Watson. It has been so pleasant meeting you. My wrap is just here, James. Robbins will be in the car."

She had detached herself from me and was gone, with Lord Belmont hastening after her. I heard her motor car's engine being started up by the alert chauffeur.

As I picked up the fallen table and retrieved the unbroken decanter and glasses from the floor, my memory darted back full fifteen years to Holmes's rebuke, astonishing because it was totally undeserved: "You've done it now, Watson! A pretty mess you've made of the carpet!"

The incident had happened at a Surrey house, near Reigate. His accusation had followed his own deliberately knocking over a table and the carafe standing upon it. It had worked as a distraction then. As the resourceful Lavinia Glanvill had shown, an old trick may work as effectively as a new one if it is well performed.

I remained standing, wondering what to make of it but having little success. When Lord Belmont came back into the sitting room, he made no move to resume his chair. He made no comment upon the contretemps, nor apologized for his insulting diatribe against Holmes. His air was that of a man who has finished his business and sees no purpose in prolonging the interview. It was nearing midnight. He called the red-faced butler.

"Edwards will show you to your room, Doctor," he said dismissively. "We shall not meet in the morning. The dogcart will take you to the station. Goodnight."

We did not shake hands. He gave a curt little bow and stalked out. The stout butler inclined himself more courteously and showed me to a winding flight of wooden back stairs. He lit our way with an oil lamp that cast writhing shadows upon the whitewashed stair walls. A door at the top opened upon a broad and deeply shadowed landing with a single gas sconce flickering on its wall.

"A poor summer on the whole, sir," remarked Edwards, leading me to a bedroom nearby.

"Hardly Coronation weather," I agreed.

"Don't trouble about any sounds you might hear in the night, sir. Some of them keep odd hours."

" 'Them'?"

"His lordship's guild people, sir. We have quite a number of them living in. There is a nightshirt and dressing gown on the bed here, sir, and I have put out whisky and soda on this table over here."

"You have thought of everything, Edwards."

"His lordship's instructions, sir. He wishes you to be comfortable."

A whisky and soda, sipped in the snug comfort of the big bed, would do more for my comfort than any effort by his lordship, I thought as I undressed. The butler returned shortly with a can of warm water for the washbasin and took away my suit and boots for pressing and polishing.

Thankful to be alone at last, I went to draw back one of the curtains and open a latticed window for the refreshment of a breath of air after what had seemed a long, oppressive evening. The night upon which I gazed was pitch black. Its rainy coolness made expected contrast. I breathed deeply and relaxed my muscles, determined not to spoil my night's sleep with concern for my host's overwrought condition, which could be the only explanation for his gratuitous rudeness about Holmes.

The country silence was profound; yet as I leaned farther out, to extend my palm and feel the rain spatter upon it, I began to realize that neither silence nor utter darkness was a fact. Vague clatterings, of an almost rhythmical nature, sounded from somewhere within the house. I thought it might be laundrymaids working upon my clothes. I imagined my blue suit under the sponge and the iron, and some fellow in baize apron giving new lustre to my boots. Then I remembered the crafts workers and their "odd" hours. The sounds were more likely made by them.

I was about to close the window when I heard another sound which did not come from the house. It was a little way off, but approaching. Ahead of it swung a pair of faint yellow lamp beams. They touched the darkness from side to side, just enough to pick a way steadily through it. A motor car was coming.

A glimpse of it was all I had as it turned across my line of sight and passed just too far for me to keep it in view. It was still quite near to my vantage point when it stopped and the engine coughed into silence. A shaft of light sprang from the house. Someone had opened a door and was carrying a lamp out. I heard a man's voice, too muffled to be distinguishable. The voice which replied, though, was clear and plain and as familiar to me as if I had been accustomed to hearing it for years. It was Lavinia Glanvill's.

I heard her quick footsteps approach the house. The shaft of light was swallowed up as the door closed again. Instinct caused me to turn from the window and hurry across the room to my own door. As my hand closed upon its iron latch I fully expected to find it locked from outside.

It jerked open with a loud creak and clatter. I froze to the spot, listening hard for some moments before tiptoeing out into the corridor and along it to the door opening upon the back staircase. I did not think to reach for a lamp. I could not have risked one anyway.

I soon found the door and opened it carefully, to stand listening. Like a funnel, the plaster-walled stairwell carried up the faint murmur of the tones of Mrs. Glanvill and Lord Belmont. Their voices were too muffled for me to make out clearly what they were saying, but I was sure it concerned me. Something to do with me had made her interrupt him in mid-speech, and now had brought her hastening back at this midnight hour. My guess was that she had had to stop him saying something that I ought not to hear. Something arising from Belmont's behaviour needed discussing urgently between them. I determined to overhear what it was.

I groped my way in pitch darkness to the foot of the winding wooden stairs, my teeth gritted all the way in case they should creak. My plan was to creep into the dining room and listen at the door connecting it with the sitting room. I knew they were in there from the new aroma of Egyptian tobacco reaching me. Unfortunately, I was foiled by the door at the staircase foot. It had evidently been locked for the night.

Momentary alarm seized me. The butler on his locking-up round might secure the landing door, too. I hastened back up and was relieved to find that it still gave to my push. No one was in the shadowy corridor. I emerged and stood hesitating, not sure whether to hurry back to my room or risk exploring further.

Curiosity won. I felt certain now that Mrs. Glanvill and Lord Belmont were some way in league. The day's events had the distinct air of a rehearsal. I wondered, even, whether the most recent drama had been staged, too. Not stopping to work out any reasons, I set off along the corridor toward the main landing at the front of the house. My new idea was to go down by the main staircase and reach the dining room. From there I ought to be able to hear what was being said in the sitting room adjoining. Using the main staircase would expose me to the risk of being seen, but at least I could pretend to be coming down openly, upon some innocent errand.

I made my way quietly, alert for the slightest sound of

anyone approaching. I could not fail to notice that there was a great deal going on in the rest of the house. That rhythmical clattering I had heard earlier came from a corridor on the far side of the landing. There was something oddly familiar in its slap-slap regularity. I recognized it as I was making my way to the head of the stairs, half lit by gas jets. It was the sound of an engine-driven flat-bed printing press. Obviously, the printing craftsmen at least were not those sort of dogmatic idealists who rejected machinery of any kind.

I was about to set foot on the top tread of the broad staircase when I heard a door open and a man's voice speak. I skipped back swiftly, to press myself into the shadow beside a towering grandfather clock. I saw two men crossing the landing to the stairs. One was rubbing his eyes.

"I reckon," he was saying in a grumbling tone, "a mass-production run would be good enough. It's ruining my eyesight."

"Dead boring, more like," commiserated the other. "Still, it's steady work, and growing. Can't ask more'n that these days."

It was hardly the conversation of dedicated handicraftsmen in pursuit of noble perfection. Their accents were not what I associated with romantic or philosophical utopians. As they passed my hiding place I saw that they were middle-aged men in rough working clothes. They resembled factory hands coming off a shift.

They had not come from the printing room, for no surge of the press's sound had accompanied them out of the door. The machine continued to slap-slap away steadily. The men were about to go down the staircase when the one who had first complained hesitated.

" 'Ere. Did you see me turn out the blessed gas?"

"I left it to you."

"I know. But *did* I do it?"

"Best go back and make sure."

The doubter half turned. I shut my eyes so that he would not catch their gleam. He would see me if he came back, though.

"Nah," said he dismissively. " 'Course I did. Force o' habit."

"Come on, then," urged his mate. "My throat's parched."

They went down together, presumably toward some source of ale and supper in the kitchen regions.

Now was my chance to get back to my room without further risk. I had lost so much time that there was probably nothing much left to try to overhear down there. Before I could move from the shadow of the clock, though, the sitting room door below opened suddenly and noisily. A shaft of light from the room fanned forth across the hall floor. From my viewpoint above I could see between the banister rails as Mrs. Glanvill came hurrying out, followed by Lord Belmont.

I could hear her loud sobs. He leaped forward to try to bar her way to the front door. She shook him aside and wrenched at the doorknob. He seized her arm and tried to pull her back. A brief struggle took place in a silence broken only by her gasps and sobs, as she tried to get out of the house and he sought to prevent her.

I started forward, instinctively drawn to the aid of a woman in distress. Before I had given myself away, though, she had made it unnecessary. Drawing back her free hand, she delivered a loud slap to Lord Belmont's cheek. It surprised him enough to set him back on his heels, releasing his grasp of her. Before he could recover she had torn at the doorknob and was safely out into the night.

He took two or three strides in pursuit. I heard her summon Robbins, her chauffeur. Lord Belmont halted in the porch. The car door closed and the engine was started.

Belmont turned back into the hall, pushing the front door

shut behind him. He uttered some sound between an oath and a growl, shrugged his shoulders, and went off back into the sitting room, as I heard Mrs. Glanvill's car drive off.

I kept still for a little longer, in case the butler or anyone else might appear on the landing to investigate the slight commotion below. No one came. I set off back to my room, but paused again on the way.

A good deal that was odd seemed to be going on in this strange house. I had no inkling what any of it might be, but I should never have a better chance to find out. I would like to have something other than my own suspicions to tell Holmes.

For one thing, I was deeply curious to know what work those men were doing who resembled so little my conception of "Artful Crafty" types. They seemed to favor mass production, which I had thought was anathema in those circles.

I retraced my way to the landing, crossed it and peered round into the corridor from which the workmen had come. Nobody was about. Guessing the nearest door to be theirs, I took big strides to reach it. I put my ear to it and listened briefly. There was no sound within. The door opened unresistingly upon a room in darkness.

The atmosphere was stuffy from their presence and the lamp's fumes. There was a sharp chemical and metallic smell. A matchbox was in its place directly under the gas lamp over a bench. I struck one of the matches, before closing the door quietly and lighting the gas.

The broad bench took up much of what must once have been a small dressing room or closet. The men's white aprons lay draped across the seats of their respective wooden stools.

It was the tray of material lying there that drew my closer inspection. At first glace I took it for a mass of slips of silver, awaiting engraving with the tools which lay neatly arranged at each man's place. I leaned closer and picked up one of the slips. It was little more than two inches long and a quarter of an inch broad. Its lightness showed me that it was nothing more precious than tin, finished to a silvery hue.

I could not help gasping aloud upon recognizing what it represented.

Although I was not expecting to see Lord Belmont in the breakfast room the next morning I hoped at least to be given a message from him, telling me that Mrs. Glanvill would be sending her motor car to take me back to her house before I returned to London. I had ascertained that Alkhamton had no telephone. That would explain innocently enough her return midnight visit.

At her house she would hand over what I had come to fetch. Her cheerful young chauffeur would drive me on to Canterbury to catch an early train, with a mind cleared of some of the dark suspicions that had been waiting to jostle it as soon as I had awoken.

There proved to be no message of any kind, although I inquired casually of Edwards, who attended me alone. Remembering vividly the midnight quarrel, I wondered whether a communication had in fact been left, but either forgotten or even deliberately withheld. I dared not question the butler too pointedly, and his aloof manner gave no sign of anything untoward.

The breakfast dishes lined up on the cumbersome sideboard of a cheerless, high-ceilinged room matched the austere decorations and furniture. Kedgeree, curried mutton, bubble

195

and squeak, and crumbly, near-white scrambled egg came nowhere close to Mrs. Hudson's robust fare. I made do with cold toast, marmalade and stewed tea.

I saw nothing of any of the guild workers. I had listened from my bedroom window, though, and heard the steady thrum and clatter of the printing press. For all I knew, it could have been working through the night.

I left the place thankfully. The rain had passed, leaving a washed blue sky that seemed to promise better prospects once I could be well away from the depressing and even grim household.

Deal, the little naval town looking onto that notorious graveyard of thousands of wrecks, the Goodwin Sands, was on the railway line from Dover, a separate one from that over which I had travelled down to Canterbury. I could not command the driver of Lord Belmont's dogcart to take me the many miles across country to Mickleden. I saw no alternative to going directly to London and awaiting Holmes upon his return from the East End. While I waited for him, I could telephone Mrs. Glanvill from our rooms. I had every excuse to telephone her and ask her decision about returning the King's letter.

I should be curious to note how she would sound across the wire in the aftermath of the latter drama. I wondered whether there had been any connection between it and the reason for my going to visit her. These would be deep waters indeed, as Holmes would say, if Belmont knew about the letter, and deeper still if she had confided its contents in him at any stage. Great heavens, could they even be plotting together to use it for some purpose—blackmail for money or for privilege, or even worse, for some form of subversion! I could not imagine it of her, but I was not at all sure about him, with his volatile nature and potentially violent manner.

He was handsome, in his way, and artistically inclined. Mrs. Glanvill was alone a great deal, married to a man who seemed to live only for his ambition. Perhaps she had been tempted into a rash affair with Belmont, or had fallen under his influence, like Trilby under Svengali's.

My mind whirled with such speculations as the train rattled through the flat Kentish countryside. During the halt at Dover I had bought several of the morning newspapers, but I was too restless to read them closely. The only headlines that caught my eye related to the previous day's sweep of Hampstead Heath in search of the hound. It had lasted from dawn until dusk, but no traces had been found. The "well-known detective, Inspector G. Lestrade, of Scotland Yard," was praised for having assumed personal direction of the large body of police and rangers involved. He was widely quoted:

> *There can be no doubt that the attack was an invention by the "victim," Chapman. As his sort unfortunately will, he had been drinking freely and got into a fight with other vagrants, who left him injured. Seeing his opportunity to throw responsiblity upon the local authorities, he had the ingenious idea of imitating the cry of a wild animal, by which he would claim to have been attacked while in a public place. His impersonation proved doubly effectual, in driving his fellow vagrants from the Heath in terror and attracting the attention of the passing beat officer, whose evidence added plausibility to Chapman's tale.*

"The fact of Chapman's having absconded without pressing the intended claim," explained Insp. Lestrade, "indicates his suspicion that his story had not been wholly believed and would be subjected to keener scrutiny. His description has been circulated to other constabularies throughout the Home Counties, and I am confident that an early arrest will follow. Meanwhile, I am happy to give my personal assurance that Hampstead Heath is completely safe for use by all persons, of all ages and sexes."

I was able to smile at the final comment, and made a mental note to draw it to Holmes's amused attention.

One of the accounts ended with the announcement that the August Bank Holiday Fair on Hampstead Heath would now be able to take place as usual. Large crowds were anticipated, especially in view of the publicity arising from "the recent, happily unfounded, sensation, and the fortuitous propinquity of the Coronation festivities."

It prompted me to a further resolution, which was to take Coral to the fair on one of its three days. It was always a glad sight to see the crowds gathered in such thousands that it became almost impossible to see parts of the Heath for people. From early morning until late at night the multitudes ascended to the Northern Heights, emptying slums and middle-class neighbourhoods alike to join in waltzing to jangling piano organs, riding donkeys, skipping, fishing and swimming in the ponds, rushing and chasing and teasing and shrieking, shying at coconuts, shooting at targets, testing strength, screaming at the dizzy motion of roundabouts and swings, gaping at the caged animals in the travelling menagerie, buying and consuming sticky sweets, ice cream, pop and stronger beverages, getting lost and found, and generally letting off steam; for the long-established fair, and others like it, acted as a safety valve for the pent-up feelings of people bound by poverty or over-respectability to the monotony of never-changing surroundings and routine. Without such diversions, that revolution which Holmes had prognosticated might have happened long since.

It was almost midday by the time I reached Baker Street, where Mrs. Hudson greeted me excitedly. She had a scrap of paper in her hand.

"Oh, Dr. Watson, I'm glad you're back! There was a call on the telephone for you!"

Our worthy housekeeper still regarded each incoming call as an event of greater magnitude than anyone's coming to the door.

"A lady, sir. Quite early this morning."

She read from the paper. " 'Mrs. Hubert Glanvill says to say that she wishes to come and see Dr. Watson this afternoon and hopes that he will be at home, if not she will wait for him or Mr. Holmes.' I hope that's correct, sir."

"I'm sure it is, Mrs. Hudson. I believe I know what it is about."

"I had to write it down very quickly, sir. The lady sounded quite bothered."

"Bothered? In what way?"

"More nervous, Doctor. Like when something frightens you, you go a bit short of breath, if you know what I mean."

"Yes, yes. Early this morning, you say?"

"About ten, I think, sir."

"Did she say what time she would be here?"

She consulted the paper again.

"No, sir. Just this afternoon."

"Very well, then. I will see her at once, of course. Holmes is not back yet, I take it?"

"Not all night. No word, either."

"Well, that's nothing new to us, is it, Mrs. Hudson?"

"No indeed, sir!"

"While I wait for Mrs. Glanvill I think a spot of lunch might be indicated."

"Hot or cold? Did you have a nice dinner last night, sir?"

"Dreadful. So was breakfast. *Hot* lunch, if you please, Mrs. Hudson. All the courses."

"Very good, Doctor. It won't be half an hour."

I went up and exchanged my blue suit for town clothes. I went through into our sitting room and treated myself to a glass of our Old East India Madeira, which I sipped in my chair beside the empty grate. It was good to feel myself back in civilization again. I would telephone Russell Square later in the afternoon, by which time I thought Coral and her aunt might be back. A jolly evening in their company would exorcise the memory of the uncomfortable one at Alkhamton House.

Mrs. Hudson's reference to Lavinia Glanvill's having sounded troubled gave me some concern. Our housekeeper was by no means an experienced telephonist, though, and perhaps Mrs. Glanvill had been merely out of breath from bustling about. There was no point in my telephoning her house. She would have left already, and might be pausing to lunch somewhere in town before coming to Baker Street. I was fairly confident why she was coming. She had made up her mind, after all, to return the King's letter, and would naturally not entrust it to the post.

It was not Mrs. Hudson's stately tread upon our stair that presently interrupted my reverie, but a thunderous stampede, accompanied by a strident shout from a voice which I had no doubt was Holmes's. Our door burst open and in he flew, panting and dishevelled. I had just time to register the fact that the roughly dressed sailor of the previous morning had since changed himself into some sort of dockland labourer, with corduroys tied below the knees and a gaping black waistcoat over a collarless flannel shirt, before he had virtually pounced upon me and dragged me to my feet.

"Watson! Thank goodness you're back! A cab is at the door. Hurry, man, hurry!"

He propelled me downstairs so fast that I nearly lost my footing and plunged headlong. His grip on my collar, and the banister, saved me. Mrs. Hudson was just emerging from her kitchen door with a laden tray. I was shot straight past her and the savoury aroma surrounding her.

"Tell . . . the lady . . . to wait!" I had scarcely time to cry to her over my shoulder before being almost heaved, like a sack of potatoes or somebody's heavy luggage, into the waiting growler.

"Drive like the devil!" shouted Holmes at the cabby, who snapped his whip obediently and harangued his beasts in a tongue he and they alone shared.

"Where . . . are we going . . . Holmes?" I gasped, as we hurtled forward across the Marylebone Road at ten miles an hour.

"Hampstead Heath," came his surprising reply.

"What? Don't say there has been another!"

"Worse, far worse! Anarchy, Watson! Revolution . . . !"

We tore past Baker Street Underground station and were almost up to the "Volunteer" public house, at the corner of Regent's Park. I had glimpsed the newspaper placards ranged outside the station. They had nothing more sensational to proclaim than HAMPSTEAD HOUND PANIC. VICTIM'S HOAX.

"For heaven's sake, Holmes," said I, "tell me what has happened and what is going on."

He had dragged off his rough cap and run his fingers through his thinning hair, usually so glossily smooth on either side of his balding scalp, but now matted and dirty. He wiped his face with the ends of his neckerchief. I noticed smudges of makeup about his eyes.

"I thought I had learned my lesson over that *Five Orange Pips* case of ours," he replied. "Hurrying along the Embankment today reminded me of poor young Openshaw, whom the Ku Klux Klan assassinated there. I had failed to warn him that he was in danger. It should have occurred to me to tell Shinwell that Chapman was under threat, too. It is why he fled from the hospital. Chapman, the hound, the Chinese steward, Anderson . . . All linked, Watson!"

"Holmes," said I, suppressing rising impatience, "if we are going to Hampstead we have the best part of half an hour's drive. You might as well use the time to tell me what has been going on while I have been away. I have one or two things to tell you myself, but when you are in your self-recriminatory state you will put your mind to nothing else. My news will keep till teatime, when Mrs. Glanvill will be there."

He glanced blankly at me. Just occasionally in his great career I had seen him in this mood. He could forgive others their mistakes, but, as his own severest critic, would allow himself nothing short of excellence. Something must have happened that he considered a blemish to his record.

"Now, Holmes," I pressed him, "from the beginning, please—and pray be precise as to details."

"My first move," he explained, "was to place myself as close as possible to my quarry, Anderson. I had found out from the Channel steamer company that his lodging is near to where Burdett Road and the East India Dock Road join. I learned also that he had several days ashore before being due to sail again. I was resolved to have him safely behind bars before then. If he were to show any sign of further violence against anyone, I should prevent him and give him in charge."

Holmes tapped a pocket significantly, and I knew that this had been one of the relatively rare expeditions upon which he had gone armed.

"For the time being, however," he continued, "it suited me best to see where Anderson went and whom he met, for I was convinced that the Chinese steward's murder was neither motiveless nor isolated. Every instinct told me that it belonged in some sinister scheme of things. I began with a few inquiries into his background. Watson, I have noticed of late that you have come to appreciate more fully the value of the telephone. It remains to be seen how great a proportion of our bill will be attributable to calls to a certain number in the Bloomsbury area."

"I shall be only too pleased to stump up, Holmes."

"It is the instrument of the future, the telephone, where police work is concerned," he continued. "I envisage the day when every officer will have access to one, possibly of a kind he will be able to carry wherever he goes. Scotland Yard will be his immediate source of information or help. He will only have to call in to report a suspicious circumstance and summon reinforcements from far beyond a whistle's range. He will be at all times within his superior's call, to be directed wherever they wish him to go."

"Hardly the reactionary old quack's way of looking at things," I observed, and received his smile of acknowledgement before he went on.

"It required less than fifteen minutes of telephone calls this morning to find out all I needed from the ferry company, the Board of Trade and the British African Steamship Company. I learned that Peter Anderson is five-and-twenty years old. He was born on the West Coast of Africa, in the Cameroons, or Kamerun, as the Germans prefer to call their protectorate. His parents were both German. Their surname, before he modified his, was Andersen. His father was an overseer at the trading station of Messrs. Woermann, of Hamburg, on the estuary at Victoria. They call that part of the world the 'White Man's Grave,' though. Our man lost both father and mother while still a child.

"He was kept in the care of one of the British missionary schools, hence his flawless and unaccented English. His ambition was to become a sea captain. As soon as he was old enough, they put him into an apprenticeship with the British African Steamship Company. He spent some time in the coastal trade, then went deepsea. He got his mate's ticket three years ago, and stayed in cargo ships as fourth or third officer. Little more than a year ago, he was offered a berth as second mate in one of their passenger vessels. He turned it down."

"Turned it down, Holmes? It was a real leg up toward a command of his own."

"Not only refused it, Watson, but left the line as well. He paid off in London, moved into this place in Burdett Road, and soon afterward signed on as a deck officer on the ferries. That was last autumn, about eight months ago."

"Quite a comedown," said I. "Wife and family, I suppose."

"He has neither. His health is plainly excellent. There is nothing to prevent his roving the world. Apart from his own ambition, one might expect him to be urged to do so by the example of Captain Bassett, consigned to a backwater with the spectre of the Company glowering constantly over his shoulder."

"Did Anderson state any reason for giving up ocean-going?"

"None that is recorded. I drew the logical conclusion as to why an aspiring young man with a burgeoning career should throw it over. Anderson needed, or wished, to base himself upon London for some specific purpose. The reason is obscure to me at present, but since his practices include deliberate murder, we may assume that he is involved in some form of planned crime. Unless he is a madman, which we have ruled out, or the killing of the Chinese steward was a 'Yellow Peril' atrocity, which we have also excluded, we must find ourselves wondering whether he is acting upon his own account, or as hired assassin for someone else."

"What about his associates?" I suggested. "Is there any way of linking him with the steward, John Sweh?"

"Exactly what I wished to ascertain," said Holmes. "It was the reason for my first port of call, our old friend the Bar of Gold, in Upper Swandam Lane."

"You don't say that place still exists!" cried I, remembering it as the deplorable centre of an investigation some fifteen years earlier which figures in my chronicles as *The Man With the Twisted Lip.*

"You may well wrinkle your nose, Watson. The opium den is under new management, but its atmosphere remains quite as unsavoury and the bill of fare unchanged: rum and cigars for those who like to occupy their time smoking and yarning; Ya'pian Kan and the *majoon* for seekers after oblivion. One is unlikely to pick up any direct information there, but it is as near as one can come to the company of Orientals without arousing suspicions. The police have never seriously considered closing it down because it is a capital place in which to ask a question or two and listen to involuntary murmurings."

"What murmurings did you hear there, Holmes?"

"None. The Malay owners professed never to have heard of John Sweh. I though it prudent not to mention Peter Anderson in the same breath, as it were. I left empty-handed and made my way farther eastward, to the Free Russian Library, in Church Lane, off the Commercial Road. I don't believe our exploits have ever taken us there together?"

"I have never heard of it. What use could a Russian library be to you?"

"It is not the books and newspapers in it that are an invaluable source of information, but the company gathered there. That whole neighbourhood, you know, is more Russian than English. Orthodox and Roman Catholics, Talmudic and Karaiim Jews, Christians, Raskolniks and Mennonites are its populace. They are united in poverty, exile and the Russian tongues. They step straight off the ships and commingle there. They find one another work in the docks, the skin warehouses, the bamboo furniture workrooms, the engineering factories, the clothing sweatshops. News, especially concerning politics or crime, spreads among them like bush fires. It is a prized commodity of people who own so little. It gives the informant instant prominence. Nowhere in all of London, not even Fleet Street, is news assimilated quicker than in the Russian Library. The men who sit and smoke there from eleven in the morning till ten at night range from the most scholarly of exiles, avid for native periodicals, to the illiterate seaman wanting a letter written. They hear everything."

"We have touched upon Russian affairs in a few of our cases, Holmes, but I was never aware that it is yet another of your languages."

"Alas, Watson, it is not. Apart from some knowledge of the Cyrillic script, and a nodding acquaintance with ikons, Slavonic subjects remain beyond my ken. I do, however, maintain some curiosity about anarchism and its ideologies. It is that which, from time to time, makes this unofficial intelligence service valuable to me.

"Every educated Russian shares my ability to speak fluent French, and that is my entrée to the library. I am known there as Anatoli, the son of Russian Socialist exiles in Tangiers. No one questions me any more, or evinces surprise that my reappearances are brief and infrequent. Some of them come and go also, on business far more mysterious than mine."

"Do you suppose that Anderson frequents the place as well, on the strength of his German, perhaps?"

"It would not suffice him. No, it is unlikely that he is

known there. It was not so much regarding him that I went, but to catch what drift I might of the way things are shaping generally: what new rumours are in the air, what coups are being plotted, what political jokes are going the rounds—one can learn as much from what men laugh about as from their most earnest discussions. Much of it is in Russian and means nothing to me, but actions and expressions speak a language of their own, which I understand perfectly. I simply sit at one of the long tables, leafing through the French-language newspapers and keeping my ears open."

"Did you hear anything worthwhile?"

"It was not so much what I heard as what happened," replied Holmes, drumming his fingers impatiently on the seat between us. Our vehicle had reached the tree-lined steep slope of the fashionable Fitzjohn's Avenue, and had slowed to walking pace as the horses strained their breasts against the harness.

"What, Holmes? What did happen?"

"I noticed two men come in together and take seats near the door. One was bearded and patriarchal, the other young and with the wide cheekbones of the Slav. After they had been there some minutes, I saw a man rise from his place and cross to speak with them. He handed them a slip of paper, and they questioned him keenly in tones I could not overhear. At length the elder one nodded what seemed to be approval. The younger one gave the third man what looked like instructions, from the obedient way he kept nodding his head. Then he touched his hat and left the premises quickly. Some minutes passed, and then the pair were approached by another man. The same sequence followed. I'm sorry to have to confess that I had evidently not been keeping my curiosity about this as unobtrusive as I had supposed."

"They spotted you, Holmes?"

"A man next to me at the table addressed me in French,

and speaking in barely more than a whisper, said: 'They're taking a risk, working in the open like that.'

"I glanced at him from the corner of my eye. He was a youngish fellow, shabby but intelligent-looking, of the student type. I was, of course, instantly upon my guard, lest he should be testing his suspicions of me.

" 'Who are taking a risk—of what?' I asked him.

"He raised his eyes in the direction of the men near the door.

" 'It only needs some damn' police agent to come in here and see them at it,' replied he.

" 'At what?' I repeated. He looked at me keenly.

" 'Are you an agent?'

" 'Far from it, my friend.'

" 'But no one's spoken to you?'

" 'I don't know what you're talking about,' said I. 'This is my first time out for over a month. I've been keeping off the street. You know what I mean.'

"I added a wink and leer, which seemed to convince him. He glanced about before asking, 'You're for the Revolution, comrade?'

" 'Back at home?'

" 'Here.'

" 'When it happens.' I nodded.

" 'It's happening,' said he 'You want to enlist?'

" 'In what?'

" 'You ought to know not to ask questions like that.'

" 'Do I get paid?'

" 'That's not the right attitude!'

" 'It's mine. I need boodle quickly.'

" 'They'll give you some, once you've been sworn. You need to get enlisted first.'

" 'So that's what they're doing?'

" 'It's plain you've been lying low,' my companion observed. 'Things have started moving fast this last week or so, or they wouldn't risk working in the open like this. They've been told to get quick results.'

" 'You think they would take pals of mine, too?'

" 'As many as they can get. Look, any member can put others forward.' He slipped me a piece of paper and a stub of pencil. 'Write down your pals' names and your own. I'll hand it over to those two fellows. Then I have to leave. They'll tip you the wink when to go across to them.'

" 'You're not a damn' agent yourself, by any chance?' said I. He laughed, and I wrote down our names, Watson."

"You did what, Holmes!" I expostulated.

"And a few others, too," he added blandly. "Of course, I thought it tactful to use pseudonyms. My own is that by which I am known there, Anatoli Vernet. You yourself, strictly for revolutionary purposes, are Jack Hudson. I picture you as an anarchist of the deepest dye and vilest antecedents."

"*Thank you,* Holmes. Have you any further tidbits of surprises in store for me?"

"Only that we and the other traitorous scoundrels whom I named are to present ourselves for oath-taking at the Old Moore public house, off the Archway Road, at nine tomorrow evening. Those were the instructions given me by the recruiting officers after I had undergone my brief interview."

"Who might these other pals of ours be, Holmes?"

"Our old colleague in crime, Chief Inspector Gregson, of Special Branch, and three subordinates of his. I advised him to choose men whose faces are not known in anarchist circles and will match the names I provided for them."

"You've been to see Gregson?"

"He was delighted to receive me, once I had explained who I was under my seafaring rig. Of course the Branch is only too aware of subversive rumblings, ahead of the Coronation. Various protests, leaflet-throwings and so forth are considered inevitable. This particular organisation, which seems to be mustering its forces swiftly and with signs of some overall leadership, is a more serious issue."

"Well, Holmes, you seem to have stumbled upon yet another urgent matter to involve you—I might say *us*. At this rate, I shall find myself too old to get married, and you will be long past retirement! But, seriously, what about Anderson? You cannot place him to one side, as you seem prepared to do your other concerns. And what of Chapman and Shinwell? Why are we on our way to Hampstead? What is going *on*, Holmes?"

His face had clouded when I mentioned Chapman and Shinwell Johnson's names. The momentary buoyancy with which he had recounted his success in the East End had deserted him again when he answered.

"You are right, my dear Watson. There are other things on hand, and it is not meet that I should crow. I have gambled, and may well have lost."

"How?"

"After I had been to Scotland Yard, to lay my findings before Gregson, I returned to the East End. I passed the whole of last night in dockland haunts. I assure you that Anderson was my sole concern again, but I could find no trace of him. His lodging appeared deserted. I considered paying it a visit of inspection, but it is situated on the inside of the building. Its windows are visible from balconies which teem with humanity at all hours. Its door opens onto one of them. It is impossible to approach without someone noticing, and I particularly wished that he should not be alerted to my interest in him. It was imperative to keep him believing that he deceived us aboard the ship and got clean away with his crime."

"So what was your next move, Holmes?"

"I slept a little at one of my dockland bolt-holes and was up soon after dawn today, to try various other places where he

might be. I had changed my nautical gear for the dock labourer's outfit which you see on me. The change brought me no
luck, and by noontime I was fast running out of inspiration. As
you will recall, I was due to visit Shinwell this afternoon, in
order to interview Chapman. It occurred to me that I might as
well call upon him earlier than arranged, on the off chance that
he had returned already. Having eaten no supper last night and
no breakfast this morning, I was feeling a trifle lacking in energy, so I paused at a workingman's eating house for a pie and
a mug of tea. Watson, you will bear witness that I have never,
over the years, allowed hunger, thirst or any other bodily de-
mand to come before my work!"

"I have warned you often enough about neglecting yourself in that way. You place too much burden upon your body
and nerves."

"But," cried he in a sudden renewal of agitation, "see what
happens when I pause to pamper them! Five minutes earlier at
Shinwell's and I should have been in time!"

"For what?"

"To stop them taking him."

"Shinwell?"

"No, Chapman! Even as I knocked at the door I could
hear the struggle going on. I put my shoulder to the wood. It
did not give at once, but I believe the noise I made saved
Shinwell from being snatched, or badly injured. He was out
cold when I got in, but otherwise unharmed. They had left him
and rushed Chapman out by the back way."

"Did Shinwell know them?"

"He did not, but Chapman did. Shinwell told me, after I
had brought him round, that he had had the sensation of being
followed ever since laying hands on Chapman at Aldershot. He
had gone there to look for him upon my suggestion that, as a
former soldier of the Royal Mallows, Chapman would have a
crony or two in the vicinity—girls, most likely. He would nat-

urally have turned to one of them to help him lie low for a few days after his experience on the Heath. Soldiers are so predictable in that way. So much so, it seems, that these other men had the same idea. They tracked him down, but Shinwell had just beaten them to it."

"But the trail was warm enough for them to follow Shinwell and Chapman back to Shinwell's house," said I.

"Precisely. Chapman had begged not to be brought back to London, where he would be in danger. Shinwell told him that he would be safe enough with him and would soon be under my protection, provided he spilt any beans in his possession. He had not reckoned upon the astuteness of the opposing force. Obviously knowing where Shinwell lived, as almost everyone in the East End criminal fraternity does, they broke into his house and waited there for him and Chapman to turn up. To think, Watson, that if I had been a few minutes earlier, Chapman would be in my hands now. Instead, either he is dead, or soon will be."

"*Dead*, Holmes! You believe they are out to kill him?"

"He had told Shinwell they would, if they got him again. He knows too much and has to be silenced."

"About the hound being a hoax, you mean? Is it serious enough to kill for?"

"Undoubtedly. I told you that it was no lighthearted prank."

"Had he told Shinwell what happened, and what was behind it?"

"The bare details only."

"And what are those, Holmes?"

He did not answer immediately. We were passing through Hampstead Village and the cabby was turning round to Holmes.

"Whereabouts, guv'?"

"The Vale of Health. Where the fairground people are."

"What are we going there for, Holmes?" I asked, as it occurred to me to wish that he had told me to bring my revolver again. "Is it where you think they have Chapman?"

"Our luck will be in if it is," replied he dubiously.

"What, then? Whom are we looking for? Did Shinwell recognize the men who attacked him and took Chapman?"

"There were two. He recognized neither. He is not as young as he was, although he fought hard until they knocked him over the head. I caught a glimpse of them making off, however."

"Anyone you know, Holmes?"

His surprising response was to beat his fist upon his thigh.

"Too well! It makes it all the worse that I was not in time to save Chapman."

"You can't blame yourself for that. You were not due to go to Shinwell's till hours later. Anyway, whom did you recognize?"

He turned to give me a bleak, troubled stare.

"Anderson," he said.

CHAPTER SIXTEEN

The fair returns to Hampstead Heath on every Bank Holiday, whatever time of year. It never fails to draw crowds of thousands to that highest corner of the expanse which lies nearest to Whitestone Pond and Jack Straw's Castle, handy to the Underground, the buses and other means of escape from the metropolis.

Most of the showmen travel the country throughout the year, from town to town and village to village. Some regard Hampstead Heath as the fixed point in their transitory world, and store equipment in a compound in the sheltered enclave of artists' and writers' cottages called the Vale of Health. This point forms the hub of the fairground, which grows out from it, colourfully and noisily, several times a year.

The menagerie was not among the year-round fixtures. The effluvia and melancholy cries of its occupants, animal and human, would have been too utterly distracting for the artistic dwellers to bear. It moved after each visit, a procession of iron-barred wagons full of resigned beasts, dull of coat and eye and spirit, who perforce suffered themselves to be tugged from place to place by old nags which they would eat when the horses became worn out and had to be replaced.

Mrs. Annie Dodds, of Dodds's Beasts of the East, proved to be a widow woman in late middle age. She had obviously

once been handsome in an exotic Romany way. She still favoured an incongruously youthful dress of flamboyant design.
Its predominant colour was purple, which she had dyed her
hair to match, making an odd complement to her well-worn
complexion.

She was attending to her animals' feeding, whose awesome
serving we watched after getting down from our four-wheeler,
which Holmes instructed to wait for us. There were a pair of
tigers, a lion and lioness, a leopard and one or two other felines
that might have been anything from pumas to jaguars. She saw
us watching her and eventually came over, wiping bloodied
hands on a piece of old purple dress material. Her leathered
expression was unsmiling and wary.

"Mrs. Dodds, I believe?" Holmes greeted her, with a bow
that scarcely went with his labourer's outfit and made her look
even more suspicious.

"Who's asking?"

"Police business. This gentleman"—Holmes indicated me
—"is a veterinary surgeon."

"We've not asked for any veterinary."

"No, madam, but I am required to have one in attendance
as I go about my duties."

"Wot duties?"

"You'll have heard about the rumpus on the Heath a few
days back?"

"Not 'arf! Bloomin' nuisance. They was talking of banning
the fair."

"Well, the Heath's been declared clear of any wild animals,
but with the fair due next week we've orders to make doubly
sure of public safety. Routine check of your cages and locks,
Mrs. Dodds, if you'll be so good."

"Nothing wrong with 'em. We don't want closing down."

"Quite right, Ma," said Holmes, relaxing his manner and
giving her a grin. "So it'll just be a step round for me and the
vet here, and we'll leave you in peace."

She turned with a shrug and led the way to the first of the cages. Holmes peered at the bars and massive padlocks. They looked to me to be in excellent order.

"May I ask where you came from last, Mrs. Dodds?" said I, seeking to justify my newly acquired status.

"Barnet. Hertford, Barnet and Hampstead's our reg'lar round, this time of year."

"Business good?"

"Middlin' to rotten, with the weather."

Holmes had passed on rapidly from the lions to the jungle cats. I still had no notion of what he was looking for or why we had come here.

"All shipshape, missis," said he at length. "Not that you'd risk any of 'em getting loose."

"They wouldn't stray ten yards from their dinner pails, any of 'em," their owner returned. "They know where they're cared for. Lot o' rubbish talked about animals preferrin' to run wild."

"The hound rumours didn't put you off coming back here?" I asked.

"We was here already. The beasts like to get settled in before the fair."

"I expect our lads—the coppers—were round to you pretty smartly," said Holmes, smiling.

"It's always the travellin' people you suspect first."

"Well, I'm sure all was in order here. By the way, what's in that cage by itself?"

Holmes had indicated the occupant of the last and smallest of the trailers, which was largely shrouded in tarpaulin, as if to keep off the sun's rays. It was a species of dog, rough and gray, only a great deal larger than any I had seen. It had been lying down when we approached, with its rather fox-like muzzle on its paws, whining and sighing in a mild enough manner. When Holmes went near, though, it rose to its feet, showing its true size, quite the equal of a small donkey. It was extremely ferocious-looking, especially when it bared its fangs upon Holmes testing the lock on its door. It uttered several low, menacing growls, but when he turned away it subsided again and resumed its almost melancholy posture.

"That?" said Mrs. Dodds, and I noticed that she avoided Holmes's eye. "Gray Siberian wolf."

"Pretty fierce?"

She only nodded, showing impatience to move on.

"Sounds a little off-colour," said I, hearing the animal whine again. I regretted the remark immediately. She might invite me to step inside and examine the brute.

"Hot weather," she explained. "Perishin' cold, Siberia. That's why we keep the sun off. Right, gents, I got plenty to be gettin' on with."

"Such as," Holmes surprised her, "telling us where this unhappy animal's companion has got to."

"I dunno what you're on about, I'm sure!"

"I think you do, madam. You have two of these wolves. We see only one, and he looks and sounds distinctly lonely," He turned to me. "Shouldn't you say so, as the expert?"

"Oh, yes. Absolutely. Definitely pining."

Holmes rounded suddenly on the woman.

"In view of recent happenings up on the Heath, Mrs. Dodds, it is my duty to ask where your other wolf is at this moment?"

The hitherto truculent-mannered widow placed a hand on his arm. A pleading look had come into her faded eyes.

"Honest, sir, I'd have reported it sooner. I thought they'd have fetched him back long ago. Now you'll go and close us down, and jest with the fair comin' on. I've never had anythin' like this 'appen before. I knew I ought never to have listened to 'em!"

Holmes spoke quickly and seriously.

"The animal is missing?"

"Like I say . . ."

"Someone else has him?"

She nodded her head.

"Do they know how to control it?" I asked.

"I dunno. Do anything for me, they will, but that's different. They might turn savage if they're not treated proper."

"How long has he been gone?" snapped Holmes.

She began to wail, and pressed her hands to her face.

"Last night. It was only to be an hour or so."

"Please listen to me," persisted Holmes. "*Listen,* for this is extremely urgent. Was it the same people who hired him last time—that night the tramp got attacked?"

"The last time? Then you know, sir. They said it was only a lark. They was going to get something in the newspapers wot'd make more folk come to the fair. Ten quid they give me, as much as I reckon to take in a week. I went with 'em, in case they couldn't manage. They only wanted him walking up and down a bit of ground, so as his paws would leave marks. I asked what they was doin', but they jest laughed and said it was a stunt."

"Who were 'they'? How many?"

"Two of 'em. No names. Well, three, counting the drunken chap with 'em. Drunk as a mute. They was half carryin' him."

"You didn't see him attacked, of course?"

Mrs. Dodds stopped moaning abruptly. I shared her surprise.

"You mean *he* was that one!"

"Without doubt."

"Well, look, mister, whatever 'appened to 'im, my Boris had nothing to do with it!"

"Boris?"

"The wolf I lent 'em. I swear it wasn't him."

"I am aware of that," Holmes told her. "Did either of the two men have a megaphone with him?"

"Like a ringmaster's? I chivvied him about what it was for, but he wouldn't say."

"You didn't see it used?"

"No. Funny thing, though. When they'd said I could take Boris home, and him and me was crossing the Heath, he stopped sudden and pricked up his ears and turned his head this way and that. Then I listened and I heard a kind of howling."

"From more or less the place where you had left the men?"

"I don't know how you coppers know all this, but that's what I reckoned."

"Did you guess it might be that man using his megaphone?"

"I didn't then, but I've wondered since."

"So you came straight back here," Holmes resumed.

"I was glad to get Boris back safe without none of the fairground folk seein'. There'd have been hell to pay if they'd thought we was goin' to get shut down. Then while I was in the Vale pub some tramps come rushin' in, goin' on about being set on by a bloody great hound. I was splittin' to laugh and tell me mates how it had bin a stunt, only I didn't dare."

"Because your friends would have been angry?" said I.

"Because I'd have had to blow me ten quid on drinks all round!"

The recollection was agreeable enough to restore Mrs. Dodds's spirits briefly. Then she relapsed into despair and begged Holmes, "You're not goin' to close us down, are you, sir? It's me only livin, and think o' the pore beasts!"

I asked her, "Why didn't you own up to the police—us, I mean—when you read next day about that man being injured?"

"Read? Me? Somebody told me about it in the pub, but I didn't want no part of it. I tell you, I didn't know it was that feller. My Boris didn't hurt nobody. They said it was a stunt."

"You're in the clear over that, Mrs. Dodds," Holmes told

her sternly, "though you did wrong to keep quiet. Be quick and tell us who has got your wolf now. It cannot be the same men."

"No, that's right. They was two others, and without the drunk one this time."

"As I thought," murmured Holmes.

"What's that you say?"

"Nothing."

During this conversation, she had been gradually sidling toward her caravan, which stood at the head of the line of cages. She mounted the steps and entered it, Holmes and I following. The littered interior reeked of butcher's meat, tobacco, gin and other essences about which I did not care to speculate. She reached down her gin bottle and poured measures for us all into some fancy fairground-prize glasses. A sip was enough for me, but she drank copiously and refilled her glass. Holmes left his untouched.

"At what time last night did these second two men come here?"

"Gone ten. I'd just got back from the pub. It was to be a tenner on the nail again, but I says, 'Oo do you take me for? You're not out to puff the fair. You're up to something, you are!' Well, you wouldn't credit how nasty they turned. Things I'd never thought to hear from a gentleman to a lady. They said the cops—you lot—is in their pay, and how you'd come and shut me down. And 'ere you are! They've sent you to do it, 'aven't they?"

"Nothing of the sort, madam," replied Holmes. "What else did they tell you?"

"That if I told on 'em they'd come back in the night and poison all my pore beasts. Vicious. Crueller than animals, humans are!"

"So you had to give in?"

"I didn't dare not. They made me keep the ten quid. I said I'd sooner jest go with 'em, like I had before, only the cheeky devils said they could see as I'd been in the pub, and they'd manage theirselves. They promised to bring Ivan back in an hour."

"Ivan?" said I.

"The wolf."

"You mean Boris."

"No I don't. Ivan's his brother."

"You lent them a different animal this time?" said Holmes.

"That's right. Boris was half asleep, like, and I didn't want to bother 'im. Besides, either would do for what they wanted."

"You mean to say that two strangers could walk off with a Siberian wolf, just like that!" said I, incredulously.

"He was on a lead—a chain."

"Did you hear anything again?" Holmes asked. "Any more howling?"

"I thought I did, but I couldn't be certain, I was that upset. I jest sat here and had a little glass or two while I waited for them to come back, only they never did. I could wish Ivan had turned round and given 'em a good mauling, only somebody would hunt 'im down and shoot 'im for it, poor lamb!"

She would have wept again but for men's voices outside and a heavy hammering upon the caravan's wooden side.

"Police!" shouted a voice. "Open up!"

"Cripes! More of you?" Mrs. Dodds exclaimed. She opened the door, revealing the burly uniformed figure of Sergeant Roberts.

"Sorry to trouble you, missis . . ." he began, but broke off in open amazement at the sight of us. "Mr. Holmes . . . and Dr. Watson! How in blazes . . . ?"

"Good day to you, Sergeant," said Holmes, stepping down the outside stairs. I followed him, thankful for the fresh air. "What brings you here?"

"Same as you, sir, I expect. But how did you hear about it so quick?"

"About what, Sergeant?" asked I.

"Why, what I thought you had come about—the stiff we've got on the Heath."

"A body?"

"Yes, sir. Over Highgate way, just outside the Cemetery."

"Is crime involved?"

"Well, Doctor, strange to say, it looks more as if that hound's still on the loose, after all. It's the same sort of injuries, though far worse."

I heard Mrs. Dodds's sob from the top of her steps. Holmes said quickly, "You had better take us to the scene, Roberts. We have a cab waiting on the road. Mrs. Dodds had better come with us."

"If you say so, sir. Before we go, though, missis, the reason I stepped over here was to make sure all your pets are locked up safe. What we call a process of elimination."

Mrs. Dodds sobbed again. Holmes nodded to me to assist her.

"There are one or two details which you must hear as we drive, Sergeant," said he, leading off toward where our cab waited. "Watson, you, too. Believe me, this is no more a case of a hound than last time. It is undoubtedly a crime. It is cold-blooded, sadistic, deliberate murder."

To prevent her overhearing, Mrs. Dodds was placed in Sergeant Roberts's police vehicle, while he rode in ours. Holmes came straight to the point, detailing for the policeman how the first wolf, Boris, had been hired from Mrs. Dodds by two strange men with a drunken companion.

"The latter was, of course, Chapman, the victim of the first crime. He told my associate Shinwell Johnson how he had been approached by the men outside Jack Straw's. They offered him drink and money if he would help them in a publicity stunt for the fair. He was with them when they made their transaction with Mrs. Dodds, though he was too fuddled to understand what was going on. He could hardly stand up, and the men had to help him along. They all went to the spot on the Heath, and the wolf was then led up and down so that its prints impressed themselves on the ground. Then the other men told Mrs. Dodds they had finished with the animal and sent her off with it.

"Chapman only vaguely understood what was going on. He was told a story he was to tell if questioned, and threatened with dire trouble if he welshed in any way. He remembers the man producing the howling noises through the megaphone. While he was wondering what came next, he was suddenly attacked from behind. He had accepted that he must allow himself to be injured slightly, to make the stunt look real, but he didn't anticipate anything like the ferocity of the actual assault. It scared him so much that he screamed out. Something was ripping at him. He told Shinwell it had felt like a set of great claws."

"Claws!" interjected the sergeant. "That just about describes this new chap's wounds. You'll see if it doesn't. Torn half to shreds!"

"Perhaps it was the screams that made the other vagrants run off in panic," I suggested. "Not so much the howling."

"The mixture of the two," replied Holmes. "The howling effect had no point otherwise. It was his screams, however, which frightened Chapman's attackers away, or he would not have lived to tell the tale."

"Yet he stuck to the other story—the one they had told him to use."

"After an experience such as his he would not wish to risk their wrath upon reading a true report. All he wanted was to collect his money from its hiding place and disappear."

"Holmes, you said that Anderson was one of the men you saw dragging Chapman away from Shinwell's place. Can you be certain?"

"Beyond doubt. He was the man I had been seeking for two days, and his features were ever-present in my mind's eye.

Obviously, I had not been able to find him in the East End because he was out of town, tracking Chapman down."

"Lucky for you that Shinwell got that out of him about the old lady and her wolf. Where else could you hope to search?"

"Although I spotted Anderson as one of Chapman's abductors, I doubt that he recognized me, what with this disguise and his haste to get away. It is just possible that Chapman was taken back to Anderson's lodging as a temporary measure, but he would not be kept there long. I went there at once, of course, but there was no sign of life. I fear very much, Watson, that the corpse we are about to inspect will prove to be Chapman's own. They have finished off this time what they began last."

Our carriage was turning out of Highgate South Grove into the steep, narrow Swain's Lane, leading down to the famous Highgate Cemetery.

"Through the Cemetery's our best way," Sergeant Roberts explained. "The body's lying just outside it. The cab can take us most of the way. Then it's only a matter of climbing a wall."

He stood up to give an instruction to the cabby.

"Holmes," said I quietly, "you can't keep Anderson to yourself any longer."

"I know my limits, Watson. There is a point at which pure detective work must give way to action. Chapman's abduction carried us beyond that point. I called at the Yard on my way to Baker Street. There will be a full hue and cry after him by now."

"Thank heaven for that!"

Being on police business, our two carriages were waved through the Gothic entrance by attendants in tail coats and gold-braided top hats. We drove at a reverent pace along broad, curving avenues, past weeping and soaring angels, winged cherubs, arches, obelisks, urns, stone trumpets, scales of justice, crossed swords, anchors, inscribed stone scrolls, vaults bearing family names and every manner of headstone, cross,

tablet and railed tomb: the route of the last stage of life's journey for so many eminent and rich Victorians, going to their
rest in the prestige and even ostentation to which they had
been accustomed. Highgate Cemetery has always been one of
the most impressive of burial places, on its hilltop slope overlooking London. I hesitate to term it a "sought-after" place, but
one might be dead there with greater prestige than almost anywhere outside Westminster Abbey or St. Paul's.

When we had gone as far as the looping driveway could
take us toward our destination, we dismounted and I went to
help Mrs. Dodds from the police vehicle. She was still upset at
the dire prospects for her missing wolf. I gave her my arm for
the stiff pull up a grass slope, accompanied by one of the
London Cemetery Company's employees. He sought to divert
us with instructive commentary.

"Up that path there—you oughter fit him in while you're
visitin'—there's Tom Sayers. You know, drew the world title
against the Yankee, Heenan. Thirty-seven rounds, bare
knuckles, over two hours. Got his dog on his tombstone with
him. Over that way's old Selby, the coachman—Brighton and
back in under eight hours. Then there's Wombwell, the circus
man, and Lillywhite, the cricketer, and Charles Dickens's old
ma and pa. Rossetti's wife's just along there, who he had dug
up again to get his poetry book back. They say her hair was
like the day she died, only longer, 'cos it had gone on growing.
Yes, we're got 'em all here. That there, where the stiff is, is
called Traitor's Mound. They reckon that's because Guy
Fawkes and his mates stood on there to watch for Parliament
blowing up."

"All right, that'll do." Sergeant Roberts silenced him, and
we negotiated the rest of the way to where the corpse lay,
enclosed by the police with low barriers of sacking. Uniformed
officers and civilians were there. I recognized the young constable who had impressed me on the Heath that first time. He
looked distinctly green about the gills, and I soon saw why.

The body uncovered for us from under a sheet lay spread-eagled on the earth, face down. The skin had been literally torn off his back. It hung from him in ribbons, tangling with his exposed ribs. Blood had congealed thickly in black cakes.

I had told Mrs. Dodds to hold back until called, but I found her beside me and heard her sudden gasp. She clutched my arm again, quivering. A wilder shudder shook her as she exclaimed, "Thank Gawd!"

"What for, Mrs. Dodd?"

"My Ivan never did that. They can't blame him and shoot him for it."

"How can you tell?"

She was not too distressed to return me a look of scorn.

"And you a veterinary! Anybody could see that no wolf or hound or anything like did that. They only bite. This poor b———'s bin tore to ribbons with *claws*!"

Holmes was kneeling beside the body, examining it with his usual minute interest. He called me over.

"The face is quite intact," he told me. "It isn't Chapman."

"Who, then? Some other vagrant?"

"Do you think the old lady is up to taking a glimpse?"

"She is over the worst." I told Holmes what she had said. He nodded and I beckoned her over.

"The face is not mutilated, Mrs. Dodds," he assured her gently. "I wish you only to tell me if you can identify the man."

I held her firmly while he turned the head. It was that of a youngish man with a stubble of gingery beard.

"No," said she definitely. "Never set eyes on him."

"None of the men who have been bothering you?"

"I'd know any of them."

"Name of Spurrier," said a familiar voice behind us. We looked up to see Inspector Lestrade, thumbs hooked in his waistcoat pockets, looking knowingly down upon where we crouched.

"Matthew Spurrier," he amplified. "Petty political agitator

and general pest. Well known for spouting rubbish at Speakers' Corner."

"Currently wanted for defacing the statue of Charles the Second at Victoria Station," supplied Holmes.

"That's him! Here, how do you know that, Mr. Holmes? It's not been in the papers."

"A little bird told us," replied Holmes, standing up. "Or rather a big one, nowadays. The Gregson Bird."

"Oh, him! Special Branch poking their long noses in as usual! This looks a sight more special to me. I knew there was no smoke without fire in that hound business. I told them to keep me notified of any further development, and here I am, posthaste, as you see."

"This was not the work of any hound," Holmes retorted, "though the 'hound business', as you call it, might well prove relevant."

He introduced Mrs. Dodds to Lestrade, who gave her a perfunctory nod.

"They tell me this chap wasn't killed where he's lying," he continued to Holmes.

"Definitely not, Inspector," I confirmed. "There would be blood all over the place. He was killed somewhere else, and many hours ago. The rigor has worn off completely. He was brought and dumped here quite recently, I'd say."

"What was all that about a hound, then?" Lestrade demanded of Sergeant Roberts. "I can see its footprints myself!"

"That's as may be, sir, but it isn't here that it did him in."

"Garn!" snorted Mrs. Dodds suddenly, causing us all to turn to her. "First thing you can think of is blamin' my pore Ivan!"

"Her poor who?" Lestrade asked Holmes, who proceeded to explain the nature of her involvement.

"All right!" she defied Lestrade's outraged glare. "Put me into clink—only don't go makin' out it was Ivan wot did it."

"What did, then?"

"A cat."

"A *cat!*"

"Big one. Like in the jungle."

"Do you stand there, my woman, and tell me that we've to start all over again, looking for a blessed cat?"

"Yes, if you want to find wot done him in."

"I see. Then let's start with this establishment of yours. Any cats there?"

"Couple of old lions. Benjy—he's the tiger. There's Sammy and Tiddles. They're—"

"All right, all right. Been hiring any of *them* out?"

"There's no need to talk sarcastic!" returned Mrs. Dodds spiritedly. "This officer here's been a proper gent—and his veterinary friend, too."

Lestrade's face was briefly a picture as he stared from Holmes to me and back again. Holmes cleared his throat.

"Lestrade, I have been telling Sergeant Roberts various details of the earlier hound case that prove to impinge upon another investigation of mine. There is some urgency, and the killing of this man Spurrier increases it. If you will allow me, I will repeat it all to you, and then I have a small experiment to propose."

"I know your experiments, Mr. Sherlock Holmes! A death of this kind calls for straight police work, not fancy theorizing."

"A mixture of both, Inspector. We shall also require this good lady's further cooperation."

"Beg pardon, sir." Sergeant Roberts spoke up. "After what you've told me about her part, it's my plain duty to take her in."

"What's this?" demanded Lestrade, as Mrs. Dodds gave a cry of fear and clung to me again.

"All will be explained." Holmes soothed the two policemen. "I beg you to trust her for a little longer. Meanwhile, might I suggest placing an officer at her caravan door?"

"Ho!" Mrs. Dodds exclaimed. "What was that about trustin'?"

"He will not be there to stop you running away," Holmes assured her. "It will be his function to guard you from the men about whose affairs you know rather too much. Sooner or later, they will turn their attention to you."

He spoke with such menace that her face paled and her hands shook.

"I'd be safer in quod, after all," she wailed.

"Not at all," Holmes snapped. "Remember that you brought this trouble upon yourself in the first place. But for your willingness to make some gin money, this man might not be dead nor your animal missing. Besides, it would be inconvenient to have you in jail. I have work for you."

"Me work for the Special Branch!" she cried, to Lestrade's renewed consternation.

"Have you any mourning things?" Holmes asked her.

"Any *what*?"

"Come, come! Clothes you would wear to a funeral."

"As it so happens, I have, from pore Dodds's passing, rest his lazy soul."

"Then get them out ready, only don't let anyone see them. Change into them later, in good time for us to collect you from your caravan at seven sharp."

"Where're you takin' me to?"

"To a funeral, of course. Simply do as you are told, and say nothing."

It was my turn to interrupt him.

"Holmes, we ought to be getting back. We have a visitor, and I have urgent things to tell you."

He gave an impatient exclamation, but acquiesced.

"Very well, Watson. We will take the Hampstead route back and drop Mrs. Dodds and her guard on our way. It will enable me to have one more look at those noble beasts of hers."

"Just a minute, Mr. Holmes," protested Lestrade. "I haven't agreed to anything yet!"

For answer, Holmes took him aside, beckoning Sergeant Roberts to join them. He spoke earnestly, silencing Lestrade's attempts to interrupt. At length I saw the inspector shrug resignedly. I knew that my friend's persuasive powers had prevailed once again. He came back to me, with the young constable in tow.

"All fixed, Watson. Now, Officer, you're to come and guard this lady closely. I have more uses for her alive than dead."

"I'll see to the old girl, sir." The young man grinned.

"*Lady*," Holmes corrected him, and she gave him an almost coquettish smile.

So we returned the menagerie keeper to her vile abode. I was anxious that Mrs. Glanvill would be waiting at our rooms, but Holmes insisted upon strolling along the line of animals' cages. He paused the longest before the tiger and the lions, peering down at the latter's claws, with his face so close to the bars I almost feared for his safety.

"Hm!" he mused aloud. "Could you possibly conceive of a lion upon Hampstead Heath, Watson?"

"Scarcely, Holmes. A Siberian wolf is quite enough to be going on with."

" 'A hound by any other name,' " he mused aloud. "Yes, my dear Watson, I am inclined to agree. The proposition is an outré one, from any viewpoint."

He moved lastly to the small cage where Boris the wolf lay like a coiled-up dog. It did not trouble to stand up this time, or raise its muzzle. It only lifted its eyelids and returned Holmes's stare with a melancholy gaze.

I took Holmes by the arm and led him firmly to our waiting cab.

As soon as we were alone and spinning along, downhill all the way to Baker Street, I insisted that Holmes put the most recent events aside and pay attention to my news. He did not do so without some objection.

"Cannot you see, Watson, how quickly things have begun to move? At every stage a new link is forged. The original hound scare introduced us to Chapman, who has now been abducted by Anderson, the very man we are after for the murder of John Sweh. Now we have the death of Spurrier, who appears to have been a revolutionary crank but was obviously worth someone's trouble and risk to kill. Yes, Watson, some-*one,* for, mark my word, a human killer was responsible. The fact that it was preceded by yet another borrowing of the "hound" from Mrs. Dodds points to the same gang, which we now know has at least four members—two sets of two— among whom is Anderson. You spoke recently of the number of mysteries lying concurrently upon my plate. It is rapidly turning out that they are all, in fact, one, and that Anderson is the common denominator."

He gave his sharp, mirthless laugh.

"All we need now is to find a connection between this and the King's billet-doux and Cromwell's bones. Then we may declare what I believe the gamblers term a 'full house,' and I may retire with all my affairs wound up!"

I reached into my jacket pocket, and then held my hand out to him, clenched fingers uppermost. He looked curiously at it and then at me.

"What is this, Watson?"

"The completion of your full house, Holmes."

I opened my fingers, to reveal in my palm two of the little tin replicas of Oliver Cromwell's battle sabre, which I had brought back from that workshop room at Lord Belmont's.

"My *dear* Watson!" he exclaimed. "Remarkable!"

For once, Holmes listened in amazed silence as I told him how I had come by them.

"There was a tray full of discards," I concluded. "They must have got spoilt during engraving. I felt sure these would not be missed."

He examined them again keenly. One was in the name of Petrus Priest, the other of Simeon Wartski. There were scratches where the tool had slipped and flawed them. The rest of the engraving, common to both, was a superscription: OLIVER'S MEN.

"My dear fellow," said Holmes, straightening up, "you have excelled yourself! In all your exploits on my behalf, you have never obtained more valuable results. These are obviously tokens to enable their holders to identify themselves to fellow members of this organization. It would be too much to hope that you are able also to furnish the engravers' list of names?"

"I'm afraid not. I searched for as long as I dared. There was a locked safe. I expect the list was in it."

"Never mind. We shall know where to look, if it should come to it. Quick, and let me hear the rest of your odyssey."

I told him swiftly the details of my visit to Kent: of my impressions of Lavinia Glanvill; of Lord Belmont's suspiciously coincidental call at her house; his pressing invitation to me to visit him; her warning about his volatile moods; the uncomfortable supper and its embarrassing aftermath, when his access of offensiveness had verged upon hysteria and she had so dramatically cut him short; of her return by midnight, and their quarrel; and, lastly, of my stealthy expedition, the spoils of which lay in his hand.

"Wonderful!" he cried. "Do you see why I sent you? Picture Mycroft undertaking anything like that!"

"You don't suppose, Holmes," said I, voicing a notion that had struck me in the train, "that your brother suspected something down there, and wanted to find a way of persuading you to investigate it?"

"With Mycroft, anything is possible. What you suggest, however improbable, is not beyond credible bounds, where he is involved. Remember how he turned out to have been using me in the Dreyfus Affair? I should not even put it past him to have persuaded the King himself to be his accomplice in persuading me. He should know that I would have to obey."

"Is it possible that your brother suspects something about Lord Belmont in which Mrs. Glanvill may be involved? To use the King's letter as an excuse for approaching them would be diabolically subtle."

"Nothing, my dear Watson, is too subtle for Mycroft, nor too diabolical. It is why they say of him that he does not merely work for the Government—he *is* the Government."

"On the other hand," said I, "either or both of them may be entirely innocent. We have nothing to link these membership tokens with them except that they are being made on Belmont's premises. Those engravers I overheard may be working clandestinely on the side."

"No, no. We know of Belmont's interest in Cromwell's bones, and of his association with Garside, who, of all people, was best situated to purloin them."

"That's true, Holmes. And Spurrier was a Cromwellian crank. But why should he have been killed, and by whom?"

Holmes leaned toward me. "Executed might be a more accurate term. Spurrier was executed both as punishment to him and as an example to others—*'pour encourager les autres,'* as Voltaire puts it. He had stepped out of line, acted without orders. His impatience for action had made him a dangerous nuisance."

"Nuisance to whom?"

"Most likely to fellow members of some anarchist or revolutionary gang."

"Oliver's Men themselves!"

"Very probably. We know Spurrier had aroused public hostility at Speakers' Corner by praising Cromwell and uttering threats against the King. The police were after him as a result. Then he carried out that symbolic execution of Charles II's statue, bringing Special Branch into the picture. Assume that Oliver's Men are organizing a coup, of the kind I predicted to you. They are well advanced, but not wholly ready. Their last wish is to attract the authorities' notice. An uncontrollable maverick of Spurrier's kind could not be allowed to jump the gun on his own account. He had to be eliminated, and incidentally made an example to anyone else who might threaten their security. Did you note what they call the spot at which his body had been dumped?"

"Traitor's Mound! Someone's idea of aptness?"

"Secret societies thrive upon such metaphors. These tokens you have brought back are typical of the sort of regalia created to bind their members to their aims. The elaborate trappings which they employ, their oaths and symbols, all manifest their inherent distrust of one another. True fellowship makes do with an honest handshake."

"I see now, Holmes, why you thought those bones would be better left where they were."

"Depend upon it, Watson, of all possible fetishes for veneration by members of an organization calling itself Cromwell's

Men, nothing in this earthly world could be more evocative for them than their 'martyred' hero's remains."

"And you believe Garside took them?"

"He had the best opportunity of anyone."

"Well, that's one point in Mrs. Glanvill's favour, at least. She dislikes him heartily. I say, though—he and Lord Belmont are close associates. Belmont is interested in the bones, and these tokens are being produced on his premises. Holmes, it means . . . !"

"The inference is obvious, my dear Watson. It only wants proving."

"If only I had searched his house more thoroughly. I say, Holmes, do you think Belmont himself has the bones?"

"Yes and no. I do not believe that you would have found them at Alkhamton."

"What makes you say that?"

"I believe they are still here, in London. Unless I am much mistaken, we shall be seeing them this very evening. Or, rather, Anatoli Vernet and Jack Hudson will be seeing them when we present ourselves at the Old Moore tavern, Archway, to pledge our revolutionary oaths."

"I had almost forgotten that! You don't suggest that the gang we are joining is Oliver's Men?"

"Would you care to wager?"

"Not against you, Holmes. But how on earth have you reached that conclusion? There might be a dozen or more such movements in existence just now."

"At least. Our friends at Special Branch have their eye on the majority, all of which, mark this, belong in the East End. It is the traditional spawning ground of revolution and anarchy, and not only that which is directed against our own country. Our laws are so free and easy, with so little provision for political repression, that the most violent radicals of Europe and Asia can do their plotting and recruiting here with near impunity. London is known to them all as the 'open city' and *poste restante* for their activities. Their natural centre is the East End, where, I have shown you, men may come and go freely, with no questions asked."

"I can see that, Holmes, but it doesn't answer my question."

"Does it not? Is it not significant to you that our recruitment parade this evening has been called, not in dockland, not in Whitechapel, not in a room above the Russian Library, but at a pub on the edge of respectable, bourgeois Highgate?"

"Because it is one of the last places the Special Branch might be watching."

"True. But does nothing else occur to you? Do you know who is supposed to have lived in Highgate Village, for instance?"

"Sir Francis Bacon, I think."

"Correct. Anyone else?"

"One or two poets. Coleridge. Marvell . . . Didn't Nell Gwynn have a house there?"

"So it is said. Just one more, please, Watson."

"You win, Holmes."

"Oliver Cromwell."

"Cromwell lived in Highgate!"

"So the story goes. His daughter certainly did. She was married to Henry Ireton, who was one of those whose body was strung up and beheaded with his at Tyburn. Their house is still there in the High Street. It is even called Cromwell House. It's said to have had a platform on the roof, where 'Old Noll' would stand and survey the capital which was now his."

"Are you saying it is the headquarters of Oliver's Men?"

"Not necessarily the house itself, but the locality is as good as any, and more appropriate than most. You know my theory of circumstantial evidence. The more arrows there are found to be pointing in the same direction, the more possibility becomes probability. Where Highgate is concerned we have this Cromwell connection, and the choice of a local pub for this evening's meeting. We have deduced the symbolic inference of Spurrier's corpse being placed on Traitor's Mound, just adjoining Highgate Cemetery. The original attack on Chapman occurred on the Highgate side of Hampstead Heath. Have I omitted anything?"

"The hound. Where does it come in?"

"Ah, yes. If my theories are correct, that detail will prove to have been fully as subtle as the choice of locality."

"Too subtle for me, Holmes."

"Perhaps I might recommend a book?"

"A book? Is it one I know?"

"Better than most people—*The Hound of the Baskervilles.*"

"Oho! Any part in particular?"

"Chapter Two, I believe, wherein the reader's blood is chilled by the seventeenth-century story of the original hound, which gave Stapleton his idea of a reincarnation. That first hound is depicted as an almost spiritual instrument of awful revenge against a tyrant. It savages the evil Sir Hugo, who has persecuted an innocent maid to her death. Imagine a messianic visionary who feels himself divinely called, in the way that Cromwell felt, to lead an uprising of the oppressed against their persecutors. Would not the legendary and universally known Hound of the Baskervilles make a perfect mascot with which to awe his following?"

"Wouldn't something to do with Cromwell be more to the point?"

"There is that, too. It is why I suggest you re-examine that portion of the narrative, especially the scene where Dr. Mortimer brings us the manuscript containing the Curse of the Baskervilles."

"You pooh-poohed it as a fairy tale," I reminded him.

"Never mind that. What else do you remember about it?"

"You guessed the document's date as 1730, whereas it was actually 1742. Only twelve years out. Not bad at all, Holmes."

"It was merely the date when the legend was written down. The period to which I would draw your attention is that at which the hound made its first appearance. Here we are at Baker Street. Do look it up when you get a moment, my dear Watson. It will be a revelation to you."

"About this funeral, of which you spoke to Mrs. Dodds," I reminded him. "I presume I am expected to attend."

"Pray excuse a verbal summons, my dear Watson. There is no time to get cards printed."

"Did I know the deceased?"

"By reputation and posthumous acquaintance only. His name was Spurrier. Our purpose is not to bury him, but to find out precisely how he died, and where."

Our cab was pulling up outside 221B. He would add no more.

"Alexandrians, Number Five," commented Holmes, without needing to sniff the air in our Baker Street hallway. "The lady has been waiting for some time and is clearly agitated. Watson, do you go up and greet her, while I commune with Mrs. Hudson and use the telephone. We are in for some busy hours, and the instrument is going to have further opportunity to demonstrate its value."

I was accustomed enough to finding our sitting room thick with tobacco fumes, but the heavy pungency of dark shag was more usual than the incense-like Eastern perfume that met me. Its density bore out both of Holmes's downstairs deductions.

"Thank heaven you have come at last!" said Mrs. Glanvill, getting up from my armchair. "Is Sherlock Holmes with you?"

I explained that he had an urgent telephone call to make before coming up. I found myself apologizing over-elaborately for keeping her waiting so long. The suspicion which I could not help attaching to her made me less at ease with her now in my own surroundings than I had been on her home ground. I felt constrained to guard my tongue.

She did not look anything like a conspirator, still less an incipient revolutionary, but I had been well indoctrinated by Holmes about women's deceptive appearances. She was quietly dressed for railway travel: a light-gray skirt and ivory blouse, without any jewellery, and a plain straw hat. She was paler than I had seen her, with an absence of that schoolgirl-like freshness. She seemed to have left her theatrical mannerisms down in Kent.

We made desultory conversation until Holmes joined us, ushering in Mrs. Hudson with her tea tray. He greeted Mrs. Glanvill with his usual easy courtesy, then dismissed our land-lady and made the rare gesture of pouring tea for us himself.

"You'll take some now, Mrs. Glanvill? Capital! Pray excuse these working clothes. You have caught my friend and me in mid-occupation. As you may judge from our boots, we have been on Hampstead Heath—following the hounds, so to speak."

He was bending over the tray, and did not watch her as he spoke, but I knew that he was listening keenly for the slightest reaction. I watched her covertly, but detected nothing. After only a token sip of tea did she set down her cup and saucer and address herself to him.

"Mr. Holmes, I am very worried. I have done something foolish. I need advice and perhaps help."

Holmes pulled off his workman's neckerchief and tossed it aside. He lowered his long frame into his chair opposite the lady, who was occupying mine while I sat upon the sofa. He leaned toward her, elbows upon knees, steepling his long fingers.

"Go on, madam," said he gently. "From the beginning, if you please, and pray omit none of the particulars."

I expected her to waste no time in producing the King's letter from her raffia bag, but she did not do so. She repeated briefly the particulars of her marriage to Hubert Glanvill, a dozen years her senior, adding the new detail that it had been in defiance of her family. She and her husband were perfectly suited, but there were no children to occupy her, and his growing transatlantic business took him more and more from home. He had had their house designed for her, and had let her furnish it to her taste, no expense spared. She was content with her country life. She did not long for the city or for the "Society" rounds.

They had got to know Lord Belmont when he inherited Alkhamton from his late brother. He had told them he was going to start a journal for the Arts and Crafts movement and run it from there. He also founded a small crafts guild, some of whose members lived in his house.

"What is the magazine's name?" asked Holmes.

"He just refers to it as 'the journal.' I don't know exactly what it is to be called."

"Then it is not yet on sale?"

"Oh, no. He has been planning it for almost as long as we have known him."

"Has he never invited you to help him?"

"I have offered. He seemed willing to let me, but nothing has come of it."

"Pray go on, madam. You were about to tell me of your personal relationship with Lord Belmont."

Holmes's assumption surprised her, but proved correct.

She had come to see a good deal of James Belmont in her husband's long absences. He was a bachelor, but never mentioned any intention to marry. He seemed to have only the artistic and literary interests which she shared. In what seemed a frank answer to a blunt question from Holmes, she said that Lord Belmont had made no advances of any kind to her. I remembered her offhand way when she had told me that she and her husband were "good chums." It made me even more curious about her reputed "association" with the King. My suspicion deepened that it was all a tactical fabrication by Mycroft Holmes, yet she had shown no surprise at the King's note when I had brought it to her. I concluded that the royal association must be the "foolish thing" which had brought her to Holmes. Perhaps, in spite of her blameless aspect, it was one subject upon which she could not consult her husband. How does a woman admit to her husband the attentions of the Prince of Wales?

"After we had known each other quite some months," she was continuing to Holmes, "James Belmont seemed to change. Most of our talk had been about art and literature and such things. Now, though, he began talking only of politics and social questions. He would go on endlessly about the Government not doing enough for the working people, and how it was wasting all our money on war, and how the people who own the factories and businesses exploit their workers to feed their greed."

"Can you say approximately when this change began?" interrupted Holmes.

"It was during the war, I should say not long after the Queen's death. James seemed very concerned about how we should fare under the new King."

"In what way concerned?"

"He has often said it is a bad prospect for us that the King had such an affection for France and that he and his nephew, the German Kaiser, are at such loggerheads. James thinks it would be better for us the other way about. He says it needs a German mind to understand problems of capital and labour. He idolizes Karl Marx. He persuaded me to read things by Marx and such people. He is always quoting them."

"What did you make of them yourself, Mrs. Glanvill?"

"I have always felt sorry for poor people and those who never seem to have any chances. I know there is a lot needing doing for them, and I feel guilty sometimes that we have plenty of everything, while so many people have not enough. I am afraid I am not the kind of woman who goes in for what Dr. Watson calls 'good works.' But, you know, my husband came up from nothing. He made all his own opportunities. I don't see how anything would be improved if he were to be 'dragged down' and made to grovel in the dust."

"Is that one of Lord Belmont's notions?"

"Very much so. He would have the so-called workers taking over everything—the factories, business, the newspapers, the law, even the Government and the police and Army and Navy."

"That sounds a curious point of view for a peer of the realm!" I could not help intervening. "Surely he doesn't say such things in public?"

"No, Doctor, but I am afraid it is only a matter of time before he will. It seems to burst out of him at certain moments when he loses control of his tongue. I thought he was simply exaggerating when I heard him speak like that for the first time, but it has happened two or three times since. Now I am conscious of it all the time, only just under the surface. It is why I warned you not to provoke him. The most innocuous remark seems enough. He turns sarcastic and provocative, as you heard, and says any wounding things that come to his mind. That in turn seems to work like some quick-acting poison on him, and takes away his reason. Then he begins to rave uncontrollably about the way the country and the world have to be changed while there is still time to save people's souls."

"Was that why you stopped him last night, Mrs. Glanvill?"

"You saw that I did it deliberately? Of course, you would. I could not let him break out like that in your hearing."

"Why, madam?" asked Holmes sharply. "Why were you at such pains to cover up for him?"

"He and I have been good friends for quite some time, Mr. Holmes. I could not stand by and let him reveal that side of himself to Dr. Watson. It is very painful to me to witness, but at least I am accustomed to it. I have told myself that it is some form of breakdown that he is experiencing, some awful tension he is under which he has never mentioned. I thought that perhaps these fits give him some release, and that I might be doing him a kindness by letting him use me as his hearer. Surely, any woman's instinct would be to shield a friend who was so obviously in distress?"

"Are you in love with Lord Belmont?" Holmes asked, dropping his coaxing manner so suddenly that even I was taken off guard.

"No," she replied without flinching. "I have told you."

"Have you *been* in love with him?"

"I have been fond of him as a friend."

"Aside from your feelings, have you been lovers in any sense?"

She struggled out of the armchair, as Holmes stood up to confront her.

"I came here, Mr. Holmes, because I believed you were a well-wisher and would help me. I did not expect to be insulted."

For answer, Holmes shot out his right arm toward her, fingers clenched into a fist, making her gasp and draw back momentarily. He opened his fingers. On the flat of his upturned palm I caught the silvery gleam of the sword-shaped tokens.

Mrs. Glanvill stared at them, then raised her eyes again to Holmes's.

"What are those?" she asked in a surprised tone.

"You do not know?"

"I have no idea."

"They bear an inscription on the other side. Do you know what it is?"

"How can I?"

Without shifting his gimlet stare from her face, Holmes flipped the tokens over with a jerk of his hand. She bent to look closely at them.

" 'OLIVER'S MEN'? What does that mean?"

"What does it mean to *you,* madam?"

She returned his look again.

"Nothing whatever."

With another flip of his palm Holmes tossed the little pieces into the air. He caught them again and shut his fist firmly around them.

"Mrs. Glanvill, I owe you my apology," he said, with a little bow and smile. "Pray sit down again and let us hear the rest of your story."

She hesitated, though.

"You have been testing me, Mr. Holmes. You think I have come here to lie and try to deceive you."

"Unfortunately, madam, there seemed to be that possibility. There is dangerous business afoot and it was imperative that I establish your involvement. My friend will support me, I am sure."

"I'm sorry, Mrs. Glanvill." I hastened to add my share. "After you had knocked over that table to prevent Lord Belmont blurting out something which you didn't wish me to hear, and then came back to see him afterward, I couldn't help feeling curious, to say the least. Then, after finding those things at his house . . ."

"You found them at Alkhamton?"

I glanced at Holmes, who nodded. I told her how I had come across the tokens.

"But what does it all mean?" she asked wonderingly.

"In a moment, madam," Holmes replied. "Pray sit down and smoke one of your cigarettes while you finish your own story."

"But you know it all."

"You have not told us why you had informed Lord Belmont that I had made an appointment to come and see you, or why, when you learned that Watson was coming instead, you went to Alkhamton to advise him of the change. You have not accounted for his 'chancing' to visit you while Watson was there, and inviting him to dine. Most importantly, you have not said why you went back there at midnight, or what caused the fracas between you and Lord Belmont which my friend witnessed from the landing. It is obviously something connected with that which has made you come here so urgently today, to reveal details of Lord Belmont's condition which you had been at pains to keep secret. In short, Mrs. Glanvill, it is we who should ask you 'What does it all mean?' "

"To answer your first questions, Mr. Holmes, I was trying to humour James, to set his mind at rest. For some time, he and his friend Dr. Garside have been after Hubert to sponsor the museum which they plan to build in London. It will cost a great deal of money. As I told Dr. Watson, my husband refused to go in with them. It resulted in rather a painful scene. James began to have one of his fits. He was becoming very sarcastic about big business, and how the country is in danger of being taken over by the Americans."

"Is that so?"

"According to James, the King listens to everything his financier friends tell him, and does just as they advise him. They want to mortgage us so heavily to the Americans that they will get complete control of all our manufactures and trade. Then our workers will be even more ground down than now."

"Presumably your husband told him he was talking rubbish?"

"He was quite polite about it, but it set James off on one of his tirades. He said that something has to be done quickly to make the people see where the country is going, before the King and his friends can do too much harm. Hubert said he thought the workers might actually *like* the idea of new investment, *like* getting rid of their dangerous old machinery, and having bright new factories and better wages and conditions.

James said the workers don't know what is best for themselves. He said that if they haven't the will to shed their chains, then someone will do it for them. As Oliver Cromwell said, 'Not what they want but what is good for them.' "

"Lord Belmont quoted that himself?"

"Yes. He quotes Cromwell as much as he does Karl Marx. Mr. Holmes, does this mean that this 'Oliver's Men,' whatever it is, has something to do with James?"

"A great deal, I fancy, Mrs. Glanvill. Please finish your story."

"Well, there was no actual quarrel between them. Hubert simply walks away from anything he has no patience with. This was shortly before he went off on his latest trip to America. A day or two afterward, James called on me and said that he had been to London to see his friend Garside and that Sherlock Holmes had come snooping after them, as he put it."

"What he meant," I explained, "was that Holmes and I happened to visit the Tyburn excavation and met Lord Belmont and Garside there."

"I know that now, Dr. Watson. The way James put it, though, was that you had gone there deliberately to spy on them."

"Why on earth should we do that?"

"That was what I asked him. He said you were obviously in the pay of the capitalists against the workers, like those Pinkerton detectives in America. He accused Hubert of having hired you. When I said it was nonsense, James insisted that at least Hubert must have reported what James had said to him, and that you had been sent to find something that could be used against him."

"Nothing could be further from the truth, madam," replied Holmes, "though, to judge from what you have told us of Lord Belmont's mental state, I can readily see how he came to imagine it."

"Then imagine also his reaction when, in the midst of his visit to me, you yourself telephoned, asking if you might come and see me."

"He was actually with you!" I exclaimed.

"I was so taken aback by the call that I did not think to conceal who was making it. I had no reason to refuse you, Mr. Holmes. Naturally, he was convinced by then that what he suspected was true."

"Were you, Mrs. Glanvill?" asked Holmes.

"I didn't know what to think. I don't know how you detectives go about such things. James was positive that you were coming to ask me questions about him. I said I was sure you were not, and that it was nothing to do with him. I could not convince him, and he was growing more agitated by the minute. I had to get him to leave my house before there could be a scene that my servants might overhear. They might put any sort of misinterpretation upon it. It was not until after he had gone that I remembered your saying that your errand was for the King."

Holmes was regarding her again at his most intent.

"What did *that* mean to you?" he asked.

Only now did she reach down for the raffia handbag beside her. She opened it and drew out an envelope.

"It meant this," said she, holding it out to Holmes. "I knew it to be my only personal connection with His Majesty. The note which Dr. Watson brought with him confirmed that I had guessed correctly."

Holmes took the envelope and glanced at it. Making no move to open it, he reached up and propped it on our mantelpiece, among the general clutter.

"Don't you intend to read it?" said Mrs. Glanvill.

"No, madam. I am merely its collector. The contents are private to the writer and yourself. Should you have second thoughts about handing it over, and wish you had not, you are free to take it back when you leave."

"Mr. Holmes," she said in a soft, sincere tone, "I was surprised at being asked to return it. I was flabbergasted, though, that a third party should be involved—perhaps I should say a fourth party, Dr. Watson. Now you have shown me why you were chosen, Mr. Holmes. I'm most grateful and relieved."

"But it was not worry over this which has brought you here, I believe."

"You are right. I can be brief now. You can imagine what state of mind James was in when he left me after you had telephoned. I was concerned for him, and thought of going over to Alkhamton to set his mind at rest. I almost determined to tell him what must be the reason for your coming, which could have no possible connection with him. Then you telephoned again to say that Dr. Watson was coming in your place."

"Then you went across to tell him of the change," said I. "You did not go to Folkestone at all."

She showed surprise at my knowledge of her movements, but admitted, "You are quite right, Doctor. With all due respect to yourself, I thought that it would set James's mind completely at rest to know it was you, not Mr. Holmes, who was coming to visit me after all. If he was still not convinced, I was prepared to tell him the real reason."

"You seem to have shown Lord Belmont more consideration than he has returned you," said I.

"You mean, what you saw last night?" Her features hardened into sudden grimness. "Yes. That is what has altered my attitude to him. It is why I am here."

"A moment, madam," Holmes interrupted. "You have not yet told us whether Lord Belmont's visit to your house while Watson was present was a wholly unexpected one."

"If you mean to ask whether it had been prearranged between us, the answer is certainly not. I did *half* expect him to come because I sensed that, in spite of all my persuasion, he still suspected that he was the subject of the visit."

"A paranoiac would certainly think that," I told her. "There is not much doubt that that is the nature of his malady."

The news did not distress her. It was plain that whatever had happened between them had driven sympathy for him out of her completely.

"He came to my house because he could not make himself keep away," she confirmed. "He had to try to find out what was being said, but there was no way he could think of approaching it. He needed time, so pressed you to dine with him. I wished you would not accept, because I guessed it would lead to an embarrassing scene, but I couldn't refuse for you. Even then, I suppose he found himself at an impasse. He could not bring the conversation round, but could only hope that a natural opening would occur. I could see him becoming increasingly nervous. I knew that he must break out, sooner or later."

"You dealt with the situation admirably," I praised her. "I suppose you came back later to make sure we were not at each other, hammer and tongs."

"Doctor or no, I could not leave you exposed to him in that state when you knew nothing of the background. I had no idea what he might say to you. When I came back I was quite ready to take you away to Mickleden."

"But there had been no further talk. I had gone off to bed peacefully enough. What happened to make you quarrel?"

She answered simply, "I told him of that letter—that one on your mantelpiece there."

"You told him after all!"

"I felt it was necessary. I was genuinely anxious for you, Dr. Watson. Suddenly, for the first time, I saw how affected his mind had become. It frightened me. Violent language might lead to real violence. I pictured you sleeping innocently in that house, unsuspecting that he was convinced you were Mr. Holmes's spy."

"Great heavens! I should not have slept many winks if I'd thought that!"

"I thought the truth might protect you."

"Mrs. Glanvill," Holmes directed her yet again to her narrative, "we are to take it that Lord Belmont knew nothing of the letter until that moment?"

"Nothing at all."

"Nor of any association between you and . . . a certain person?"

She shook her head emphatically.

"No one knows, except that 'certain person' and myself, though I suppose I must now include you, your brother, Mycroft, and Dr. Watson—and, I'm afraid, James Belmont. That was my foolish act, Mr. Holmes. I was not to suspect what telling him about it would do."

"What was that?"

"He was delighted. He seemed almost triumphant. I was to bring the letter across first thing this morning, then he would have it photographed and give it straight back for me to send to you. You can imagine how baffling it was, hearing things like that!"

"Did he tell you his reason?"

"No, and I've racked my brains to think of any."

"It will become apparent soon enough," replied Holmes grimly. "So you refused him?"

"Absolutely. I said I'd never heard anything so monstrous. He began to get very excited again. When I said I had only mentioned the letter to try to help him, he said that nothing could help him better. He even said the whole country would have cause to thank me! I saw that he was raving again. I was starting to feel frightened. I wished I hadn't gone back. I saw what a mistake I'd made, but it was too late. I wanted to leave, but he barred my way to the door. He said he shouldn't let me go until I'd promised to bring the letter to him. Then he said he would come with me in my car, and I should hand the letter over and Robbins could drive him back."

"You still refused?"

"I should not have dreamed of agreeing. But I was becoming very frightened indeed. I thought of calling out, hoping you would hear me, Doctor. It seemed futile in that great place, though, and I was fearful what he might do. So, at last, I said I would do as he wished. I would bring him the letter this morning."

"That was very wise." Holmes nodded.

"Very," said I. "Otherwise, you might not be telling the tale."

"I think I knew that. If he had insisted on coming to Mickleden with me, I don't know what I should have done. Tried to escape, perhaps, and locked myself in somewhere until the servants could get rid of him—anything rather than give him the letter."

"But you managed to make him believe that you would deliver it today!" I wondered. "That was an achievement. Paranoiacs are excessively suspicious of anything that is told them."

"He safeguarded himself," she answered bitterly. "As I was about to leave the room, he told me that if I failed to keep my promise he would reveal my secret to Hubert, and I should be a ruined woman."

"The scoundrel!" I exclaimed. "No wonder you slapped his face."

"Yet in seeking to bind you with that threat," Holmes pointed out to her, "he destroyed the vestiges of your sympathy. You owe him no further loyalty now." He jumped to his feet. "You are a brave and resourceful woman, Mrs. Glanvill. If you had acted in any other way the outcome could have been disastrous for both yourself and my friend here. But you must recognize that you have made a deadly enemy."

"It is why I hurried to consult you, Mr. Holmes. As to my reputation with my husband, let him do his worst to destroy it. The only proof is there in that envelope. I will defend myself against his word."

"It is not that against which you need defending. The more immediate danger is to your life."

"My life!"

"Depend upon it. You have cheated him, thereby confirming his fear that you might do so. What is your prognosis of his state in consequence of that, Watson?"

"Homicidal," I had no hesitation in answering. "You have not only defied him, Mrs. Glanvill. You have snatched away something that was almost within his grasp, and which he saw as setting the seal upon his mad scheme."

"What mad scheme, Doctor? I still don't know what is behind all this."

Holmes was crossing to the window. I saw that he took care to avoid showing himself.

"There is no time for explanations now," he told Mrs. Glanvill. "Suffice it to remind you that Lord Belmont spoke to you of implications for the country as a whole."

Holmes was peeping round the curtain, looking down into the street. "Ah! I expected as much!" he exclaimed. We moved to join him. He motioned Mrs. Glanvill to keep back, while I took up position behind the opposite curtain. Across Baker Street, two roughly dressed men with their backs to us were staring into the bespoke tailor's shop window. They did not appear to be conversing and made no move while we watched.

"See the beauties?" said Holmes. "It is not their own reflections that they are contemplating in that glass."

"What is it?" our visitor asked. "What is happening?"

"Our front door is being watched by two men. They are waiting for you to leave."

"You mean James Belmont has sent them? They have followed me?"

"Luckily, they did not catch up with you. You did well to come here and wait so patiently. If you had come after they had taken up their position, or had stepped out again, they would certainly have had both that letter and yourself. It would be a simple matter to contrive an accident in all that traffic."

Lavinia Glanvill shuddered visibly. Even her resolute spirit recoiled at the proximity of such danger.

"Holmes, Mrs. Glanvill cannot leave these premises," said I. "I had better tell Mrs. Hudson to make some arrangements."

"No, Watson, that will not do. We ourselves have to go out shortly, and again this evening. We dare not risk her being here in our absence."

"You mean I may not go home?"

"On no account, madam. Your husband is still away presumably? You see how vulnerable you would be there. We must have recourse again to our friend the telephone. However did we manage without it, Watson?"

"Call the police, Holmes?"

"No, my dear Watson. I wish no attention which will alert those watchdogs down there that we are planning something for tonight. Are your ladies back in town yet?"

"I imagine so by now," replied I, surprised by the question.

"Then pray call them up and ask if they would be prepared to receive a young man to stay the night."

"Young man, Holmes?"

"Dear me, Watson, you don't suppose that Mrs. Glanvill can simply leave here as herself and calmly take a cab to Russell Square? Remember how Irene Adler took us in in her male clothing, greeting us outside our own door? If the trick could be worked on us we may confidently reverse it upon a pair of plug-uglies."

"What if they see through it? You can't expose Mrs. Glanvill to that risk."

"I will do anything you say, Mr. Holmes," she interposed. "I place myself in your hands."

"You see, Watson? You will be the one exposed, as escort. Now, make haste and ring for Mrs. Hudson. While you are making your telephone call, she can be looking out whatever outfit we can furnish that will turn our client into a handsome young gentleman setting forth early for an evening with you upon the town."

"Very well, Holmes."

"By the way, you won't mind if I urge you to ensure that your revolver is fully loaded?"

"No, Holmes."

"I might go so far as to advise you to keep it better to hand than you had it the other evening upon Hampstead Heath. I let you live to fight another day. These present villains might prove less accommodating."

"*Yes,* Holmes! By the way, reverting to this 'funeral'—"

"Your city black will suffice, my dear chap. You had better take it with you to Russell Square and change there. Be at Albany Street Police Station by six o'clock."

CHAPTER NINETEEN

C oral and her aunt had just returned to Russell Square. They were delighted at the prospect of my calling upon them so soon, and intrigued by my request. The telephone still being a novelty, we none of us knew how vulnerable it might be to eavesdropping. When Coral asked if I had caught a cold, because my voice sounded so strange, I realized that I was whispering into the mouthpiece.

Half an hour later Mrs. Glanvill and I left openly by our front door, raising our top hats ostentatiously to Mrs. Hudson, who saw us off. Obedient to Holmes's instructions, we did not dash to the nearest cab, but sauntered some way in the Oxford Street direction, swinging our evening canes and puffing our cigars.

We continued almost as far as Portman Square before I suggested to my companion that we might take one of the cabs waiting there. "He" made a gesture of agreement, and we went leisurely over to the rank. We were soon jogging upon our way, having done nothing to denote urgency.

"All clear," said I. "They only followed a few paces, along the other side of the road. They daren't leave their post for fear of missing the lady they have been told to expect."

"May I get rid of this cigar?" was the response, accompanied by a grimace.

"Throw it out of the window. Everyone does."

Coral's and Henry's faces were pictures of amazement when I introduced my evening-suited and cloaked friend as "Mrs. Glanvill." Henry's eye showed something more than simple surprise, and I hastened to explain the successful trick. She beamed relief.

"I was going to say 'Any friend of John's . . . ,' but then I wasn't all that sure. I'm Henrietta—Henry for short. This is my niece Coral."

"How do you do? Please call me Lavinia. You, too, Dr. Watson."

"You must be longing to change out of those things!" Coral exclaimed, looking disparagingly at the mixture of Holmes's and my evening clothes that their guest was wearing. "John, why don't you go through and sit down with Henry while I fix Lavinia up with some of my clothes?"

I explained that I could not stay. I told them only that Holmes and I had a busy evening ahead of us. In the cab I had requested Lavinia not to worry them by speaking of the danger she must have gathered might face us, though she still knew little of the ramifications of what was happening. I did not try to enlighten her, because I did not know them all myself.

"I must just change one or two of my own things," I told Coral, indicating the small parcel I had brought with me. She indicated the bathroom, where I changed quickly out of the black and white of evening dress into something that was black all over, and made them exclaim when I showed myself again.

"Why, John, whatever have you gone into mourning for?" asked Henry.

"I'm off to a funeral. I must fly, or I might miss it."

"Whose funeral?"

"Just a man. No one you would know."

"I think this is a case of 'The game is afoot, Watson,' " said Coral.

"You will let me . . . *us* . . . know what has happened?"

said Lavinia Glanvill, with a note of genuine anxiety that made the others look curiously at her.

"As soon as possible."

"Do we wait up for you?" asked Henry.

"I hope not to be too late," I replied.

I made my escape before they could question me further, or any of them could remark upon the bulge which the loaded Webley No. 2 was making in my coat. Its sagging weight reminded me that this was no game, and that I had no inkling of its result.

In order to evade the eyes of the sentinels opposite 221B, Holmes had arranged by telephone to Inspector Lestrade that our rendezvous should be at Albany Street, not very far from us on one of the borders of Regent's Park. He would have no trouble leaving our rooms undetected by the rooftop route that had served him on other occasions when our movements were being watched.

I arrived by hansom cab just before the appointed six o'clock. The bizarre sight which greeted me when I entered the police station was of Lestrade, dressed like myself in funerary black from head to toe, and looking for all the world like a professional mute. A heavily craped hat was beside him on the counter, where he leaned, smoking one of his rank small cigars, chatting with the duty sergeant. They stared at my costume.

"I told Holmes that this sort of thing's gone out," Lestrade complained. "He would have it, though. I'm glad they can't see me like this down at the Yard."

"Ah, Watson!" came Holmes's high voice as he bustled in, in mourning weeds also, by the side door from the compound in which police vehicles were kept. "Capital! Come along. Our cortège awaits."

Within ten minutes we were travelling Hampsteadward once more. Our vehicle was a black four-wheeler, drawn by two black horses with black knots in their manes and tall black plumes bobbing on their heads. We made quick time, our black-clad police driver attracting a few censorious glances for whipping up so purposefully and cutting out any vehicle in our path. Eventually we pulled up outside the premises of one of the several Hampstead undertakers. A low-slung hearse, with its curtains closed, stood waiting for us, with two more black horses in its shafts. Another black four-wheeler, similarly drawn, waited behind it.

Our young constable friend, up on the box of the hearse beside the driver, touched the brim of a black-ribboned top hat in salute to us. Sergeant Roberts, also sombrely outfitted, was beside the driver of the carriage, whom I recognized as another policeman. The carriage contained two pairs of mourners, whose physique and aspect suggested to me that the men were constables and the women wardresses, borrowed from one of the gaols.

The undertaker's manager, red face shining like a polished apple, approached us, rubbing his hands.

"Inspector Lestrade? How de do, sir? Quite the part you are, sir. Afternoon, gentlemen. Here's the cemetery plan you requested. Strictly on loan, you understand."

"Can we just get on?" growled Lestrade, not troubling to introduce us as our carriage was manoeuvred into the procession. "Are we ready, Sergeant Roberts?"

"All aboard, sir."

"Then let's be off."

"You'll sign for everything afterward, sir?" called the manager as the cortège moved away. "Twenty pound, seeing there's no shell provided."

"Send a bill to the Yard," Lestrade told him. "Might get paid this side of Christmas," he murmured to Holmes and me as we were borne in the hearse's wake.

"No flowers, Lestrade?" remarked Holmes.

"That'd look good on the expenses!" Lestrade snorted. "I've let you lead me some capers, but there was never one to match this."

"If things go as I expect them to you will have plenty to satisfy you for this night's work. By the way, you will excuse my pointing out that it would not look seemly to be puffing a cigar while riding in a funeral procession."

"I forgot," said the Scotland Yarder, nipping out the weed with thumb and forefinger and returning it to its packet. "Is it any wonder?"

I, too, was experiencing a feeling of unreality. A respectful gentleman removed his top hat, to stand with bowed gray head as we passed. I hoped that the Widow Dodds, presently hidden from sight in the leading vehicle, had not been calming her nerves too freely with gin. If curiosity were to cause her to part the hearse's curtains and peer out, a fresh Hampstead sensation would shortly be galvanizing Fleet Street.

The news of Spurrier's death had been kept from the press so far. Lestrade had put the Cemetery employees under dire threat to say nothing. I gathered that Holmes had brought him up to date with as much as it was now his duty to tell him. He had also been in touch with Gregson, at Special Branch.

As we rode he unfolded the London Cemetery Company's plan of Highgate Cemetery. The layout, with its looping avenues, resembled a diagram of the great intestine. Scattered little blocks in a variety of colourings could only denote plots in differing price categories. Some bore ticks, other crosses, and some a sinister "?." Holmes's searching finger swung like a compass needle to the feature marked Traitor's Mound, just outside the western boundary. It was not far from the top gate adjoining St. Michael's parish church, near which a section was more elaborately marked in concentric circles and radii, resembling a clock face without hands.

"The Circle of Lebanon and the Catacombs," he interpreted. "The pick of the Cemetery, by all accounts. It is said to be the highest viewpoint over London, though what use that is to those who are in permanent residence is somewhat questionable."

We turned into Swain's Lane. The gatemen, who had been primed to expect us, doffed their gold-braided hats to the hearse. Two of them joined the procession on foot. The drivers stared solemnly forward and the horses' heads nodded with the effort of drawing us up the winding slope. The smell of new-cut grass was rich upon the air. A gardener, doing some late trimming and watch-keeping near the farthest point we could attain, removed his cap and at the same time nodded us an all-clear.

We all dismounted and went quickly to the hearse. Lestrade opened the veiled door at its rear. He recoiled slightly as the fearsome gray snout of the Siberian wolf poked itself at him. It blinked at the light, after the interior gloom, and looked back within.

"All right, Boris, love," came Mrs. Dodds's voice. "Jest let your Ma get past."

She clambered forth, in a plenitude of black flounces. Sergeant Roberts helped her to the ground.

"Cor, the 'eat in there!" she complained, shaking out her skirts with one hand and adjusting a vast black bonnet and veil with the other.

"Never mind that," said Lestrade. "Just you keep hold of that animal before he goes escaping."

"*Boris* won't go escaping, will he, pet?" she cooed at the great beast, who would have licked her but for the veil. " 'E knows 'e's all right with 'is Ma."

She retrieved her end of the chain lead and tugged gently. Everyone fell back a pace as the wolf jumped out. It stood looking about uncertainly.

"You sure nobody's been snooping round?" Sergeant Roberts asked the gardener sternly.

"Not a one, sir. Last funeral was five o'clock. They was all out an hour or more ago."

"Right," said Lestrade. "On to where the body was."

"Ought we to make a procession, Sarge?" murmured the young constable, keeping his face straight.

"We'll have none of that lip, my lad," Sergeant Roberts rebuked him. "This is serious work. Lead on, Ma."

"Come on, Boris love." She ordered the wolf up from his haunches. "Little walkies."

Preceded by them, we all trooped up the path and across from it toward where Spurrier's corpse had lain.

"*Can* wolves follow trails?" I asked Holmes as we went. "I thought they just went where the pack goes."

"In terms of Dodds's Beasts of the East," replied he, "two must be held to constitute the pack. Lestrade was going to use a bloodhound, but I persuaded him that a bird in the hand is worth two in the bush. It is just possible that Boris might lead us to two, anyway."

"What was that, Mr. Holmes?" asked the inspector, catching his name.

"Just telling Watson how sharp it was of you to think of using the wolf to lead us to the place where Spurrier was actually killed."

"Oh! Oh, well, quite so, Mr. Holmes." Our old friend said, smirking.

As we approached Traitor's Mound, I was interested to see Boris starting to show excitement. His nose went often to the ground. Incongruous little whines seemed to be emanating from deep inside his formidable body. Mrs. Dodds had to hold on hard to the chain. Sergeant Roberts signed to the constable and the other male mourners to be ready to jump to her assistance.

The body had been removed, together with the makeshift enclosure, so as to avoid attracting public notice. The paw prints were still clear, though. It was when he encountered this area that Boris became truly agitated. He pulled Mrs. Dodds in circles as he ran round and round, nostrils constantly to the earth, and then ultimately jumped upon the very spot at which the body had lain. Straddled there, with the evening sky behind him, which made him look as if carved by a monumental mason, he raised his head to bend back as far as it would go and uttered a prolonged and blood-chilling howl.

" 'Strewth!" exclaimed the constable, and went unrebuked; the awe which showed in his expression was reflected by every other one of us present.

"Quickly!" Holmes instructed. "Before we start drawing attention to ourselves. Mrs. Dodds, see if he will lead us."

Something remarkable occurred then, which I can see still with memory's eye. The raffish old woman, looking as incongruous in her mourning weeds as a pantomime dame, squatted down beside that great beast, generations of whose ancestors must have made the Siberian wastes the more terrible from their threat, and began whispering into its ear.

What it was that she confided I could not hear. Doubtless it was spoken in some unrecorded tongue, shared only between wild animals and those humans who enjoy some sort of intimacy with them and have been trusted with a few of their age-old secrets. As she whispered, she fondled the powerful neck, burying her fingers in the strong gray fur, and stroked the back of the erect ear.

We men watched transfixed in silence and respect. I am sure that my companions were as moved as I by the mystic spectacle of woman and beast from the wild. No one intruded with an impatient word or movement. At last she got up, stiffly, yet with a kind of grace.

"He'll take us," she said quietly.

She resumed her end of the chain. Boris stepped down from the mound and lowered his nose to the earth again. Without even momentary hesitation he led us back toward the Cemetery grounds.

The gates had been closed to the public, so we were free to go openly wherever Boris took us. All the same, Sergeant

Roberts's men kept their eyes peeled, upon Holmes's orders through Lestrade, for observers within or without. I am sure a few were expecting a hound as well.

The wolf's progress was unhesitating. He took us diagonally and upward, with the spire of St. Michael's ahead. We crossed the wall, then veered abruptly to the right along one of the paved walks. Boris was drawing us on toward a fantastic entrance, cut into the steepest part of the incline. Twin obelisks, like smaller versions of Cleopatra's Needle, flanked a massively solid stone arch of what seemed to me inappropriately Eastern design. Spiked iron gates barred the way to a steep street, dark and narrow, with rows of niches or doorways on both sides. In response to the wolf's impatient whines, one of the Cemetery attendants with us hurried forward with the keys. He, like the rest of us, seemed to be no longer afraid to go close to the great gray beast who was for the present our leader. Boris showed no interest in us. His eyes searched only toward where his sensitive nostrils were impelling him.

"The Egyptian Avenue," Holmes murmured to me, sounding fearful of breaking a spell existing between us and the animal. "Leading into the Valley of the Kings and the Circle of Lebanon."

"What is all this Egyptian effect about?" I hissed back.

"The architect as showman. Death and burial as the final act of life's drama. Overdone, yet effective."

The intended dramatic effect worked potently enough on me as we passed into that narrow way. The shadow of death was about us, literally. Behind each of the implacably shut doors along its sides I knew there were cubicles lined with shelf upon shelf of coffins and urns. The dusty, dank stillness of those airless interiors whose occupants needed no air exuded an atmosphere that was almost tangible. It seemed as if there were reaching toward us chilly, ghostly arms, coaxing us to go in, and lie down in their embrace, and be still.

We moved on into the Circle of Lebanon. It was like a

fortification, with a circular stone parapet all round. A similarly shaped mound was at the centre, with a circular trench separating them. A vast cedar tree, rooted in the middle of the mound, spread its branches densely above us. Circumnavigating the entrenchment, we were in semidarkness still. Some long-dead sentry, in tattered red coat and with a Brown Bess musket over his shoulder bone, should have paused in his eternal pacing there to challenge us.

The stone face of the outer wall was pierced again with iron doors, bigger than those we had passed, each with an Oriental pediment. Anybody might have been forgiven for expecting the vaults behind them to contain highly ranked Egyptians mummies in painted and hieroglyphed cases, instead of mundanely coffined Victorian English bourgeoisie.

A flight of broad stone stairs took us once more into lighter, less oppressive air. To my relief, the trail Boris was following with such sureness did not lead us down yet again, this time into what Holmes had pointed out on the plan as the Terrace Catacombs. The very name gave me shivers, to add to the chill with which the atmosphere in this place had already dispelled for me the summer evening's mildness.

The unlovely, gray neo-Gothic pile of St. Michael's soared above us, and we were at the Cemetery's upper edge. Backing onto the wall dividing it from the church was a vaulted, square-bodied edifice, with a pyramidal roof. A square iron door in the front had pillars for its sides and a massive stone lintel above, flanked with identical coats of arms.

Holmes stopped in his tracks, clutching my arm to halt me.

"Watson! See!"

In a plaque forming part of the lintel was carved the name of the family whose burial vault this was.

"Belmont!" I gasped.

The wolf, without pausing or even raising his head to consider with his fierce eyes the verdict of his nose, threw himself at the heavy metal door. Mrs. Dodds was nearly jerked

off her feet. But for a quick move by the strong young constable, the chain would have flown out of her grasp. We all
dashed forward. To my relief, Boris had no notion of escaping.
He was up on his hind feet, his raised head far above the head-
height of anyone there. With all the weight and muscle of his
broad shoulders behind them, his forepaws scrabbled toward
the door.

"Hold him back!" ordered Holmes. The powerful beast
remained on his hind legs, straining at his chain, forepaws
flailing.

"Take him away!"

I could not understand the urgency in his fresh command.
The young constable and two of the others relieved Mrs. Dodds
of the chain. With main force, they hauled the writhing wolf
away. Holmes moved swiftly to press his ear against the iron
door, motioning to us to keep as quiet as possible.

After some moments he shook his head and stood back.

"Not a sound," he said. "Who has the keys to this vault?"

"Head of the family, sir," answered a Cemetery man. "The
present Lord Belmont."

"Arrange to get it forced," said Lestrade.

"No, no." Holmes turned to him, shaking his head. "We
do not wish to enter yet. All must get away from here quickly,
before anyone sees us. Quickly, and quietly!"

We all turned to disperse to where we had left our cortège.
The men grappling with the wolf's chain needed all their
strength to drag Boris reluctantly away.

Suddenly, though, the wolf ceased to resist. He sank
down, to stand on all four feet, then turned to face the vault.
His ears were as sharply pricked forward as they could go. He
raised his head once more and uttered another of those blood-
chilling howls.

This time there came an answer. It reached us almost as a
muffled echo: a long, wailing, dismal cry. It was the howl of
another wolf—and it came from within the tomb!

CHAPTER TWENTY

The burial vault's massive stone walls would have prevented the imprisoned Ivan's cry from being heard at a greater distance. His brother Boris's blood-chilling howl, to which it had been the response, must have given our presence away to anyone keeping watch in the vicinity, and struck renewed fear of the hound's return into neighbouring residents. There was nothing for it but to return to our funeral vehicles as swiftly as possible, reinstall Boris and Ma Dodds inside the hearse—I envied her even less this time—and drive away with unhurried unconcern.

"Belmont's family vault!" I exclaimed to Holmes as we rode again in our black carriage. "What do you think of that?"

"I think that this Cemetery plan is half useless," replied he tersely, casting it on the floor. "You might expect it to name family vaults. It might have saved us that expedition, and the risk of showing our interest in the place."

"You weren't expecting it, then?"

"It had never occurred to me. I associate the Belmonts with the country, and a vault in some country churchyard, if not their own grounds. But you had told me that Alkhamton House had been rebuilt so tastelessly in the middle of last century. I might have guessed that the delusions of grandeur would have included paying for one of the biggest vaults in the most envied section of the newest of cemeteries."

"If it is Belmont who has the missing bones, then that is where they will be, don't you suppose, Holmes?"

"Without a doubt. Sharing the last resting place of the Belmont dead. It will seem wholly fitting to that madman."

"Stealing a wolf to guard over them seems pretty mad," I agreed."

"I fancy there is rather more to poor Ivan's captivity than that. At least, though, we have our solution to the hound mystery."

"Have we?"

"You know the age-old smuggler's trick of starting some local fright to deter sightseers?"

"Oh, that! It is the explanation for half the so-called ghost sightings ever claimed."

"Belmont admitted to being one of your readers, Watson. It is not hard, then, to see him seizing upon the legend of the hound which kept Dartmoor folk safely home at nights. Have you looked up that reference which I gave you, by the way?"

"When have I had the time, Holmes? You haven't given me a moment's peace."

"Perhaps you will have remembered it by the time you come to look for it. I shall not spoil your anticipation by explaining further. The idea of a hound struck him as both symbolic and practical. The practical use of it was to ensure that the skeletons stolen from the Tyburn excavation could be brought to the vault without anyone noticing. There would be no question of smuggling them in a portmanteau. A considerable degree of reverence, and even some ceremony, would be involved. Activity at Belmont's vault would have been noted and questioned by the Cemetery staff. He did not wish them to know that anyone had visited the vault lately. He is the keyholder, and must have become implicated."

"You mean to say he coolly hired Mrs. Dodds's wolf to impersonate the creature, and paid Chapman to be its victim?"

"He wanted footprints of something that could not be mistaken for any ordinary domestic animal, and would be of an impressive size. The idea of the fairground wolf was truly inspirational.

"Mrs. Dodds did not know what was to be the true price of her gin, and Chapman was only too ready to let himself become soaked in whatever it was. Amazing what a thirst for strong waters will lead some people to do, is it not? But, seriously, Watson, though to be forewarned is to be forearmed, the most dangerous part of this proceeding still lies ahead of us. Any slip-up this evening could cost lives, and I do not exclude our own. Here is Albany Street. It will have to be a case of a rooftop entry to 221B, in case those two are still on watch. Another quick change, a bite of Mrs. Hudson's cold victuals, and Messrs. Vernet and Hudson must be off again, this time to consult Old Moore."

The Old Moore public house, named after the sixteenth-century astrologer and quack Francis Moore, was near the North London road junction known as Archway. Half a dozen busy routes converge there at the foot of Highgate Hill, close to the spot at which, in about 1390, Dick Whittington, setting out with his cat from an ungrateful capital, paused to listen to the distant peal of Bow Bells:

> *"Turn again, Whittington,*
> *Thrice Lord Mayor of London."*

The Old Moore stood in one of the narrow cross streets linking the Archway Road and Highgate Hill. Holmes and I presented ourselves at its side door, as the recruiting officers had stipulated. A narrow-eyed man in what I suspected was a wired-on false beard took our names, checked them by a list and nodded us upstairs.

Holmes had resumed his seaman's outfit, with a beard and one or two other modifications that altogether hid the hawk-like features with which the criminal classes were familiar. I was less known to them, yet there existed the strong likelihood that at least one or two of those present would have cause to remember me. After some experiment, Holmes had transformed me into what he termed a disaffected butcher, of dubious background and unsavoury habits. I had scarcely recognized myself in my own glass.

My trusty service revolver lay inside my jacket again. Holmes, too, was armed this time. Gregson and his three Special Branch men, who would be our unrecognized allies, were also to carry weapons.

There must have been fifty men in the room. Most were younger than Holmes and I. A lot were foreign-looking and some were noticeably disguised. I had expected a fog of smoke and spirituous fumes, but soon saw that no one was smoking and there was no drink. This was an occasion for strict discipline.

Holmes got into conversation with a sly-looking Slav, who I heard address him as Anatoli. Presumably he was the French-speaker from the Russian Free Library who had introduced him to the recruiters. Holmes did not introduce me, but the man must have seen us arrive together, for he gave me an unsmiling nod.

There was no seating provided. We stood about, keeping our hats on and eyeing one another from under the brims, for the most part suspiciously. There was no general conversation, although several small groups had formed. A few more arrivals drifted in. The atmosphere of impatient expectancy intensified. Then we heard the door shut firmly and a man clap his hands for attention as he mounted the small dais at the room's end.

I had to stop myself seeking Holmes's eyes. The man standing before us, clapping his hands together for silence, was the young ship's officer and John Sweh's murderer, Anderson!

He was wearing a seafarer's dark-blue wool jersey and brown corduroy trousers. He was hatless, and his hair stood out bright yellow in contrast with the darkness of almost every other man present. His eyebrows were so light as to be invisible, adding to the boyishness of his pink, unwhiskered face. His manner when he spoke, though, was anything but boyish, and totally without congeniality.

"Right, you're all here, bar a couple who haven't shown up. They'll wish they had, when someone calls on them. Excuses won't help. We've no place for backsliders. We're all equals here. The man who lets one down lets all down, so deserves what will come to him. Understood?"

There was a buzz of conversation, as ones whose English was deficient had the gist of his words conveyed to them. Anderson's grim look and hard, relentless tone were enough.

"If any of you wants out, say so now. Give your name at the door and go to hell. You might even be left alone there, if you keep your mouth shut—or you might not. We've got your mark, and we'll be watching you. The rest of you will see shortly what happens to dirty traitors. Leave this room with the rest of us, and you're in with us for life. There'll be no backing out then. Go now, or never."

The explanations soon died down, and every man glanced about him. No one moved to the door.

Anderson showed neither relief nor satisfaction.

"That's it," said he flatly. "You're all in. Now, here's what you'll do. You'll leave the room together, one by one and no talking. Outside you'll find some delivery vans. Get in them as the drivers direct. No overloading, no hanging about and no talking or smoking. They'll be taking you up the hill. You'll be set down beside a big church. You'll find a path down the side of it, and somebody to lead you where you're going. If there's anybody about when you get out of the vans, don't bunch together and attract attention. Hang about casually till they've passed, then get moving down that path."

He did not invite questions, but merely glared about him while his orders were being passed on. His blue eyes traversed Holmes and me with the rest. They seemed to settle on me, and I felt the sweat start under my collar; but the gaze passed to another conspirator.

Holmes and I got separated between two of the vans. From the way that he moved swiftly to make the last of a group being counted off by one of the drivers, I got the impression that he had acted purposely. I climbed up into the back of the van behind and sat in the stuffy hot gloom, reflecting that I probably looked as repulsive as my companions. As the horses pulled us slowly up the steep Archway Road, I speculated whether any of the Special Branch men were in my contingent, and whether any of them would know me or Holmes without our disguises. I had looked for Gregson in the crowd, but had not been able to pick him out.

We made level running at last and soon pulled up. The driver came to open the door in the back, which I had noted being locked upon us. Then we were getting out into the fresh Highgate air, almost in front of St. Michael's Church. It was obvious that our destination was the Cemetery again. From the rapidly increasing plenitude of clues linked with Highgate, and our earlier discovery, Holmes had predicted as much.

The men from the first van were already making their way into the narrow pathway at its right. It was after dusk, and the only people about were across the way, sitting at benches behind the public houses backing onto Pond Square. They were talking and laughing and drinking, and I heard music from somewhere. No notice was being taken of us. We followed the others into the pathway.

It took us to the rear of the church, into open land outside the Cemetery wall. I felt upon familiar ground now, for we passed not far from Traitor's Mound, where Spurrier's corpse had been taken from the vault in which, according to Holmes, he had met his horrifying death.

Following the others' lead, we soon turned sharp left and found a place where the Cemetery was easily entered by shinning over the wall. This time our route did not take us into the Valley of Kings, along the Egyptian Avenue and by way of the Circle of Lebanon. I imagine that if the more superstitious foreigners among our part had realized what sort of surroundings we were in, one or two might have risked the consequences of making a bolt for it. It remained to be seen what they made of the Belmont burial vault, where we were obviously being taken.

We stood outside it at last, in a whole group, observing the imposed silence. I listened for any sound from the wolf within, but heard none. I imagined, as much as saw in the dimness, the strained foreboding on some of those faces. I myself was not so much scared as anxious that our operation was going to succeed without a hitch. Thanks to Holmes's perception, and our earlier reconnaissance, we knew a good deal of what to expect. I knew that our silence was superfluous, in that the Cemetery Superintendent and his staff were under Lestrade's orders to pay no attention to anything which might occur that night. I knew that Lestrade himself and a force of policemen were somewhere nearby, and would creep closer when it was safe to do so, alert for a signal to rush to our aid.

There was comfort in this knowledge, but we did not know everything. We did not know, above all, precisely what we should find ourselves up against, or what to expect. One or two totally unpredictable elements could throw our tactics off balance. Events might move too fast for us to counter, with fatal consequences.

I saw a vertical line of light appear and broaden before us. The tomb's iron door was being opened from within. I am sure that every other man's breath was held with mine as the entry widened; then those at the front of the crowd began to enter.

Holmes's tall silhouette was unmistakable to me against the yellow light, though there were many men between us. I noticed how the first men to go in removed their hats or caps as they crossed the threshold, in instinctive reverence, and how those behind them followed suit. The vault must be of enormous capacity to hold so many of us. It proved to be so, the roof soaring to a high point atop towering walls. Of course, it occurred to me, only enough time had passed since its building for a couple of generations of Belmonts to be interred there. The capacity had been created in anticipation of further generations to come. James Belmont's bachelor state seemed to have precluded that.

It was brighter now. The light came from flaming cressets upon the end wall. There must have been ventilation of some kind in the pyramid vaulting, because it was much hotter than became a tomb, and the living greatly outnumbered the dead. Only one wall was covered with stone shelves of coffins, mostly sheathed in lead, with ornate designs. The place was surprisingly clean and undusty, and there were no mortal relics lying about.

The feature that startled me was hidden at first by the crowd. I heard it before I saw it: a low, rising, growling snarl, continuing without seeming need to draw breath. Then I saw the wolf, Ivan. I had anticipated his being there, but the reality of seeing him, so savage-looking in comparison with his gentle brother, briefly chilled my blood.

He was chained to an iron ring in the wall under a stone shelf. He had little space for movement and was straining menacingly toward the incoming men. Those ahead of me halted and swayed uncertainly. I knew that their fear at the sight and sound of this living beast was far more potent than any superstitions about the proximity of the dead.

Someone shoved us forward from behind, and I recognized Anderson's shipboard tone, commanding us to "Get on!" Those at the front of the crowd were forced almost within the radius of the wolf's chain. One tall chap, in seaman's clothing, cowered and cringed, having to stand no more than inches from the long muzzle full of bared, gleaming fangs. I realized with a start that the man was Holmes.

It seemed that the surge forward had brought us all inside, for it was followed by a doom-laden clang as the vault door was pulled shut. Uneasy glances passed among us all. We were shut inside a tomb, in a lonely part of a vast burial ground, late at night and with no passers-by to hear any amount of noise we might raise. Rows of dead people were our companions; and a great gray Siberian wolf, which had been imprisoned there and perhaps starved, was exerting its powerful tension upon a distinctly fragile-looking chain.

I saw, too, that I had been wrong in thinking there were no human remains on view. At the centre of the vault's far end, where the wolf's territory precluded anyone from going, lay a single casket, lidless and uptilted toward us to display its contents. In a cushioning of yellow, and draped with cloth of that other Cromwellian colour, buff, lay a headless skeleton. I had no doubt whose it was.

Anderson himself was shouldering his way through the crowd. With him came others, who had arrived after the rest of us. And now still more figures were entering from an alcove evidently connecting with a smaller chamber within the wolf's domain. Two roughly dressed men appeared, dragging between them a stumbling, fear-stricken form, whom I knew at once to be Chapman. He was jacketless and his wrists were handcuffed in front of him.

He was bustled to the space at the front, where Anderson had turned to wait, a little beyond the wolf's reach. I half anticipated seeing the prisoner thrown down for it to take out on him its frustration and hunger. I thought that was what Spurrier's fate must have been in this very place, perhaps before a similar assembly. My hand went toward my revolver, but I only placed my fingers across the trigger guard. Holmes's strict order was for there to be no use of weapons unless he gave the lead, or was recognized and overpowered.

The captive was not thrown to the wolf, however. His back was forced against the stone wall. His escorts wrenched his hands up above his head, to slip the manacles over a hook in the stone. He slumped there, knees buckling under him in his terror, eyes staring, sweat streaming down his face and neck and soaking his shirt.

I doubted whether he was of a mind to notice the last of all to enter, also from the side chamber, a bizarre figure, tall and majestic, shrouded and cowled from head to toe in a waxy green robe. Seeing the garment sent a *frisson* through me. For a moment I was back at the Tyburn site, picturing the exhumed corpses of Oliver Cromwell and his generals hanging there in shrouds of green waxed cloth.

An even more dramatic feature brought me back abruptly to the present. Between the hooded one's hands, brandished aloft like a talisman, was the sword which I myself had found and briefly held.

It had been in halves then, and discoloured from its long burial. Now it was repaired and burnished. The yellow flames from the sconces made it seem to glow with its own inner fire. It appeared magical, almost alive. A din arose from the crowd of bareheaded men as its holder passed slowly among us, compelling all eyes to follow.

He circled the chamber, then returned to stand facing us. With the light now all behind him, there was not so much as a glimmer from the eyeholes in the cowl. The effect heightened disturbingly the unhuman illusion, as of a visitor representative of some unsanctified region where cabalistic and impious practices held sway.

Still holding the sword before him, he stood impassively as Anderson proceeded to read out names from a list. Each man named made his way forward to face the motionless cowled figure. By a gesture, Anderson made it plain from the first that everyone was required to bow, not so much to the silent figure as to the sword. This evidently constituted the oath-taking. As each man straightened up, Anderson handed him one of the little tin replicas of the sword, which I knew would be engraved with his name.

"Jack Hudson!"

My turn had come. I felt my legs weak under me as I walked into the flames' glare. I desperately willed my disguise to stand the scrutiny of Anderson's hard blue eyes and those unseen ones behind the cowl. There seemed an endless pause while both stared at me. All movement was suspended. I held my breath, expecting a challenge. Anderson had been handed my token by an assistant beside him, who held a box of them. He thrust it into my palm. I was able to make my second bow, and then retreat on shaking limbs.

"Anatoli Vernet!"

Holmes, too, passed unchecked. I did not know the names under which he had enrolled Gregson and his men, and could not guess which they were; but if Holmes, too, had not been able to identify them before, he had been enabled to do so now, and to note where they were distributed among the crowd.

This ceremony over, it was Anderson's turn to bow to the mysterious figure, who placed the sword into his hands. Anderson took it to show to the terrified Chapman, hanging helplessly on the wall. For another chill moment I feared we were about to see him beheaded. My grasp tightened upon my revolver. Chapman cringed in his fetters and screwed up his eyes against the sight, uttering a sobbing whimper.

But it had been another ritualistic gesture. The sword was returned to the silent one's hands. I recognized beyond doubt, though, what the significance of it had been. Anderson had identified himself to the victim as his executioner. It remained only to find out what diabolical form the killing was to take;

and from the memory of Spurrier's ghastly wounds I thought that the wolf must be involved.

The whole of the proceedings except the calling out of names had been in dumb show. The portentous solemnity of the various acts spoke meaningfully enough to need no words. Now, for the first time, the cowled figure addressed us. I recognized his voice almost at once: "Comrades—*brothers!* Greetings! In acknowledging this historic sword you have taken the oath of allegiance to a noble cause, bearing its martyred owner's name. Now you are Oliver Cromwell's Men!

"That noblest and best of men, whose very bones have witnessed your enlistment, would have been proud to bless such a cause as this. He would applaud its rise, like the avenging soul out of his desecrated carcass, to soar upon the divine ether of his memory.

"It is a cause which dedicates itself, as *he* dedicated *himself,* to the regeneration of a mankind that has lost its way: crushed, corrupted, traduced, debased by tyrannical, self-seeking governments serving the monster called monarchy. It is consecrated to the raising up of every man, woman and child who is in any way oppressed by poverty, hunger, ignorance, landlordism, the overbearance of the law—those thousand stringencies imposed by capitalism and privilege to protect and perpetuate themselves through the servitude of their slaves.

"It is a cause, brothers, against the suppression of the majority by the powerful few; against governments that make few promises and keep none of them; against the pitiless exploiter and the cynical profiteer.

"It is a cause whose purpose is to forge a union of all men, whatever their birth, under a new nationality, whose only distinguishing mark shall be equality. Inherited rank, privilege, wealth, the divisive influences of religion and journalism, shall cease to exist. Equality shall be the whole of the law. The nation shall be the sole owner of property, possessions, income, commerce, manufacture; the sole educator, lawgiver and enforcer.

"The trappings of archaic tradition and ceremonial shall be abolished. All government shall be conducted by elected committees, whose decrees shall be upheld by central power, with unquestionable authority to discipline and correct. A new legal system, drafted by elected tribunals, shall purge and punish, in the people's name, all activities adjudged harmful to common interest. The paid Army, Navy and police force shall be replaced by self-accountable citizen bodies, electing their own officers and answerable only to the central power.

"Do not imagine, brothers, that these high aims can be achieved overnight. The forces of reaction, though corrupt, are strong. I hide my features from you only because I am known to their agents. They would dearly love to crush us before the moment comes to carry all with us upon the flood tide of our cause.

"That tide is almost ready to break. Others throughout this and other lands are waiting for you. Your endeavours will be matched by theirs. Go on, comrades, brothers! Go forward with all those others who have dedicated themselves.

"Go forth and fight! Fight, and, if necessary, die, that your names might live alongside *his* immortal name. You are Oliver Cromwell's Men. You have made your oath upon the blessed and martyred hero's own battle sword, under witness of his bones. Your lives are in thrall to his spirit. His spirit lives within his sword! It shall lead you as it led and conquered three centuries ago!

"Follow the Sword!

"Trust the Sword!

"Fight by the Sword!

"Be willing to *die* for the Sword!"

The diatribe had been rising in intensity and volume to a pitch of near-hysteria. The cowled frame shook at these last words. The sword was thrust ceilingward again, as high as the arms could hold it. The turning blade burned like a torch as the flames' light caught every facet.

From almost every throat there burst the simultaneous cry: "The Sword! The Sword! The *Sword*!" A rousing cheer followed, and the hitherto passive and even fearful men embraced one another in new-found solidarity.

I was forced to follow suit with those nearest me. Their eyes gleamed with savage fervour. I saw at once how mobs of hundreds and thousands and even hundreds of thousands might become hypnotized by a display of this nature. Their mass-hysteria would be self-feeding. Once fermented and incited, they would hesitate at nothing, only blindly rampage however commanded, whether the commands were idealistic, chauvinistic, opportunist or even criminal. I saw fully at last the danger and imminency of this crazed challenge to the stability of our own country and perhaps others beyond it.

Anderson, who had himself given the cue for the mass outburst, made no effort to stem it. He punched his fists into the air, echoing the Leader's cry of "The Sword! The Sword!" in a voice that carried even above the clamour; and again there came the roared response, "The Sword! The Sword!"

I noticed, in utter contrast with all else, the gibbering terror of the helpless Chapman, faced with this howling frenzy. I saw also the fresh agitation being shown by the wolf, Ivan. He snarled and gnashed defiance at the excited men who were so near to him, safe only while they kept beyond his chain's stretch.

I kept watching Holmes for any sign. He had seen where I was, but no signal came. I wondered how much further the proceedings would have to go before he would intervene, and what chance we should stand if this inflamed rabble could be turned against us.

Anderson was gesturing at last for quiet. It fell rapidly.

His least command as the Leader's deputy demanded instant obedience.

"Any movement such as ours," he said, speaking with a quiet menace which made everyone strain to hear, "is as strong as it weakest link. When the going becomes hardest, and the chances of coming through unscathed start to narrow, some of you will be tempted to save your skins, to take easy ways which are offered you.

"Your oath upon The Sword forbids it!" he cried suddenly, in a voice like a whipcrack. "No weaknesses from here on. No running away. No *treachery*!"

He spun about to point with outstretched arm at Chapman.

"Here is a traitor! A would-be informant! Look at him. Hate and revile him!"

The chorus of jeers, curses and whistles, accompanied with showers of spittle and shaking of fists, was almost too painful to hear. Chapman wrenched his head from side to side in his agony. I kept looking toward Holmes. He *must* end this soon!

Anderson was moving to the wall where the shelves of coffins mounted high. The ones on the lowest shelf, as I had seen, were brand-new, in polished elm without lead sheaths. He stooped to one and lifted its lid.

Before he drew anything out he turned to the expectant crowd and gestured toward the wolf, which now stood growling as it waited.

"This animal stands for the hound of vengeance against those who betray us. Let it be a reminder to all that certain revenge will come down on anyone else who is minded to turn traitor. The hound is our symbol of that, but he is not our executioner."

With another of his electrifyingly sudden gestures, Anderson whipped something from the casket—a blanket, or a cloak, it seemed; heavy, and tawny-coloured.

"*Here* is our executioner!"

He threw it over his own shoulders and back.

I saw that it was a lionskin—and that the forelegs, into which he thrust his arms like sleeves, retained their gigantic claws.

A scream from Chapman startled us all. The chained wolf snarled frantically as the new scent reached him. He strained his utmost, but Anderson stepped just out of his range.

His back was bent slightly from the weight of the skin, partly also from an assumed posture which made him all the more grotesque and fear-inspiring as he advanced slowly upon Chapman. The wretched prisoner screamed again, starting to thrash about, shrieking to anyone to save him.

Slowly Anderson came on. As he drew nearer to his victim he gradually raised one of the sets of razor-sharp talons . . .

Then the wolf sprang. In a gray blur he leaped in a powerful arc upon the back of the rival beast in front of him. His huge weight bore it to the ground, and he began to savage it with all the pent-up fury that his awesome fangs could express.

Instant pandemonium arose. The crowd rocked fearfully back upon me. I saw the Leader recoil, changing his grip on the sword, ready to defend himself with it.

I also glimpsed Holmes, who had been standing nearest to the wolf all through the ceremony. I knew that it must have been he who slipped Ivan's chain. He had his revolver in his hand now. I drew mine and used its threat to get through the throng.

As I was moving, Holmes stepped forward. For a split second I thought he was going to fire into the wolf's heaving gray body. He did not. He placed the sole of one boot against the side of the tilted coffin in which the headless skeleton lay, and thrust out with all his weight. The casket toppled with a crash, spilling bones everywhere.

The effect of this surprise was chilling. The clamour of the mob ceased as if at the snap of a switch. There was utter silence, apart from the wolf's snarls as it worried at the lion-skin. Anderson, beneath it, lay outstretched and motionless.

The cowled Leader recovered before anyone, making a mighty swing at Holmes with the sword. Holmes ducked beneath it. The momentum of the attempted blow was so great that it could not be repeated immediately, but Holmes was too far off to risk rushing in to grapple. At the same time he was not far enough from his assailant for me to dare try a shot.

He had his revolver, but I knew he would use it only as last resort. As the sword returned in a backhand swing, Holmes grabbed the box from the man who had assisted Anderson at the ceremony and dashed the silvery shower of its remaining contents at his attacker's cowl. The instinctive avoiding movement caused a shoulder to drop and the sword blade to flail the air. In a flash, Holmes had stepped in and seized the sword arm in a Baritsu lock. The weapon clattered to the stone floor.

Obedient to Holmes's nod, I dragged off the cowled garment. It was no surprise that revealed beneath it was James Belmont, temporarily paralyzed, wide-eyed, and mouthing insanely as handcuffs were snapped upon him. Holmes released his grip and he sank to the ground.

The struggle had lasted only seconds and the mob's anger was sounding again. Holmes swung round, pointing the revolver from his side. I saw that several other men were holding weapons, and they were in positions which contained the crowd. Someone blew a police whistle. Another answered from immediately outside. There was a clang of iron, followed by an immediate inrush of uniforms and flourishing truncheons. They drove into the crowd in a flying wedge, making passage for a small figure in woman's skirts. I realized that the incursion had been designed to get Mrs. Dodds to Ivan with the least delay.

She could not approach him at the height of his savagery. She could only call to him. Even she went unheeded. The wolf's snarls were horrible to hear as he took out upon the lionskin his revenge for his enchainment, his captivity, his misrepresented culpability in the killing of Spurrier and the attempt upon Chapman. Anderson was left seemingly untouched, but motionless and beyond defending himself. One side of his face was visible, though, and its staring wide-open eye and fixed grimace of terror told me that he was dead.

A man who must have been a Special Branch officer stepped forward and raised his revolver, pointing it at Ivan.

"No!" came a shriek. "Don't you dare!"

The smaller form of Mrs. Dodds hurtled forward, to interpose herself between the gun and the wolf.

"Get out of it, woman!" shouted Lestrade, who had appeared, gun in hand, alongside an armed and long-haired ruffian who proved to be Chief Inspector Gregson.

"Shoot my Ivan, you 'ave to shoot me first!" returned the widow's defiant cry. Before anyone could stop her she had thrown her arms about the wolf's shaggy neck and seemed to be nuzzling its ear. Police and prisoners alike fell silent to watch the astounding spectacle, and heard her utter strange whimpering noises, such as a pining dog produces.

The sound became more insistent, more urgent. Ivan lifted his head, letting drop the skin in which his fangs had made great jagged rents. He turned his head, and I raised my weapon instinctively as I saw his wild stare.

Mrs. Dodds thrust her leathery cheek into the furry one—and I saw that I should not have to shoot.

Т he next morning's headlines made bizarre
reading: DISTURBANCE AT HIGHGATE CEMETERY. TROUBLE AT
FAMILY VAULT. POLICE DENY SACRILEGE.

Few of the facts as we knew them had got into print,
however. The Home Office had issued an advance notice to
newspaper editors. It prohibited the reporting of certain matters appertaining to the peace of the realm, and had been generally obeyed. Lord Belmont's arrest went unmentioned, and
also Anderson's death, both of which had happened conve-
niently inside the vault, away from any chance of public notice.
A small item about Matt Spurrier was allowed to appear, reporting his accidental death due to a fall upon Hampstead
Heath. It attracted no special attention.

Unusual activity in and near the Cemetery, involving a
large body of police, had not gone unobserved locally and was
allowed to be mentioned in print on the red-herring principle.
That "distinguished Scotland Yard officer, Insp. G. Lestrade,"
resumed the spokeman's role, which he filled with enough
ready verbosity to satisfy any journalist. Not content with the
daytime search for the rumoured Hound of Hampstead Heath,
he stated, he had felt it his duty to the public to order a further
search by night. Once again he had assumed the responsibility
of personal supervision.

Yes, it was true that in the course of it there had been certain activity within Highgate Cemetery. It was, after all, a considerable open space, attractive to wildlife of various species, and it would have been neglectful to overlook it. No, nothing at all had been found there. Asked about a hearse being driven away in the Hampstead direction at what a witness had claimed to be "inordinate speed," the jovial inspector would only smile and observe that "all sorts of rumours get attached to cemeteries." He added good-humouredly that there were at least a dozen public houses within a stone's throw, and imagination could play queer tricks late at night.

Mr. Lestrade concluded his statement with the categorical reassurance that there was nothing to be feared on Hampstead Heath by man, woman or child. He took the liberty of wishing much enjoyment to all who attended the August Bank Holiday Fair.

There was nothing in the press, either, about a raid by plainclothesmen of the Special Branch upon Alkhamton, the country home near Deal, in Kent, of the Earl of Belmont, in his lordship's absence. Many items were taken away, and a number of men and women remanded in custody. Other addresses were visited in the course of that same night by officers, both uniformed and in plainclothes, and men were taken in for questioning. Much of this activity was in the East End of London, but simultaneous operations occurred in a number of provincial cities, especially Liverpool, Birmingham, Leeds, Manchester and Southampton. Although the fact was not published, it had been the busiest night for the police forces of England since the worst of the Fenian bombing campaign.

"Of course, Spurrier's murder changed everything," explained Chief Inspector Gregson through the smoke of one of Holmes's prize stock of La Corona Sin Igquales, crop of '93. "Thank heaven, in this country it's no crime to get up a political movement. Murder is another thing, though."

"You'd had suspicions for some time, then?" said I.

Gregson tapped the side of his nose. "Not much gets past the Branch, Doctor."

Lestrade, the Scotland Yarder, snorted cynically, making himself cough upon his unaccustomed large cigar.

We were seated in our parlour at Baker Street. It was the afternoon following that night of frenzied and widespread activity, the aftermath of which had kept the officers fully occupied all morning. Holmes had insisted, however, that Gregson and Lestrade join us for luncheon. He had taken the unconventional step of inviting a lady also; but since she was that unconventional lady, Mrs. Hubert Glanvill, there had been no inhibition to either our smoking or discussion. The air was cloyed with attar of Havana, Alexandria and Brazil. The summer meal of trout, wild duck and gooseberry fool, accompanied with correspondingly light wines, had been well judged by Mrs. Hudson to keep post-prandial drowsiness at bay. The golden, sweet, old-bottled Haut-Sauternes with which she left us after clearing away the debris served to mellow our memories of last evening's dramatic events.

"Matter of fact, Mr. Holmes," Gregson continued, looking exceptionally smug about it. "I can tell you now that we were onto you, too."

"You refer, of course, to your man in the Russian Library —the one who persuaded me to join in the Revolution?"

Gregson slapped his thigh.

"Trust you to smell an agent when you meet one! We had a real chortle at the Branch about him recruiting you and you coming here telling how you'd recruited me and some others, not to mention the Doctor here."

"I could not bear to deprive you of your innocent merriment, Gregson. The end result of our cooperative enterprise worked out very nicely for us all."

"Why were you having Holmes watched, Gregson?" I asked.

"Typical Special Branch!" growled Lestrade. "Got to have their noses into everything."

"It was your old friend, Superintendent White Mason, Mr. Holmes. Your idea of letting Anderson run free had him really rattled. He'd consented, because you were who you are, but it worried him afterward, what with coming up to retirement. He travelled up specially by train that night to tell me about it in confidence. I agreed that you should be given your head, seeing that you would be bound to lead us to Anderson again, who was the villain we wanted."

"Wait a minute!" Lestrade protested. "What's all this? Old White Mason should've come to the Yard. Chasing villains is work for the Old Bill, not for your lot."

Gregson shook his head, and his expression had become serious.

"Not that villain Anderson. Not after he'd killed John Sweh."

"John Sweh? Who's he?"

"Another of your men, Gregson?" asked Holmes, and received a grim nod.

"Do you mean a Special Branch agent?" asked Lavinia.

"One of our best, madam. A Chinese who worked as a steward on the Channel ferries. You'd never believe what comings and goings there are on them. Perhaps you've heard those stories of German soldiers dressed up as nuns?"

"Why, yes."

"It was John Sweh who rumbled them, by their boots. He telegraphed ahead from Newhaven, but we let 'em pass, and plenty more since. We knew exactly what so-called convent they were making for in the Midlands. We rounded up the lot this morning."

"Why did Anderson kill him?" I asked. "Had Sweh found out his connection with Oliver's Men?"

Gregson shook his head again. "John was onto Anderson as a Kaiser agent. Lovely cover, fourth officer on a ferry, able to come and go on both sides of the Channel. Regular organizer he was, seeing their agents safely in and out. Again, we let him carry on, so that John could keep tabs on who was involved and report back. His last message said that he was afraid Anderson suspected him. He was right, poor chap. Clever of you to get onto him so quick, Mr. Holmes."

Holmes repeated the observations and reasoning that had led him to identify the ship's officer as the steward's murderer.

"I knew that he was no ordinary ship's officer," he explained for Mrs. Glanvill's benefit. "He was young and unattached, not at all the type to quit deep-sea sailing for a humble ferry. As Inspector Gregson says, the latter was an ideal situation for a German agent. He was German-born, by the way. His original name was Ander*sen*."

"So he was serving Germany as well as Oliver's Men!" said I.

"You might say further that Oliver's Men themselves were serving Germany," Holmes replied. "I fancy Gregson will confirm that what started as a relatively small and patriotic radical movement was spotted by the Germans as an ideal cover for something far bigger. Lord Belmont was marked down as one of those enthusiastic idealists who will clutch at support from any quarter, without stopping to ask why it is being offered. You can imagine how far open he laid himself to blackmail and threats. He had become their dupe and their pawn, with no means of escaping. He found himself nominal leader of something which he had never envisaged but from which he could not detach himself."

"Poor James!" said Lavinia softly. "The strain must have been intolerable. No wonder he cracked under it. It was not wrong of me to feel protective toward him."

"Not wrong at all, madam." We heard the laconic voice of Mycroft Holmes from our doorway, where he had entered unnoticed. "He is far more to be pitied than condemned. He is completely deranged and morally blameless for what has been going on around him."

When Mycroft Holmes had been introduced to Lavinia, and had established himself upon the sofa with a glass of port, he continued.

"I have come from visiting him personally at a certain hospital where he is being detained. He is distressed and shocked, and it was out of the question to try to interrogate him in detail, but we know enough of him already."

"What . . . what will happen to him, Mr. Holmes?" asked she. "Will he . . . ?"

"There will be no criminal charges. Lord Belmont is insane. He will be put away somewhere secure to live out his life as a gentleman. He is suffering from paranoia. Such people, madam, appear and remain perfectly normal for much of the time. Many of their ideas sound plausible, but they are based upon assumptions that are quite wrong. The whole reasoning arising from them is defective. It is the odd one, such as Belmont, whose delusions become so strong that they outweigh all other considerations."

"*Poor* James," she repeated.

"Don't grieve for him, Mrs. Glanvill. He will be perfectly happy. Give him a few years, and I fancy he will grow his beard and hair long, and take to a white robe and sandals. That is his ultimate image of himself. Now, Sherlock, tell us how you knew those were not Cromwell's bones."

Mycroft Holmes's nonchalant change of topic astonished us all into silence. I noticed, though, that Holmes was smiling at his brother.

"Come along, Sherlock," Mycroft insisted. "I have heard an eye-witness's account of what happened in the vault. You are not so diehard a rationalist as to do violence to the remains of a man who is still revered by many people."

"Watson can describe the marks that distinguished the

remains of Cromwell and his henchmen," Holmes replied. "He was the first to point them out."

I repeated my observations about the state of the clumsily beheaded skeletons.

"I am certain that they were the correct ones," I added. "All the marks were present that I expected."

"Upon the bones which you and Sherlock examined in the pit." Mycroft Holmes nodded.

"But not those arranged in that coffin," confirmed his brother. "I was near enough to see that they were not the same. Mrs. Glanvill appreciates the value of a startling diversion. Kicking over the coffin was my equivalent of her upsetting Lord Belmont's table."

Lestrade and Gregson were exchanging looks of equal bafflement. They spoke simultaneously.

"Whose bones were they?"

"What happened to Cromwell's?"

"Weren't they in the vault at all?" I asked. "In some of the other coffins?"

"I doubt whether anyone has looked," answered Holmes. "They weren't found in the search at Alkhamton, then, Gregson?"

"Not a sign of them. Mind you, we weren't looking for bones, but we'd have been bound to notice any."

"What did you find there, apart from membership tokens?" I inquired again.

"All sorts, Doctor. Printed stuff mostly. Manifestos and the like. A lot of muck they'd raked up or invented about the King . . ."

"To be distributed on Coronation Day," Mycroft Holmes informed me. "Among the crowds, in public houses, to the newspapers, through the letter-boxes of Members of Parliament and diplomats. They had even planned to float balloons over the procession, showering leaflets by the ton. Everyone attending the Abbey for the ceremony was to find a set on his seat. At least Lord Belmont was able to tell me that much."

"Is that what they would have used my poor little letter for?" put in Mrs. Glanvill.

Gregson and Lestrade stared again.

"What letter?"

"Who to?"

"Least said about that, soonest mended," replied Holmes, as he rose to go to the bureau, whose secret compartment behind the pigeonholes was the temporary receptacle for valuable items passing through his hands. Shielding the process with his back, he withdrew the envelope and closed the bureau again. His brother held out a podgy, expectant hand, but it was to Lavinia Glanvill that Holmes went.

"It has been in safe custody, madam. You have my word that no one has read it." He held it out to her.

"Sherlock, I will take it, if you please!"

"It is this lady's property, Mycroft. She must decide what is to become of it."

His brother turned entreatingly to Lavinia.

"Madam, I must beg you to—"

"It's all right, Mr. Holmes." She smiled, to his relief. "Have it with pleasure."

Mycroft took the envelope and put it away inside his jacket.

"Thank you, madam. I would put a match to it here and now, if it would save further misunderstanding, but His . . . a *certain person* might not be satisfied."

I saw both Gregson and Lestrade drawing breath to ask more about the letter.

"I still wish someone would tell us about those bones," said I quickly.

"It is a question which will have to be saved for Lord Belmont to answer," said Holmes. "Either he had become so obsessed with Cromwell's remains that he could not bear to part with them to his masters, and substituted some others, or he had still enough guile to cheat them. That is, assuming his friend Garside had not cheated him."

"What, gave him some other bones and kept the real ones himself?"

"At any rate, it will be interesting to see where they turn up eventually."

The "distinguished Scotland Yard officer" had been thinking. He turned upon his colleague from the Special Branch.

"It sounds to me, Mr. Gregson, as if your people have been keeping a great deal too much to themselves, as usual."

"Didn't want to trouble you, Mr. Lestrade. We all know how overworked you lot are—chasing stray dogs, and suchlike intellectual tasks."

"Yes, Holmes," I intervened. "What about that? Where does the use of the hound come in? I can understand it on the Heath that first time, to create a scare. But why kill Spurrier as if the hound had done it, and why make such a performance with Chapman in the vault?"

"Well, as you will bear witness, it was an effective way of putting the fear of the devil into the recruits. Did you know it was an old trick of the Spanish Inquisition, scraping people to death with animals' claws?"

"How horrible!" said Mrs. Glanvill.

"From the way you were looking at Mrs. Dodds's lions, Holmes," said I, "I almost thought you suspected one of them."

"They provided me with the extra confirmatory link with Anderson. Lions, Watson. West Africa. The Cameroons, in particular, where he spent his childhood and youth. Lion-worship is quite common there still. One man in the tribe is privileged to dress in a skin, claws and all. Heady impressions for a parentless boy with perhaps latent tendencies to violence. Depend upon it, Anderson had more murder in him than any of Mrs. Dodds's poor beasts.

" 'Ere! 'Oo's that takin' Dodds's Beasts of the East in vain?"

All our eyes were attracted to the doorway again as Mrs. Annie Dodds made a somewhat unsteady entrance, half restrained and half supported by Mrs. Hudson in the background.

"Mrs. Dodds!" cried Holmes, springing to his feet. "Do come in, madam! You'll have some tea, of course?" He helped her to a seat. "Mrs. Hudson, some tea for . . . No? Ah, Watson, perhaps you'll oblige, then?"

I went to the brandy decanter. Mrs. Hudson withdrew, sniffing.

The animal keeper was wearing what I took to be her best, a deep purple outfit with exaggerated shoulders, black flounces and other trimmings, and a tremendous, fruit-bearing hat. The colour scheme was matched perfectly by her cheeks.

Having introduced her to Lavinia Glanvill and his brother, and seen her supplied with refreshment, Holmes addressed her.

"I sent for you, Mrs. Dodds, in order to assure you that you stand in no danger of prosecution arising from this case."

"Very thankful, I'm sure!" She raised her glass to him. "I may have been a mug to go hiring a wolf to a stranger, but I never meant harm to come of it."

"But for your help, madam, we should not have found out that place so soon, and Chapman would have been killed after all."

"I do hope as the pore man is all right now," replied the old lady. "Give me beasts any day, sooner than men, but that doesn't say as it's right for 'em to be murdered."

"I'm sure we all applaud your sentiments. Chapman is in

hospital in good hands. Far from blaming you, it is agreed that you deserve some reward for your help and bravery."

"Hear, hear!" said I.

Mrs. Dodds drained off her glass and put it into my hand without a word.

"It's not me as wants a reward, sir. It's pore Boris and Ivan, what they went through, missing each other so bad. But what can you do, 'cept give 'em an extra nice cut o' meat and a bowl of ale apiece? Did you know that wolves is very partial to ale, madam?"

"I hear that you have a remarkable affinity with them, Mrs. Dodds," Lavinia said.

"That's right, madam. But it has to be from the tap. No bottled stuff. Gives 'em gas. Ta very much, Doctor. Good health, lady and gents."

"You're very fond of them, and they of you," I prompted.

"You would know, as a vet'rinary, that it's kindness as does it." She nodded. "There's people too quick to call animal keepers cruel. As poor old Dodds used to say to me, 'We're all of us in the same zoo together, Ma. Only difference is the beasts is on one side o' the bars, and we're on t'other.' I married into them animals, and when poor old Dodds 'anded in 'is pail 'e left me to 'em for life. Note, left *me* to *them*. Ma Dodds is the one in the cage, never to be let out. I couldn't sell 'em off or let 'em be put down, which'd amount to the same. I'm stuck with 'em, bless 'em, and I worry sick sometimes what'll become of 'em when the Great Landlord calls Time."

She took a consolatory draught. Lavinia used the handkerchief from her sleeve to dab the corner of each eye in turn. Lestrade had to blow his nose.

"With something of that nature in mind, Mrs. Dodds," said Holmes gently, motioning me to employ the decanter again, "I took the liberty this morning of having a word with an acquaintance of mine, a Dr. Garside."

"Not another vet!" she cried, while the rest of us reacted with alarm at Holmes's casual use of the historian's name. "I told you, I won't have 'em touched."

"And it does you great credit, madam," continued Holmes. "The gentleman is connected with the British Museum. He has influence with men in certain other walks of life, including the Zoological Society, at Regent's Park."

"Oh, that's a nice zoo, that!" approved the old lady. "I used to say to old Dodds whenever we come to London, 'I'm glad our beasts can't see that Regent's Park zoo, they'd be that envious'."

"Well, they need be envious no longer. Dr. Garside, who happens to owe me rather a considerable favour, has spoken to his friends there. I am happy to tell you that, if it is your wish, they will take your animals in."

"Oh, Mr. Holmes!" Lavinia cried, clapping her hands.

"Well done, Holmes!" I congratulated him.

"Very nice, Sherlock!" His brother beamed.

"Good old girl!" said Lestrade and Gregson in unison.

"However," said Holmes, "there is the difficulty that without your menagerie you would presumably have no means of livelihood. You would not be able to go on travelling with your fairground friends."

"There 'ad to be a snag to it!" groaned Mrs. Dodds. "Isn't that jest life, puttin' in snags?"

"Life can do better than that," Holmes admonished. "My brother here, who is very high in the Government, has come to your rescue."

"Bless 'im, then!" cried Mrs. Dodds, and for a moment I thought that she was going to rush at Mycroft Holmes to embrace him. His astonished stare at my friend was probably what restrained her.

Defying him, with his gimlet eyes, to refuse, Holmes went on, "That's right, is it not, Mycroft? You have offered to arrange funds for Mrs. Dodds to replace her menagerie with a sideshow stall of her choice?"

"Oh! Oh, yes, Sherlock. Absolutely."

"Three cheers for the Special Branch!" shouted Mrs. Dodds—and stumbled out of her chair to Holmes's, to stoop and kiss him before he could recoil.

"Holmes," said I, when they had all left us and we were at our customary ease once more, "do you suppose that the King really will go to the United States?"

"Certainly not. The Privy Council and his Ministers would never allow it. He will have found already that he is even more restricted as King than ever he was as Prince of Wales. Besides, as recent events have shown, there is enough awaiting his good intentions nearer home. If he must try overseas diplomacy, I fancy that France will serve as his oyster. He is as popular there as he was in the United States, and the kisses and pinches of the Parisian girls will be as agreeable as his remembered New York ones."

"I suppose we shall never know what passed between him and Mrs. Glanvill. What a delightful woman, Holmes!"

"We never knew what was in the photograph of Irene Adler and the King of Bohemia," he reminded me. "It would have made no difference to my admiration for her quite exceptional qualities."

"True enough. My faith in the sex would have been quite shattered, though, if Mrs. Glanvill had proved to be in with Belmont and his schemes."

"It might have brought you back to earth before you commit yourself irrevocably," said he, but I knew by now that he was no longer in earnest.

"What about yourself?" I asked. "Are you really bent upon retiring?"

"If your intentions are serious, so are mine. With so many matters cleared up at one fell swoop, I cannot imagine a more convenient or appropriate time to depart."

"After the way you have handled this latest business, Holmes, you can scarcely go on saying that you have outlived your use, or that your methods are old-fashioned. You have always maintained that you would never allow investigations to overlap, for fear of their impinging upon one another. I have just seen you juggle brilliantly with several at once."

"Thank you, Watson! However, the best artist takes his exit when the applause is at its peak. 'Leave them wanting more' is the principle behind it."

"But without you there can *be* no more!" I protested. "You have trained no apprentice. You have not founded a school."

"Then the sooner I set about doing so the better. My proposed magnum opus, *The Whole Art of Detection,* is intended to synthesize my complete experience and the practical and theoretical conclusions which it demonstrates. Your urgent reminder convinces me that its composition must be delayed no longer."

There was clearly no moving him.

We sat smoking silently for some minutes in that comfortable depository of our memories. The familiar sounds of Baker Street lent their familiar accompaniment to our thoughts.

"Holmes," said I again.

"Yes, Watson?"

"One more point . . . "

"My dear chap!" he groaned in mock protest.

"Oliver's Men adopting a hound as their badge of revolution. You said there is a key to it in *The Hound of the Baskervilles.*"

"So there is."

"Chapter Two, you said."

"Unless memory fails me."

"Then it does!"

I picked up the open volume from beside my chair. I had taken it down from its shelf as soon as I had returned from escorting Lavinia Glanvill to her train back to Kent. A telephone message from her butler had told her that her husband would be arriving that very evening.

"I have read several times the scene where Mortimer brought us the story of the curse, and I find nothing relevant in it. It is high time you explained, if you can, Holmes."

"Watson, there are moments when you cause me acute embarrassment."

"You are admitting you were wrong?"

"Not at all. The words are, I think, 'Know then that in the time of the Great Rebellion . . . ' "

I soon found them on the page.

"Exactly right, Holmes. What about it?"

"The *Great Rebellion,* Watson!"

"Something to do with James the First or Monmouth, wasn't it?"

"Nothing whatever. The Great Rebellion was the old name for the English Civil War, when the people rose up, and King Charles was executed, and there was no more monarchy, and Oliver Cromwell ruled in his place. How often have I said to you that there is nothing new under the sun? Now, kindly pass me the *Evening News,* and let us enjoy an hour of peace after our endeavours."

There was one further extraordinary scene remaining, to round off the series of interlocking events which made that Coronation summer of 1902 so memorable to me; and in many ways it was the most extraordinary scene of all.

When I had telephoned to Russell Square that morning, at Holmes's behest, to invite Lavinia Glanvill to join Lestrade and Gregson at our luncheon table, she had tried to insist that her "dear new friends," Coral and Aunt Henry, should come, too, as they were owed a full explanation of what had been taking place. I put this to Holmes, over my shoulder with my hand across the instrument's mouthpiece, but he demurred firmly. The meeting was to be confined to the principal actors in our drama.

I told Lavinia this, and heard the unintelligibly muffled murmurs as she in turn consulted the other ladies. The outcome was an ultimatum: She would come to 221B to luncheon alone, on the sole condition that Holmes and I would dine with the three of them at the Hotel Russell. Fully anticipating his indignant refusal, I put this to Holmes. To my great surprise, he heard it with a smile, and nodded consent.

Thus it was that, at nine o'clock, we presented ourselves at the house in Russell Square, and Sherlock Holmes, Esq., and Miss Coral Atkins, soon to be Watson, met for the first time.

"Such a pity that dear Lavinia couldn't be with us, but she wished to be there when her husband arrived," remarked Henry again, as we strolled across to the hotel, she upon Holmes's arm and Coral upon mine. "She is just the nicest woman. I made her promise that if she ever happens to be passing through Nebraska she *must* make a point of stopping by."

Like a grape being pressed of its juice, I was persuaded and forced during the long meal to yield up to the ladies every detail of our exploits. Holmes was at his most co-operative and agreeable, readily lending his commentary to my narrative.

"Oh, Lavinia would have just loved to hear all this!" exclaimed Henry at several points. "We had such a laugh over that letter of hers from King Teddy. She wished she had it to show us, but she had to tell us instead. Didn't you think it was a hoot, John?"

I explained that we had not read the letter.

"You didn't? Well, I guess it's no secret between the four of us. Coral, darling, why don't you tell it?"

She did, and a droll tale it was, of a country house party not long after Lavinia's marriage. Her husband had been called away and she had stayed on alone. True to the custom of such occasions, the then Prince of Wales, who was the principal guest, had set his sights upon one of the other married ladies. She had left her shoes outside her bedroom door, as the signal that the coast was clear, but the practical joker among them had struck. He had moved the shoes one door along, to where Lavinia had her room.

The Prince of Wales had duly arrived. Upon finding his mistake, he had apologized with customary courtesy and withdrawn. The letter, written a few days later, had renewed his apology and added another, to the effect that he would not wish it thought that his hasty retreat implied anything lacking in Mrs. Glanvill herself. Perhaps they might meet again one day, by which time her husband would be a great tycoon and she in consequence a countess or something of that nature; and then, who knew what might eventuate?

"It was all a charming compliment, of course," Henry explained, "but I guess that if it were read in a certain way, with a word or two changed, it could have sounded dead serious, as if Teddy were offering to set them up with a family title in exchange for you-know-what."

"But as Lavinia said," Coral put in, "the real joke is that her husband would never accept any kind of title —not if one were offered him on a gold plate."

"He wouldn't?" said I, astonished.

"He turned down a knighthood already. He told Lavinia he wouldn't want anything that would put him out on a limb from the Americans. Plain 'Mister' is good enough for them, and that's how he prefers to stay himself, so as to be like them."

"And do you know what?" added Henry. "That James Belmont wanted to give his title *away!* He said all of them ought to be abolished, along with the monarchy and the court and all. Can you beat that? It strikes me Hubert Glanvill is right—'Mister' is good enough for any man."

"Holmes would agree with that," said I. Coral turned to him.

"But what's all this we hear about you going to retire, Mr. Holmes?" she asked. "From all John's just been telling us, there seems to be more than enough for you still to do."

"You think so, Miss Atkins? I am rather hoping that they will see it otherwise. I hope they have done with me, and are ready to let me go."

It was that rarest of moments, at which he seemed to be asking a question of which, for once, he did not know most of the answer. I caught my breath as Coral reached out to him and placed her hand upon the back of one of his. She engaged him with her frank eyes.

"I don't believe that 'they,' or 'we,' shall ever have done with you. We shall go on needing you. Even if you do retire, we shall need to feel that you are always there, in case we should have to call you back, Mr. Sherlock Holmes."

The gray eyes seemed to mist slightly. Perhaps it was my imagination that provided the merest quiver of his lip as he answered:

"Pray, Miss Atkins—call me . . . Holmes."

MICHAEL HARDWICK is the first man since the late Christopher Morley to be honored with the investiture of The Sign of the Four by the Baker Street Irregulars of America, one of the most prestigious honors possible for any Sherlockian. His novel *Prisoner of the Devil* is considered by many to be the finest of all the Sherlock Holmes adventures written since Conan Doyle's death. He is also the author of *The Complete Guide to Sherlock Holmes, The Private Life of Dr. Watson,* and *Sherlock Holmes: My Life and Crimes,* a Sherlockian autobiography. He was for years a leading writer and drama director for the BBC. He also successfully adapted, with his wife, Mollie, the *Upstairs, Downstairs* series and Billy Wilder's film *The Private Life of Sherlock Holmes* into book form. The Hardwicks live in a beautiful, five hundred-year-old house in Kent, England.

STERANKO, internationally acclaimed artist, succeeds such famous Sherlockian artists as Sidney Paget, the original illustrator of Sherlock Holmes, and Robert Fawcett, whose marvelous pictures of the great detective were featured in *Collier's*. Steranko, whose experiences as an escape artist brought him early fame, is an award-winning graphic artist, painter and designer. He is the author of *Chandler,* a graphic novel highly regarded by mystery readers and illustrators alike. He also publishes *Prevue,* a popular magazine of film and entertainment.